# FOOL'S GOLD

BOOK ONE

THE SKINNERS OF GOLDFIELD

# FOOL'S GOLD

## STEPHEN BLY

CROSSWAY BOOKS • WHEATON, ILLINOIS

A DIVISION OF GOOD NEWS PUBLISHERS

*Fool's Gold*

Copyright © 2000 by Stephen Bly

Published by Crossway Books
    A division of Good News Publishers
    1300 Crescent Street
    Wheaton, Illinois 60187

Cover illustration: Paul Bachem
Cover design: Cindy Kiple

First printing, 2000

Printed in the United States of America

**Library of Congress Cataloging-in-Publication Data**
Bly, Stephen A., 1944-
    Fool's gold / Stephen Bly.
        p.    cm. — (The Skinners of Goldfield ; bk. 1)
     ISBN 1-58134-155-5 (alk. paper)
     1. Gold mines and mining—Nevada—Goldfield—Fiction. 2. Family—Nevada—Goldfield—Fiction. 3. Nevada—History—Fiction. 4. Goldfield (Nev.)—Fiction. I. Title.
PS3552.L93 F66  2000
813'.54—dc21
                                      99-089568
                                        CIP

| 15 | 14 | 13 | 12 | 11 | 10 | 09 | 08 | 07 | 06 | 05 | 04 | 03 | 02 | 01 | 00 |
|----|----|----|----|----|----|----|----|----|----|----|----|----|----|----|----|
| 15 | 14 | 13 | 12 | 11 | 10 | 9 | 8 | 7 | 6 | 5 | 4 | 3 | 2 | 1 | |

*For my friends and neighbors*

*in Ivanhoe, California,*

*in the 1950s*

*who taught me the*

*strength of ordinary people*

*For ye see your calling, brethren,*

*how that not many wise men after the flesh,*

*not many mighty, not many noble, are called:*

*But God hath chosen the foolish things*

*of the world to confound the wise.*

1 CORINTHIANS 1:26-27A KJV

# FOREWORD

Dear Readers,

Last Sunday evening I sat, like millions of people all over America and the world, to watch Mr. Armstrong take that first step on the moon. I didn't know whether to shout for joy or break down and bawl.

I ended up doing both.

It was a victory for mankind's ingenuity, tenacity, bravery . . . and spirit of adventure. In some sense I stepped on the moon's surface with those two intrepid astronauts.

But progress, even glorious progress in space exploration, comes with a cost. The past must be set aside. Old ideas get discarded, old ways reformed. And old memories are swept away to make room for the marvelous new ones.

For me it wasn't the first time I had gazed at men who possessed uncommon ingenuity, tenacity, bravery, and a spirit of adventure. I was only ten years old when I arrived in Goldfield, Nevada, in 1905. We were on our way from Oklahoma to California. Daddy took a shortcut, and we decided to stay a day or two.

I ended up staying there for eleven years.

Few people in the late 1960s can imagine what life was like in a boomtown. For most it would be as foreign as walking on the moon. Not many mothers today have inadvertently crushed a stink bug and had to live with that stench for days. Or glanced down at the baby on the living room rug and watched in horror as a scorpion crawled up his arm. They've never had the pleasure of tearing up newspapers into tiny scraps, then wetting them and sweeping the floor with them because that was the only way to pick up the alkali dust. They've probably never sliced tomatoes for lunch and seen them curl and dry up at the edges within minutes, if not seconds, in the dry desert wind.

Some now praise the solitude and the stillness of the desert as they drive through it in their air-conditioned automobiles. They have never experienced the terror when the desert takes on an identity of its own and chases you back into the house like an animal stalking its prey.

Goldfield was the last gold rush in the United States. It attracted not only every prospector and want-to-be prospector in America, but also every gunman and outlaw that lamented the Old West's passing, every crib girl who wanted one last chance to marry a rich mine owner, every gambler who had been slaving away at dying little Western towns, every speculator and huckster who ever dreamed up a get-rich-quick scheme, and every college graduate who could find enough gasoline to fuel his Thomas motorcar across the roadless wastes of places with names like Weepah Hills, the Montezuma Range, and the Ralston Desert.

It was, for a brief few years, the finale of the Old West. And nearly every character of that era still alive made the pilgrimage to Goldfield. According to many, the strike was the richest concentration of gold ever found in the world. Whether or not this is fact, I can only tell you that the people on the street corners of Goldfield in 1905 thought it was true.

I know.

I was there.

Daddy (Mr. Orion Tower Skinner, called O. T. by everyone but Mother) was forty-one years old when he drove our old farm wagon pulled by Ida and Ada, our mules, down off the hill at Tonopah and across the desert to Goldfield. Mama, the former Dola Mae Davis, sat next to me. She was eleven years his junior. Rita Ann was twelve. Tommy-Blue was nine. Silas Paul was two. We called him Punky.

I still do.

He and I are the only two left of the Skinners of Goldfield.

The world has changed almost beyond belief since that hot, dusty June day in 1905. The future will undoubtedly captivate our imagination, our time, and our hearts. But we must never forget that the spirit of adventure, exploration, and survival against all odds is an old instinct.

We are rushing through the years of this century as if they were pocketbook change, best if quickly spent. There are not many left who can tell the story of America's last gold boomtown.

Some will complain that an old woman has a faulty memory, at best. But I tell you some images never fade.

All of us will forever envision those daring men walking on the moon's surface.

And I can never, ever forget the moment we rounded Columbia Mountain and stared at the mysterious, adventuresome . . . bleak and dusty place called Goldfield.

Corrie Lou (Skinner) Merced
August 4, 1969
Dinuba, California

# ONE

*Tonopah, Nevada, June 11, 1905*

Mama told them not to look, but Corrie Lou Skinner peeked between her fingers. She knew that her sister Rita Ann was spying also but would never admit it.

As soon as the fight poured out of the freight office into the street, O. T. Skinner yanked their team of mules to the right and parked the wagon at the edge of the rutted dirt street in front of Edwards & Cutting's Building and Mining Hardware Store.

A tall, thin man wearing a bowler took a roundhouse swing at a dirty-faced man with thick eyebrows and mustache. The sound of knuckles hitting chin caused Corrie to flinch. Her bangs bounced over her fingers.

Both men tumbled out into the hard-packed dirt street. Fine gray dust fogged about them as they rolled to their knees. The dirty-faced man slammed his hand into a pile of dried horse manure and wiped it off on the sleeve of his suit coat. Then two more men, in worn three-piece suits and scuffed boots, began a shouting and shoving match on the wooden sidewalk only a few yards away from the Skinner wagon. At least a dozen men crowded around to watch.

Nine-year-old Tommy-Blue Skinner climbed up on the canvas-covered steamer trunk strapped to the back of the farm wagon and peered over his father's shoulder. His denim coveralls were patched with used brown ducking at the knees. "What are they fightin' about, Daddy?"

Mr. Skinner pulled a wooden toothpick from the slight gap between his two front teeth. His chapped lips tasted of alkali dust and breakfast bacon. "Don't reckon I know, son. Some men don't need much excuse to throw punches."

"Are you going to make them stop it?" Tommy-Blue queried.

"Nope. They're too big to scold and too foolish to protect."

The man with thick eyebrows kicked the tall, thin man. The tall man caught his foot, and both tumbled onto the street in front of a freight wagon pulled by six pair of oxen. The wagon squeaked to a halt as the bullwhacker joined the audience to watch the fight.

As the two men in three-piece suits stumbled along the wooden sidewalk, the shoving turned into a wrestling match. They took turns throwing one another against the front of the freight office, until someone's elbow shattered one of the small panes of window glass. Both men staggered out into the street and wrestled each other to the ground.

Corrie chewed her tongue as she leaned against her father's left arm. Her gray cotton dress hung straight off her shoulders to her ankles and was sprinkled with cherry jam stains from breakfast. "Are they going to use pistols?" she asked.

Dola Skinner smoothed her hair down from its part in the middle to the soft coil under her black straw hat with its faded red silk poppy. *Lord, you certainly must have a higher purpose for these men than public brawling.* Without looking down, she gave her youngest daughter a hug. "Are you peeking, young lady?"

Corrie kept her smudged hands over her eyes. "No, Mama."

"She is too!" Rita Ann insisted, her purple gingham bow riding up and down her Adam's apple with each word. She clutched a thick, ragged book in front of her.

Corrie rubbed her nose with the back of her sticky hand and tried to hide a grin. "I was sort of looking," she confessed.

The fight seemed to be expanding. A black man leaped onto the back of a round-bellied man with a full black beard. They crashed into a post that held up the porch roof, and the entire hardware store vibrated.

Mr. Skinner rubbed the back of his neck just below his neatly trimmed gray hair. "I reckon them gun-totin' days are over." *When I promised Mama that this southern route would be easier on the mules, I didn't figure the town was still this rough.* "I can't tell if they are even carryin' guns."

"Maybe one of them is Wyatt Earp!" Corrie speculated. "I heard he's in Nevada. Maybe he'll make some more history. I'd surely like to see some history."

"I doubt if he's here." Mr. Skinner continued to pick his teeth and stare at the struggle near the front of the wagon. *Course, Lord, I don't reckon any of us know when we're makin' history.* He reached over and fingered Corrie's bangs out of her eyes. "Earp's an old man. These men look young."

"Daddy, are you an old man or a young man?" Tommy-Blue asked.

"Daddy is only forty-one," Rita Ann informed him. "There are many men older than that."

O. T. pulled out a blue bandanna and wiped sweat off his forehead and neck. Desert dirt streaked the bandanna. "This heat makes a man feel old—that I know."

"Well," Rita Ann continued, "you haven't reached the point where Shakespeare said 'every part about you is blasted with antiquity.'"

"Thank you."

"You're welcome," she replied, with a triumphant look at Corrie.

"I wish we could see a gunfight. We've been travelin' for months, and we haven't seen one gunfight," Corrie complained.

"Corrie Lou!" her mother scolded. "We will not sit here and watch a gunfight. Besides, those days are over." Her long, strong, callused hands continued to rock the sleeping toddler.

Tommy-Blue made no attempt to hide his eyes. "How many are fighting?" he asked.

"Only six so far," Rita Ann replied. "That is, I think there are six. . . . If I had my eyes open, I could see more."

Corrie peeked at her sister huddled behind their mother. Gold wire-framed glasses accented Rita Ann's pinched-shut eyes. "You can see six of them with your eyes closed?" Corrie chided.

"I can hear them," Rita Ann snapped back. "I have very good ears."

Dola clutched the sleeping toddler in her left arm. She pulled off her straw hat and fanned her face and the toddler's. "Orion, I told you we should cross the mountains at Carson City. We have no business exposing the children to such a town as Tonopah."

"Darlin', we're on our way out of town. We'll just park here until these fellas are done. I don't reckon five minutes will cause the children any permanent damage."

From out of the crowd a large object was hurled at the tall, thin man. Wood shattered as it hit the back of his head. He crumpled to the street.

"That looked like it would cause permanent damage," Tommy-Blue shouted and held his hands on top of his hat.

"It all depends on whether that wooden bucket was filled with nails or old newspapers," Mr. Skinner commented.

Dola shaded the toddler's face with her hat. "Orion," she scolded, "I want you to turn the wagon around right now and get us out of here."

"That dark-skinned man has a bloody nose!" Tommy-Blue cried.

"He does? I can't see! Let me see." Corrie Lou climbed up on the trunk next to Tommy-Blue.

Over fifty people now filled the street and watched the brawl. Shouts and bets came from every side. The more the crowd closed in on the combatants, the less those in the farm wagon could see.

"Hey, that big guy hit the other man with a chair!" Tommy-Blue called as he leaned forward and clutched his father's arm. "That ain't fair!"

Dola rubbed the dust-filled creases next to her eyes. "That isn't fair," she corrected.

There was a thundering noise behind them. The crowd in the street parted for an approaching stagecoach, and the Skinner family, except the one sleeping, turned to watch its arrival. The six men involved in the fight continued to slug away with fists, chairs, and buckets.

The stage driver was a huge man with a mustache that drooped past his chin. When he stood up, tobacco stains showed down the front of his rattlesnake skin vest. He shouted at the crowd, but no one could hear him. Finally he raised a short-barreled shotgun above his head and fired it in the air.

Thick, white gun smoke drifted straight up, like half-hearted prayers. The stagecoach horses danced forward.

Ada and Ida, the Skinner mules, lurched sideways, their front hooves perched on the wooden sidewalk.

Corrie threw her hands up over her ears.

Tommy-Blue ducked behind Corrie.

Rita Ann crossed her arms, clutching the thick book to her chest.

Red-faced and sweating, the toddler sat straight up in his mother's lap and cried.

"Boys," the driver roared, "we're loadin' up this stage. If you fightin' men have settled up who gets them last three tickets, I'll take—"

Rocking the bawling toddler on her hip, Dola stood up in the wagon, shoved her hat back on her head, and waved a finger at the driver. "Mister, don't you ever do that again!" she hollered.

With shotgun still in hand, he pushed his hat back and stared down at the Skinner wagon as if inspecting a basket of eggs for a cracked one. "What did you say?" the driver bellowed.

Dola's small mouth narrowed, and her eyes danced. "The reckless discharge of a firearm within city limits endangers the lives of innocent people, let alone disturbing the peace of infants!" she shouted. "Don't you ever do that again!"

O. T. Skinner continued to pick his teeth and lean back in the wagon seat. *You have incurred the wrath of Dola Mae Davis Skinner. The host of heaven would be a less dangerous foe.*

"There was a riot in the street, lady!" the driver called down.

"Yes, but it was your gunshot that woke little Punky! I'm sure you were taught better than that. You should be ashamed."

"'Oh, shame, where is thy blush?'" Rita Ann blurted out, then ducked down behind her mother.

"Isaac, you cain't ever beat a mother and child, especially them that's quotin' Shakespeare. You might as well just give up now!" a man shouted from the crowd in front of Butler's Saloon. In the outbreak of laughter that followed, the Skinner wagon became the center of attention.

The driver of the battered Concord stagecoach doffed his hat. His bushy, wild gray hair sprayed out as he bowed to Mrs. Skinner. "My sincere apologies, ma'am, for disturbing you and your little one," he blustered. "My mother, bless her soul, did teach me better than that."

Mrs. Skinner balanced the wide-eyed but now-silent youngster on her left hip and shaded her eyes with her right hand. "Thank you, sir. Your apology is accepted. And, if I might suggest, your appearance would be much more comely if you would get a haircut." She promptly sat down as the crowd of men hooted and roared at the stage driver.

Her face flushed with embarrassment, Rita Ann stayed behind her mother. But Corrie watched the man's reaction with open blue eyes.

The tall, thin man whose head had encountered the wooden bucket shuffled over to the rig and guided the mules back down off the sidewalk. He wore soiled khaki britches and a collarless cotton shirt.

The stagecoach driver held up his shotgun to quiet the crowd. Corrie clamped her hands over her ears. Tommy-Blue held his breath and pinched his nose shut.

"Settle down, boys," the driver shouted as he jammed his wide-brimmed felt hat back on his head. "Or I'll be forced to disturb that youngster again. I'm heading down to Goldfield in three minutes. I'll take the eleven men who have today's tickets. The twelfth man who tries to board will be shot on sight. Is that clear enough?" He glanced toward Mrs. Skinner. "I'll shoot him in a dignified and discreet manner, ma'am."

There was a near riot as eleven men in suits and ties tossed duffel bags onto the top of the stage and shoved their way toward the open door of the coach. Within seconds seven men crammed inside, with four crawling up on top, crowding the driver and the baggage for a place to hold on. Then, with no more conversation, the stage lurched forward, heading south out of Tonopah, leaving a flock of men on the street milling around and mumbling.

The tall, blond man attempted to brush off his shirt. "Ma'am, I'm sorry about fighting in front of your children. It wasn't a very good example."

Little Punky squirmed out of her arms and back to the canvas-covered trunk with Corrie and Tommy-Blue.

Dimples appeared for the first time in the tanned face of Dola Skinner. "I appreciate your apology. I trust your outrage was for a noble cause."

"Yes, ma'am." He stepped up closer to the wagon. A faint scar ran from the side of his mouth to his ear. "Me and Wasco and Charlie Fred won today's stage tickets in a knife-throwin' contest, and then they wouldn't settle up. They said we cheated."

Rita Ann crawled up on the front seat between her mother and father. She wrinkled her nose, forcing her glasses higher. "A knife-throwing contest?" she gulped.

"Yep. I'm Lucky Jack Gately."

"I think I've heard that name before," O. T. replied.

"Are you thinking of the Gottleys in Fort Smith?" Dola probed.

"Could be," O. T. mumbled.

"Well," Lucky Jack continued, "among other things, I used to have a knife-throwing act for Buffalo Bill Cody's Congress of Rough Riders. These old boys here claimed I was a professional and tricked them into a contest they couldn't win."

Rita Ann peeked around her mother and studied the man. "Did you?" she quizzed.

"Of course I did."

"I wish I could've seen that knife-throwin' contest," Tommy-Blue put in. "Mama don't let me throw my Barlow knife."

Lucky Jack Gately ambled to the other side of the wagon near Mr. Skinner, surveying its contents as he went. "I reckon you folks are headed down to Goldfield to see the elephant?"

Corrie Lou Skinner's blue eyes widened, and her full, round mouth dropped open. "We saw a camel down in Bisbee, Arizona, but we haven't ever seen an elephant!" she said.

O. T. Skinner rubbed the back of his neck, which was as brown as his dust-covered felt hat. "I surmise this man is talkin' about the town of Goldfield itself, not a real elephant, Corrie Lou."

"Do they have elephants in Goldfield, Daddy?" Tommy-Blue asked.

"Of course not," Rita Ann declared. "That's merely an expression for all of those rushing to the mining location to see the gold that has purportedly been discovered."

Lucky Jack tugged off his bowler and brushed rocks and bucket splinters out of his hair. "That's a precocious little girl you have," he offered.

"I'm twelve years old," Rita Ann announced. "You would hardly call me a little girl. I'm the eldest child."

"Mr. Gately, let me introduce us all. I'm O. T. Skinner; this is my wife, Dola, and our children—Rita Ann, Corrie, Tommy-Blue, and we call the baby Punky."

Lucky Jack studied Corrie. "You look a lot like your brother."

"We ain't twins," Tommy-Blue protested. "Corrie likes carrots, but I don't."

"Well, you certainly aren't twins then." Lucky Jack grinned.

"And I have adorable dimples when I smile," Corrie bragged. "Just like Mama."

Gately leaned on the faded gray wood of the farm wagon. "Mr. Skinner, I'd like to ask you an imposing question that I have no right to ask."

"Are we supposed to cover our ears again, Daddy?" Rita Ann called out.

Mr. Skinner slipped his strong arm around his daughter and hugged her. "I reckon you can listen."

Gately's voice lowered as if relaying directions to a lost mine. "Mr. Skinner, would it be possible for me to hitch a ride with your family down to Goldfield?"

Dried sweat had left a dusty film on the buttoned collar of O. T.'s long-sleeved white shirt. "It would be unchristian to turn you down," he replied, with a quick glance at his wife's reassuring nod.

Lucky Jack pointed toward the freight office. "I just have one small carpetbag."

"Go get it. We aren't in any hurry. It's only thirty miles, and we were told we can make Goldfield in about seven, eight hours. We're goin' to camp overnight and then head out in the morning."

Gately spun back around toward the wagon. "You aren't stayin' in Goldfield?"

"No, sir." Skinner reached over and plucked Punky from his

mother's arm. "We're on our way to California." He bounced the toddler on his right knee.

"Well, now I feel like old Abraham bartering with the angel of the Lord over Sodom." Gately pulled off his bowler and held it in his hand. "Can I ask you another favor? Would you have room for my two partners also? Just three of us and three bags."

Mr. Skinner glanced back at the goods piled behind him on the wagon. "Of course they can come," he said. "It isn't a very comfortable wagon, but the children can scoot over, and we'll make room."

"This is an answer to prayer, folks. The wait for stage tickets is over a week, and you can't buy a horse or mule to save your soul," Lucky Jack added.

"I trust you will rely on prayer more than on your fists in the future," Mrs. Skinner reproached him.

"Yes, ma'am." He shoved the bowler back on his head. "Now I just have one last favor . . ."

"'O! How wretched is that poor man that hangs on a prince's favors!'" Rita Ann recited.

"'And when he falls, he falls like Lucifer, never to hope again,'" Lucky Jack said grinning. "*Henry the VIII.*"

"Act 3, scene 2," Rita Ann replied with wide blue eyes.

"Nevertheless, I will ask the favor," Gately continued. "Could you swing over west of town to pick us up? Me and my friends will load up behind the headworks of the old Athens mine."

O. T. Skinner stared down the alley at the distant twelve-by-twelve-inch bleached beams that marked the top of the mine shaft. "Why is that?" he questioned.

"'Cause if some of these men find out you're goin' to Goldfield, there'll be a stampede to your wagon until the axle breaks."

Charlie Fred wore a flat-crowned, gray felt California hat and a black eye. Wasco Delmar nursed a bleeding nose with a bandanna. His bruised face managed a wide, white-toothed smile as he crawled up into the back of the Skinners' wagon. The family's belongings had been restacked, allowing two men to perch at the back of the wagon and another on the tattered green trunk behind the driver's seat, next to the canvas-covered trunk. When the wagon finally rolled down off the slopes of Siebert Mountain, it was Lucky Jack Gately who sat up front with the family.

Rita Ann scooted next to him with her tattered burgundy *Complete Works of Shakespeare* in her small, dainty hands.

Tommy-Blue just stared at the two men in the back, his thumbs looped in the front pockets of his bibbed coveralls.

Corrie played peekaboo with Punky, who remained seated between his mother and father.

Lucky Jack pulled a red bandanna from his back pocket to wipe sweat and dirt from his clean-shaven but scratched and bruised face. "Can't thank you folks enough for this ride."

O. T. stared out over the mule's ears at miles and miles of empty desert. "It's on our way."

Gately reached over and picked up the Shakespeare book. "Rita Ann, I had a book identical to this one."

Her tightly drawn pigtails made her blue eyes seem even wider. "Just like mine?"

"Yep," Lucky Jack grinned. "Only I had Billy Shakespeare autograph it for me one time when Buffalo Bill took the show to England."

"Really?" Tommy-Blue gasped.

Rita Ann pulled the book back. "William Shakespeare died on April 23, 1616, in Stratford-on-Avon," she announced with judicial authority.

Lucky Jack winked at Tommy-Blue. "I was just funnin' your sis."

"Well, I have Stuart Brannon's autograph!" Tommy-Blue boasted. "Don't I, Mama?"

"We all have Stuart Brannon's autograph," Rita Ann sighed.

"You folks know Pop Brannon?" Gately pressed.

Dola Skinner turned back so she could look at Gately's square chin and gray eyes. "My uncle, Everett Davis, was a very good friend of Mr. Brannon's. We met him in Gallup, New Mexico."

"Well, I am impressed with your autograph, Tommy-Blue," Lucky Jack admitted. "The only famous autograph I ever got, besides Buffalo Bill Cody's, was Annie Oakley's. She gave me a photograph of her and Sitting Bull and signed it: 'To my friend, Lucky Jack Gately, the worst shot, male or female, that I've ever seen.'"

"Are you telling us the truth?" Rita Ann quizzed.

"Mostly. Oh, I might be stretchin' it a little, but me and Frank Butler—that's Annie's husband—were partners in an act for a while."

"You think there are any famous people in Goldfield, Mr. Gately?" Corrie asked.

"I believe there are some that's goin' to be famous someday. But we just don't know which ones yet." Lucky Jack tried to brush the dust off the legs of his khaki trousers but soon gave up. "You folks really aren't going to stay in Goldfield?"

"Nope," O. T. declared. "I hear it's a barren place without any redeeming value except the gold." He slapped the lead lines and sped the mules down the gradual slope. Those in the back grabbed the side rail for balance.

When the wagon leveled off, Gately tried to stretch out his long legs but gave up and kept his knees tucked nearly under his chin. "Yeah, the gold is the reason ever'one wants to get there."

O. T. reached across Punky and patted the navy-blue-dress-covered knee of his wife. "Well, we already have our riches, don't we, Mama?"

Dola pushed the straw hat with its faded red ribbon hatband back and then patted her forehead with a tattered tea towel that once had a complete butterfly embroidered on the corner. "Yes, indeed, Mr. Gately. O. T. and I consider ourselves very wealthy." She slipped her fingers into the callused hand of her husband.

"I heard the children mention Bisbee," Lucky Jack said. "Did you all make a fortune down in them Arizona mines?"

"Oh no, Mr. Gately." O. T. smiled. "We weren't talking about the mines. Look around in this wagon. The Lord has given us four beautiful, wonderful, and intelligent children. Do you think there is anything in all of Goldfield worth more than that?"

A wide, easy smile broke across Gately's slightly battered face. "No, sir, I don't reckon there is. But if the Lord wanted to provide you some extra funds so you could lavish it on these handsome children, that would be all right, wouldn't it?"

"Why would the Lord want to complicate our life with riches, Mr. Gately?" Dola Skinner stared at her hands still laced into her husband's. *Lord, my hands are as rough as O. T.'s I used to have soft, delicate hands. Mother said so.*

Lucky Jack pulled off his hat and gingerly scratched his head. "I don't rightly know, Mrs. Skinner."

The only sounds were the clomp of the mule hooves and the squeak of drying hubs on the wagon. "I surmise you men are going to try your luck at finding gold?" O. T. finally ventured.

"Yes, sir. That's the plan. Wasco's our gold expert. He spent time in the Yukon. He's the one with the black eye. Charlie Fred is the one who's black all over."

"Is the Yukon in Alaska, Mama?" Corrie asked.

"No," Rita Ann lectured. "It's one of the northern provinces in the Dominion of Canada."

Gately stared at the twelve-year-old. "You surely know a lot about geography."

"We have a map of the entire world in Daddy's fishing pole case, and some evenings we pull it out, and Rita Ann reads all the names of places," Tommy-Blue explained as he stared at the big knife sheathed on Lucky Jack's belt. "Is that your throwing knife?"

Gately reached down and unfastened the sheath. "Yes, it is, son. Do you want to look at it?"

Tommy-Blue's eyes grew wide. Then he glanced up at his mother. The flash of her blue eyes banished the smile from his face. "No, sir. But thank you anyway," he managed to mumble.

Lucky Jack nudged Tommy-Blue with his elbow. "You're a smart man to mind your mama. I know a lot of men whose lives would be much improved if they had been wise enough to listen to their mamas."

"Thank you for that support, Mr. Gately," Dola Skinner said.

"Where did that black man come from?" Corrie asked. "He's the first one we've seen in Nevada."

"The black race traces its ancestry to the continent of Africa," Rita Ann announced.

Gately grinned. "What college did you say you attended?"

Rita Ann tugged on her pigtail. "Mama's been our teacher ever since we left Guthrie, Oklahoma."

"When was that?"

"The day after my birthday!" Corrie chimed in. "My birthday is February 14th."

"Valentine's Day? I bet it's nice being born on a holiday and having ever'one celebrate with you," Gately added.

"I was born on New Year's Day," Rita explained. "Tommy-Blue was born on Christmas, and Punky on the Fourth of July."

"That's amazing!" Gately replied. "I don't believe I've ever heard of a family who has every birthday on a holiday."

"Mrs. Skinner is a very determined woman." O. T. smiled. "She don't take no for an answer."

"Mama's birthday's on November 1. That's All Saint's Day, you know," Rita Ann said.

"But Papa's is on December 7, and there ain't nothin' important ever happened on that day," Tommy-Blue added.

Gately pulled off his suit coat and folded it neatly across his knee. "You've been on the road since February?"

"We're workin' our way west. It's kind of slow, but it fits our budget," O. T. explained. "Oklahoma can be a tough land to farm, especially if the weather don't treat you right."

Lucky Jack turned sideways and dropped his legs over the sideboard of the wagon. "You say you're headed to California?"

"Yes, sir." Skinner stared down at his boots and the hole near his little toe where his sock showed through.

"California is a big place. You got kin out there?"

O. T. tucked his worn boots back under the wagon seat. "My brother Pegasus got himself a little twenty-acre vineyard and plenty of ditch water out there in the San Joaquin Valley. Said he'd help us buy the twenty next to him if we'd farm it and give him some company."

"So you just packed up and headed west?" Lucky Jack said.

"Yes, sir, we did. A tornado leveled our house last May, and we lost the place to the bank. So we figured it was a sign that the Lord was leadin' us to move."

"I never considered that the Lord would use a tornado on good people. But I got to admit, you folks have the right attitude," Lucky Jack replied.

"What do you mean by that, Mr. Gately?" Dola asked.

"Well, you have your family . . . your plans. . . . You know where you're headed."

"We're going to Dinuba!" Corrie blurted out.

"See there?" Gately added. "Any money you earn along the way just helps you fulfill the plan you already have. Now me and I would guess most of the men in Goldfield are just runnin' around lookin' for money first off. Then if we happen to find it, we figure on decidin' what to do with our lives."

Dola brushed two flies off Punky's red face. "You seem to have it backwards, don't you?"

"Yes, ma'am. I believe you're right," Gately concurred. "A man ought to find his place and purpose first and then worry about riches."

"Do you want to go to California with us?" Tommy-Blue queried. "I bet they don't have any knife throwers in Dinuba."

Gately put his long-fingered hand on the boy's shoulder. "Tommy-Blue, if I had a family like yours, I'd go farm some grapes too. But I don't have anyone but me."

"You got Wasco and Charlie Fred." Corrie pointed toward the sleeping men on the back of the wagon.

"Yep. Ain't that a pair to draw to? A sourdough prospector and a black Nebraska cowboy. But you're right. We got ourselves a good prospect of a lease, so if we work hard, we could make a little money." Gately stared out at the plodding mules. "I'm just a little anxious to get there."

"Ada and Ida aren't very fast, but they've pulled us all the way from Oklahoma," Tommy-Blue responded.

The children began singing "Four-Leaf Clover" and then moved into "Little Boy Blue." "Sweet Marie" followed, but then the wind picked up and dust swirled. Their voices became mute from desert dust. For a while the men at the back of the wagon talked of rich stringers, picture rock, colored float, pay shoots, and $300 ore, but they found that the desert dust can silence even the most enthusiastic prospectors.

Tommy-Blue now wore a bandanna under his wide felt hat to keep the sun off his neck and ears. Corrie and Rita Ann wore two of their mother's faded gingham bonnets, while Mrs. Skinner held a dusty brown canvas umbrella over her head and Punky's. Red-faced and silent, he had a damp tea towel over his head.

The three passengers pulled hats across their faces and tried to find a position to sleep as the wagon creaked along the rutted desert trail. Everyone and everything was layered with fine gray dust.

The descent to the desert had been gradual. There were no trees, save the occasional spike-leafed Joshua. No greenery. No grass. No cactus. No buildings. No springs. And very little sagebrush.

When they finally came to a cluster of three Joshua trees that provided a little patch of shade, Mr. Skinner stopped the rig and slipped down. "The wind's died down a little. Everyone out and stretch. It's time to let the mules rest."

Dola Skinner studied her husband, the other men, and her children. Every inch was coated with a layer of dust. Every individual hair was encased in gray dirt, much as ice encases a telegraph wire during a spell of frozen winter fog. She knew her eyes too peered out from lashes heavy with dirt. *Lord, if it weren't for the discomfort and misery, this would be a humorous sight. It would be hard to imagine a dirtier band of people on the face of the earth. I would like to have a photograph of this moment, but not have to look at it until fifty years from now. Perhaps then I could laugh. I trust You're smiling.*

"Can we eat now, Mama?" Tommy-Blue asked.

"Yes, but we'll have a cold lunch. We don't need a fire today." Mrs. Skinner looked up at Lucky Jack, who was a foot taller than she was. "I trust you and the others will join us."

Lucky Jack stretched his long legs and then tipped his bowler. "Thank you, Mrs. Skinner, but we aren't going to eat up your larder. We can wait until Goldfield."

"Nonsense. We might not have a lot, but we would be selfish not to share it with you," Dola insisted.

On the tattered multicolored quilt with orange backing, she spread out a tin plate filled with slightly limp carrots, a long loaf of very hard sourdough bread, and a dozen pieces of rabbit jerky.

O. T. Skinner motioned toward the food. "We do have water in the barrels. I reckon we can refill them at Goldfield."

"Don't be too sure of that," Charlie Fred cautioned. His white silk shirt was a dingy gray and worn to the skin in places. "I hear they have to haul water for most of the town. Rabbit Springs, at the base of Malpais Mesa, can't hardly keep up with the increased population. You might have to buy the water. One ol' boy told me that in some of them saloons water's more expensive than whiskey."

"I reckon the Lord made enough water for everyone," O. T. murmured.

"Only He didn't put much of it around gold mines," Charlie Fred added. "Did you ever notice that?"

"Well, boys, before we all dig in, let's have a blessin'," O. T. announced. He bowed his head and began, "Lord, we thank You for these new friends—Lucky Jack, Wasco, and Charlie Fred. I'd like to ask You to turn this meager offering into nourishment for our bones. In Jesus' name, amen."

"You men help yourself," Dola invited. "Guests always go first at the Skinner house."

"We ain't got no house, Mama," Tommy-Blue reminded her.

"Tommy-Blue, don't you correct your mama," O. T. scolded. "They all knew what she meant."

Lucky Jack pushed his hat back. "You kids go ahead and eat."

"Proper hospitality is not limited to adults," Rita Ann asserted. "You are our guests, and we will wait."

"Would you all hurry up? I'm hungry," Corrie whined.

"You kin eat all the carrots you want," Tommy-Blue offered graciously.

Wasco scooped up several pieces of jerky.

Lucky Jack cleared his throat. Wasco put some of the jerky back. Soon everyone had a little something on a plate.

Dola waved her hand toward the back of the wagon. "Orion, get me grandmother's case, please."

Mr. Skinner carefully set a two-foot-square, battered blue trunk on the desert dirt next to the rear wheel of the farm wagon. Dola carefully opened the lid and brought out the crystal glasses one at a time, wiping them on the back side of her apron.

"We going to use Grandma's glasses just for water?" Corrie quizzed.

"We always use them when we have company," Rita Ann explained.

"Ma'am, there ain't no need to—" Wasco began.

"Now don't you tell me what I can and can't do," Dola fumed. "These are to remind my children that civility and good etiquette know no geographical limits."

"Even in the middle of the godforsaken desert?" Charlie Fred quizzed.

"I assure you, God has not forsaken this desert nor you," Mrs. Skinner replied.

"Are you sure my mama didn't send you out here to hound me?" Charlie Fred laughed.

The smile was tight, almost smug, but Dola Skinner's blue eyes danced. "Perhaps she did, Charlie Fred. Do you think it will do any good?"

"It just might, ma'am. I ain't seen Mama since '98. I reckon I ought to go back to North Platte someday."

"After you strike it rich in Goldfield?" Dola probed.

"That's the plan."

Rita Ann handed a carrot to Punky. He swatted it to the quilt and then kicked at it with chubby, round toes.

O. T. made a sandwich with rabbit jerky and bread crusts tossed aside by Corrie and Tommy-Blue. "Just how do you boys expect to cash in once you get to Goldfield? You can tell us 'cause we ain't interested in gold. We're just passin' through."

Gately swallowed down a bite of rubbery carrot with a gulp of water from a crystal glass. "Me and Wasco and Charlie Fred bought us a 175-foot lease on the Juniper Mine," Lucky Jack explained. "We'll push it as far as it goes and see what we have."

"I don't understand mining leases," Dola admitted. "What does that mean?"

"Well, see . . ." Lucky Jack played tug-of-war with a bit of rabbit jerky and then continued. "The man who discovered the gold doesn't want to have to do the diggin'. So he leased out a certain portion of his claim for others to work."

"What does it cost you to buy a lease?" Corrie asked.

"Darlin', it ain't proper to ask a man what somethin' costs," O. T. cautioned.

"We put some money up front and promised to give the man 20 percent of the gold we find," Lucky Jack explained.

"But we do have one problem," Wasco mumbled, trying to keep the bread from sticking to the roof of his mouth. His black left eye was almost swollen shut. "Leases have to have a name. We can't decide what to call our lease. We sat up half the night discussin' the matter. The Lucky Jack-Wasco-Charlie Fred Lease seems a mite too long a name."

"What is the length of time you bought the lease for?" Mr. Skinner asked.

Charlie Fred patted his tender nose with the blue bandanna. "It lasts until January 1."

"That's my birthday!" Rita Ann exclaimed.

Lucky Jack glanced at his partners and then back at the twelve-year-old. "Maybe we ought to call it The Rita Ann Lease."

Her eyes widened, and a dimpleless smile broke across her face. "Really?"

"Sounds good to me," Charlie Fred concurred as he reached over and plucked up a carrot with his fingers and popped it into his wide mouth.

Wasco tore off a hunk of bread with his teeth. "Shoot, ever'body knows having a purdy lady's name on your mine or lease brings you good luck."

"Then we'll call it The Rita Ann," Lucky Jack announced.

"I've never had a gold mine named after me," Rita Ann squealed.

"Not the whole mine—just the lease," Mr. Skinner corrected.

"I've never had anything named after me," Corrie grumbled.

"That ain't true. I named a vigaroon after you," Tommy-Blue reminded her.

"Vigaroons don't count," Corrie pouted.

"Well, I thought it was a real scorpion when I named it," Tommy-Blue countered.

Lucky Jack stepped over next to the Joshua trees and gazed out on the desert. "Looks like we got company."

O. T. tugged the brim of his gray felt hat down low and squinted. Three men rode burros toward them. The men's feet were almost dragging the dirt. The heat rising off the pale gray desert floor made the men look like wistful images in a fading dream.

"I should dig out some more food," Dola offered.

Lucky Jack Gately stalked out toward the approaching men. "I know these men, and you definitely don't want to feed them. Wasco, grab your carbine and find a position behind these trees. Charlie Fred, put another bean in your pistol. It looks like the Wilkins brothers are still on our trail. Mr. Skinner, you and your family stay back at the wagon. This is our score to settle."

"You know these men?" O. T. asked.

"You ever heard of the Wilkins brothers, Mr. Skinner?" Gately spun the cylinder of his revolver.

"No, sir. I reckon not." O. T. continued to size up the approaching men. "What are they famous for?"

"For packin' six-guns," Lucky Jack replied.

Dola pulled three more crystal glasses from the tattered trunk. "Whoever they are, they can use a drink of water. I have found that most men still have a few virtues left."

"Shakespeare said, 'Men's evil manner lives in brass; their virtues we write in water,'" Rita Ann proclaimed from her place next to her father.

Lucky Jack popped his knuckles as he waited for the men to approach. "I don't know if they got any virtues, but these three ought to have their vices written in lead."

# TWO

The thick layer of fine gray-brown alkali dust neutralized all colors of man and beast. Like desert chameleons, the three men blended in with beige dirt and brown burros.

Dola retied the worn silk hat ribbon under her chin and studied the trio. *They are like a vaporous mirage . . . like the last scene before a person wakes up from a dream . . . or like a scene through a cloudy pane of glass. Dirt equalizes ages. I must remember that. No one really looks younger when filthy, but their age is hidden. I think they are Orion's age. I think they might all have mustaches. I know that they are wearing sidearms. That seems to be the only clean spot on them.*

She watched as Lucky Jack Gately and Charlie Fred went out to meet the men. Wasco remained hidden, carbine in hand, behind the Joshua trees. Rita Ann scooted in next to her mother. Tommy-Blue spied things out from behind her long brown skirt. "Orion, you must stop these men from doing something terribly foolish," she demanded.

O. T. ran his fingers through his short, thin hair and re-set his wide-brimmed felt hat. "I don't know what the argument is, Mama, nor who is in the right. So I reckon we should just sit this one out." He put his hand on Corrie's shoulder and squeezed her to his side. He could feel her thin, pointed shoulder blade under the cotton dress.

Rita Ann fidgeted with the purple bow on her long black braid.

"We're on Lucky Jack's side, of course. He's our friend. I think he's a very nice man," she declared.

"That's what you said about George Parker when we met him over in Utah, darlin'," Dola reminded her.

Rita Ann's thick, dark eyebrows curled across her forehead. "How was I to know he was Butch Cassidy? Anyway, he was very nice and friendly to me," she replied.

The thought of the clean-shaven Cassidy and the fresh scent of tonic water on his face came to Dola Skinner's mind. "That's one advantage of having nothing anyone wants to steal," she said. "Everyone who rides into our camp is friendly to us. We are neither a threat nor potential victims."

O. T. jammed his hands into the back pockets of his faded blue jeans and rocked back on his heels. He could feel the dirt caked in the creases beside his eyes as he squinted into the western sun. "There ain't a whole lot of advantages," he mumbled, "but that surely is one."

Tommy-Blue timidly stepped out in front. "Daddy, do we get to see a shootin'?"

O. T. glanced at the tanned shoulders and arms of his son. "Nobody wants to shoot nobody." He tugged on Tommy-Blue's bare shoulders. "Now stay back here, son."

"I still think Lucky Jack is a good man," Rita Ann insisted.

"Just because a man ain't had an opportunity to be bad don't make him good," Mr. Skinner reminded her.

"Daddy's right about that," Dola concurred. "And this just might be Lucky Jack's opportunity."

With his dark brown hair curling out from under a tattered canvas cap, Punky tottered to his mother's side. "Mama, carry me," he entreated. Dola plucked him up and felt a twinge of pain in her lower back. She herded Rita Ann and Tommy-Blue behind the farm wagon. Corrie stayed with her father in front of the wagon. They all leaned forward to listen.

"Ace, you and your brothers look like you just walked out of Hades!" Lucky Jack called to the men on the burros as they approached. Even from a distance, O. T. could see pinkish red eyes peeking out from the harlequin costume of alkali dust. The men rode the burros bareback.

The one called Ace wiped the dusty barrel of his carbine across the sleeve of his shirt, like a fiddler drawing a bow. "Gately, finding you out here is proof enough that we're still in Hades," he yelled. "You better be packing a gun."

Corrie flinched. Mr. Skinner shoved her behind the wagon with the others. He crossed his arms and leaned against the wagon, positioning himself between the men and his family.

"Orion, you be careful," Dola whispered.

"I don't need a gun until you start sneakin' around to shoot me in the back," Lucky Jack countered.

The man stepped off the burro. He brushed dirt and dust off his shirt and trousers while keeping the barrel of his Winchester '94 saddle-ring carbine pointed toward the ground. Every individual dust-caked hair stood out as his eyes peered from under eyelashes heavy with "desert mascara." "Don't matter. Your luck's run out. It's time to get this over. You're dead. You lit shuck out of Santa Fe, Silver City, Tucson, and Nogales, and now we find you when we ain't looking for you." The man studied O. T. Skinner. "I don't know you, mister, so don't get in the way." He abruptly paused in his tirade. "Say, have you got water on that wagon?"

"You'll have to come through all of us to get it," Charlie Fred fumed, his hand resting on the grip of his revolver.

In contrast to the dirt on Ace's face, his teeth looked fairly white when he forced a smile. He yanked off his hat to reveal a mostly bald, sweating head. "I don't reckon that would slow down a bullfrog." He wiped his head with a dirty red bandanna and replaced his hat. "I presume Wasco is hidin' like the bushwhacker he is."

With his belly on the hot desert dirt, Wasco propped the carbine up with his elbows. "I'm over here with a carbine pointed at your belly, Ace. I'm surely hopin' I get a chance to use it."

Ace Wilkins led his burro a couple of steps closer and pointed toward O. T. "Who's the other man?"

"Mr. Skinner owns the wagon," Lucky Jack replied. "He, his wife, and children were generous enough to give us a ride to Goldfield from Tonopah."

Ace brushed the dirt and dust off his thick mustache. "Did you hold them at knife point?"

"They are sincere Christian people, and we accepted their charity." Lucky Jack and Charlie Fred held their ground as Wilkins approached.

Wilkins stared past O. T. at the wagon. "I'm glad to hear that. All we was lookin' for was a little water."

Charlie Fred, his hand still on the grip of his revolver, stepped in front of Wilkins. "We don't have any to spare," he snarled.

"Nonsense. We would never withhold a cup of water from any man," Dola called out as she set Punky down in the wagon.

Ace Wilkins tipped his hat in her direction. The other two men stepped off their burros and ambled toward the Skinner wagon.

"You don't know what kind of men these are, Mrs. Skinner," Wasco growled from his position behind the Joshua trees.

"Don't matter," O. T. added. "Dola's right. The Lord causes the rain to fall on the just and the unjust. Jesus said even our enemies deserve a cup of cold water. You boys come on and get yourselves a drink." *Lord, I can usually judge a man by his eyes, but these men are so dirty, it's like starin' into a hole in the ground.* "We don't have a whole lot of water left, Mr. Wilkins, but we won't turn you men away thirsty."

Lucky Jack Gately glared at the Wilkins brothers all the way to the wagon, but remained where he stood, between the wagon and the burros. Charlie Fred kept his hand on his revolver. Wasco's finger still caressed the trigger of the shotgun. All three watched the dusty gunmen's every move.

The Wilkins brothers paused near the back of the wagon. They eyed the goods and the children.

Skinner held out his hand to the nearest man. "Most folks call me O. T."

There was an awkward pause. The shortest of the Wilkins brothers pushed back his dusty hat, revealing a clean strip of forehead next to his hairline. He glanced at his brothers and then reached out and shook Skinner's hand. "I'm Trey Wilkins. These are my brothers, Ace and Deuce." His dust-covered mustache was the thickest of the three.

Tommy-Blue bounced on the toes of his worn brown boots. His eyes danced in time with his feet. "Ace, Deuce, and Trey?" He grinned. "That sounds like a poker hand!" His chin dropped to his chest. "Not that I know anything about poker, of course," he mumbled.

"Son, don't be disrespectful of a man's name," his father scolded.

Ace Wilkins propped his carbine against the wagon wheel and dusted off his shirt sleeves. "That's all right, son. Kids is honest. I like that. We got strange names, I reckon. Our daddy ran a faro layout up at Creede, Colorado. So you ain't too far wrong. I always figured they stopped at three because they didn't know another word for four."

"'I cannot tell what the dickens his name is,'" Rita Ann recited.

Ace Wilkins peered over the wagon at the tallest of the children. Rita Ann pushed her glasses up on her nose. "*The Merry Wives of Windsor*, Act 3, scene 2," she reported.

Dola pulled three crystal glasses out of the crate next to the fourteen-spoke wagon wheel. When she stood up, she brushed a strand of dark brown hair out of her eyes and waited for the men to approach. "Our Rita Ann likes reading Shakespeare."

"So did our mama . . ." Trey Wilkins reminisced. He was the only one of the three who had tucked his trousers inside the vamp of his tall leather boots.

Dola looked each man in the eyes as she handed him a spotless crystal glass.

"We don't need to use your best service," Deuce Wilkins protested. "Just a ladle will do for anyone this dirty."

Corrie laced her fingers together and rested them on top of her head. "Mama always uses our best dishes when we have company," she reported. "We have a very nice set of Dresden china also. It used to belong to my grandma."

Ace Wilkins gulped down two glasses of water and took off his hat and poured the third over his head. The rivulets cut furrows through the dirt on his face. He glanced back out at the men standing with their guns. "Don't reckon Gately told you folks about how that Mexican woman got killed down in Nogales, did he?"

Dola felt suddenly short of breath as she stared out at Lucky Jack and Charlie Fred. *Killed a woman? Lord, protect us from evil . . . and the evil one.*

"We didn't ask about his past, and he didn't ask about ours," O. T. interjected. He kept his arms folded across his chest as he spoke. "So we won't ask you about yours either, Mr. Wilkins. I figure it's the Lord and the government's job to judge people. My job is to treat folks decent."

Ace Wilkins handed the crystal glass back to Dola. "I figured you ought to know what kind of company you and the children are keepin'."

"Why?" O. T. challenged. "A man isn't limited by the mistakes he's made in the past, is he?"

Ace Wilkins shrugged and then lowered his voice. "But it does give you a clue to the mistakes he's prone to make in the future. Lucky Jack just might not be the type you want travelin' with the wife and kids."

"Wilkins! There was more than one who died that day!" Lucky Jack shouted from near the Joshua trees.

Ace Wilkins picked up his carbine. "My gun wasn't fired that day, and you would have known that had you stuck around."

Tommy-Blue darted under the wagon and crawled over to the desert side. "Did you really kill a woman, Lucky Jack?" he hollered from his hands and knees.

Gately and Charlie Fred strolled back to the wagon. "There's a lot more to the story. I'll tell you all the real facts after our company crawls back into their snake hole," he insisted.

Deuce Wilkins poured a whole glass of water on his bandanna and down the front of his dirty cotton shirt. Then he peeked under the wagon at Tommy-Blue. "Don't let him lie to you, boy," he insisted.

"You got your water," Charlie Fred hollered. "You can jist ride off on those donkeys."

Corrie crept back around the wagon to where her father was standing. "Your burros look tired," she declared.

"Ain't they somethin'?" Trey Wilkins tilted his head back and washed his eyes out with half a glass of water. He let the water drip down his face as he glanced out at the animals. "It took us two hours this morning to find and fetch 'em. But we didn't have much choice. We needed to find some way out of the hills."

Tommy-Blue climbed out from under the wagon. "What happened to your horses?"

"No horses, son," Ace Wilkins announced. "We have us a motorcar."

"An automobile? You own an automobile?" Rita Ann gasped.

Ace stared across the desert in the direction of the Silver Peak range. "We sure do, missy. But it got hot on us."

"I've never ridden in a motorcar," Rita Ann added. "Where are you going?"

"Me and Daddy rode in a motor truck in Arizona," Corrie boasted as she crawled up in the wagon.

Ace fingered the trigger on his carbine. "We've got some big-payin' jobs waitin' for us in Goldfield," Ace reported. "Our kind of work, provided we can get that rig runnin', of course."

Corrie pulled Punky over to her lap. "We're going to Goldfield too!" she announced.

Ace Wilkins stepped closer to O. T. "Mr. Skinner, I'll be blunt. We need some of your water for our automobile."

"You don't get any. There's just enough to get us to Goldfield," Wasco shouted. His carbine now lay on the dirt in front of him.

Deuce Wilkins spun around, facing the Joshua trees. He drew his revolver with his right hand, still holding the crystal glass in his left.

Rita Ann gasped.

Tommy-Blue covered his eyes.

Corrie hugged Punky close, and the baby stuck a fat, sticky finger in her ear.

O. T. pulled off his hat and cleared his throat. "Mr. Wilkins, I'll have to ask you, please, to put your gun away. It frightens my children."

Deuce Wilkins glared. "You ain't go no idea who you're talkin' to!"

Dola, with Rita Ann tagging along, stepped up next to her husband. "What difference does it make who you are or who we are? It's not appropriate for you to be threatening others with firearms in front of children. I'm sure your mother would say the same thing if she were here."

"Why did you say that?" Deuce demanded.

"That's what Mama always tells people," Rita Ann mumbled.

Dola felt a lock of hair droop down on her forehead but refused to reach up and adjust it. "Is it true?" she asked Deuce.

"Put up your pistol, Deuce," Ace ordered. "She's right. We were taught better." He turned back to Skinner. "But the fact is, we desperately need water, and we are not beyond acting desperate to get it."

O. T. stepped over to the water barrel and peered inside. "I reckon we'll make Goldfield by dark. We'll split what we have with you."

Wasco picked up his carbine. "You're aimin' to pay for the water, ain't you?" he called out.

Ace Wilkins rubbed the back of his neck and glanced at the children. "I reckon . . ." Then he stepped toward O. T. "What do you want for the water, Mr. Skinner?"

"We wouldn't think of chargin' a man for water any more than we'd charge him for breathin' air," O. T. replied.

"Well, it's a cinch you ain't never been to Goldfield," Trey Wilkins mumbled.

Ace peered down into the water barrel. "Now I need one more favor. Have you got an old three-gallon tin we could borrow? I don't have a thing to carry it in."

Dola pointed toward the large green trunk on the back of the wagon. "They can use the olive crock," she announced.

Ace stepped closer to the wagon. "The what?"

"Orion and I were given a three-gallon olive crock for a wedding present, but we never lived in olive country. So it's never been used for anything but hauling water. It has a nice clamp-down lid. You can return it to us in Goldfield," she suggested.

All six Skinners, plus Lucky Jack, Wasco, and Charlie Fred, lined up among the Joshua trees and watched the ceramic-crock-laden Wilkins brothers ride west into the alkali flats.

When they dropped over the rise in the barren desert floor, the spectators returned to the wagon. Lucky Jack helped them load up their supplies. "You know, you folks might just be too nice," he said.

"Don't be ridiculous, Mr. Gately." Dola smiled, revealing her straight, very white teeth. "No one on the face of the earth has ever been too nice."

"Except Jesus," Rita Ann observed.

"And look what happened to Him," Lucky Jack added.

"What happened to Him was the will of God. We should be so fortunate," O. T. concluded.

Lucky Jack shook his head. "You folks are . . ."

Corrie's blue eyes opened wide. "We're what?"

"Eh . . . different," Lucky Jack mumbled.

"I surely wish I could see their motorcar," Tommy-Blue added. "Ridin' in one must be like ridin' on the train. Did you ever ride on a train, Lucky Jack?"

"In 'em, on 'em and under 'em," Wasco laughed.

"Chances are we'll see a number of motorcars in Goldfield," O. T. said. "Right now we'd better pack up and get on the road. We'll be racin' sundown. And if that wind picks back up, we could strey off the trail in the dark." He helped Dola climb up into the wagon. "We don't have enough water now to make that kind of mistake."

"I don't know why you gave 'em that water," Charlie Fred fumed.

O. T.'s voice was very soft. "I believe it was our water to give."

Lucky Jack Gately was the last one to climb into the wagon. He sat next to Tommy-Blue and Corrie, behind Mrs. Skinner. "I take it you've known those men for a while?" Dola asked him.

"You folks have probably heard about the Gately-Wilkins feud?" he probed.

O. T. shook his head. "Eh . . . nope. I reckon I haven't."

"Well," Wasco inserted, "you have now."

"Did you really kill a woman in Nogales?" Corrie asked him.

"Corrie Lou Skinner, we don't ask questions like that! It's not proper," Mrs. Skinner scolded.

Corrie's chin dropped as her dusty face reddened.

"It's okay, darlin'. I don't mind you askin'. But it ain't a very pretty memory. About six years ago there was a little train trouble north of Telluride, Colorado. Two railroad companies were trying to beat each other to be the first with a line into the silver mines.

Both sides hired some guards to protect their workers. Me, Charlie Fred, and Wasco worked for one railroad company. The Wilkins brothers worked for the other. We spent most of the summer and fall takin' potshots at the other side. They called it the Rocky Mountain Railroad War. You remember readin' about that, don't you?"

"Eh, no, sir, I guess we never did," O. T. apologized.

"Did anyone get shot dead?" Corrie questioned.

"A few," Lucky Jack replied.

"Who won the war?" Tommy-Blue asked.

"Son, sometimes nobody wins. Our side got the rails built first, but then the mines played out. It's an abandoned line now. Well, the Wilkins brothers were hoppin' mad. They took it personal. Claimed we were to blame for some of the violence. So I was in Nogales, Mexico, about a year ago and . . ."

"What were you doing in Mexico?" Rita Ann asked from the wagon seat between her parents.

"Now that, darlin', is one I'd rather not answer."

"How come?" Rita Ann pressed.

"Rita Ann, don't you hound Mr. Gately," Dola chided.

"But how am I going to learn anything if nobody tells me?" she complained. "'O thou monster Ignorance, how deformed dost thou look!' Sir Nathaniel in *Love's Labor Lost.*"

Lucky Jack plucked off his bowler and plopped it down on her head. "Some things is better left unlearned," he remarked.

"Please continue your story, Mr. Gately," Mrs. Skinner urged.

Tommy-Blue reached up to grab Lucky Jack's hat off Rita Ann's head, but she held it down tight with both hands.

"Me and a pard named Tully Two-Nose were walkin' down this narrow street when—"

"Did he really have two noses?" Corrie pressed.

"Not that I could tell, darlin'. I never had a chance to ask how he got that name. Anyway, bullets started flying at us from the bal-

cony of a small hotel. Tully took two bullets in the head and fell dead.
I dove behind some 100-pound sacks of rice and shot back without
thinkin' too much about it. I just wanted to get them to quit."

The dust was blowing harder, and Tommy-Blue tied his red bandanna around his mouth and nose. "Who was shootin' at you?" he
called out.

"I had no idea at the time. I couldn't see who was behind the
balcony window."

"It was the Wilkins brothers, wasn't it?" Rita Ann quizzed.

"That's what I was told afterwards. They also claimed one of my
bullets ricocheted off something and struck a Mexican woman and
killed her."

"Oh, no!" Rita Ann gasped.

Dola watched Lucky Jack's eyes as he told the story. *Mr. Gately,
you are a convincing storyteller, but it remains to be seen if you're a truthful one. One thing's for sure, you've captured the attention of my oldest
daughter.*

"What did you do then?" Rita Ann began to slowly rock back
and forth on the wagon seat.

A sudden dirt devil made everyone clamp their eyes shut and set
Punky to coughing.

"Rita Ann," Mrs. Skinner instructed, "give Mr. Gately back his
hat. He'll need it to keep the dirt out of his eyes."

With a long face, Rita Ann returned the hat. "What did you do
when you heard that the woman was shot?" she repeated.

"I rode hard back across the border into Mexico. I didn't have
anyone to witness for me what really happened. I knew the Wilkinses
would make it out to be murder and get me shot by a firing squad.
Course, that's not the last time the Gately-Wilkins feud resulted in
gunplay. You've probably heard about that standoff at Cave Creek.
Well, don't believe those lies," Lucky Jack urged.

"Don't believe I've ever heard about that," O. T. declared.

"Good," Lucky Jack continued. "'Cause I ain't got no mind to tell you something that ain't the truth."

The dust boiled in from the northwest.

The wagon trail continued southwest.

The mules slowed down.

The sun sank toward the Silver Peak range.

The water barrel emptied into thirsty mouths.

The wagon axles creaked like a quartet of wounded geese.

And finally Columbia Mountain loomed closer as they crept across the desert toward the base of Malpais Mesa.

By the time O. T. Skinner brought the wagon to a stop at the edge of town, the electric lights had flickered on. The dust off the streets filtered a monochromatic golden tinge to every building and person and object. Stretched out in every direction were dust-covered tents, half-built dust-covered buildings, and massive dust-covered mine shaft headworks that loomed like tombstones in a giant's graveyard.

Silas Paul "Punky" Skinner lay sound asleep in his mother's lap.

Lucky Jack, Wasco, and Charlie Fred had hopped to the street as soon as the wagon slowed down. They now pulled their satchels out of the wagon.

"I'm hungry," Tommy-Blue fussed.

"Where are we going to sleep tonight, Daddy?" Corrie called from under an old bed sheet that had been her protection from the dust.

"I'm just fixin' to figure that out, darlin'," O. T. replied. He climbed down off the wagon and sauntered over to Lucky Jack Gately and the others. "It took a little longer than I reckoned, but we made it."

"Can't thank you folks enough," Lucky Jack replied. "Wasco, Charlie Fred, and I want to do a little something for you, and we—"

"We won't accept pay, if that's what you're hintin' at. No man gets money for doin' his Christian duty," O. T. insisted.

Lucky Jack put his hand on Skinner's muscular shoulder. "Now hear me out, O. T. You folks haven't been around many gold boomtowns. Prices are high, life is fast, there are few places to stay, and . . ."

Skinner stared through the shadows of the noisy, busy town. "We'll just pitch our tent in a vacant field and—"

Lucky Jack waved his arm toward the acres of buildings and tents. "Where?"

"I reckon there's an empty lot somewhere."

"That's the point. Every lot in town and all the land around town is staked off. You move in the middle of the night, and folks will accuse you of claim jumping. I tell you, there will be bullets flyin' and tempers let loose." Lucky Jack pulled a folded piece of paper out of his pocket. "You don't want to endanger the children."

O. T. pulled off his hat and scratched his head. "Claim jumpin'? We aren't interested in gold claims. We're leavin' for California tomorrow."

"We aren't leavin' until I get my olive crock back," Dola called out from the wagon seat. "I aim to raise olives in my garden when we get to Dinuba."

Gately handed O. T. the folded paper. "Here's what we suggest you do. Take this deed. It was a part of the deal when we bought the mining lease. It's the title to one giant city lot somewhere to the east on Columbia Street. You go over there tonight and pitch your tent. If anyone asks you about it, show them the deed. You folks just stay right there until those mules gain some strength and you get your crock back, although I wouldn't count on those Wilkins brothers keepin' their word."

"We can't take your place," O. T. objected.

"It don't matter to us if you stay there," Wasco insisted. "We ain't goin' to use that lot for nothing anyway."

"When you leave town, hand us back the deed," Charlie Fred added. "It's officially your lot as long as you're in Goldfield."

O. T. held the paper out toward Lucky Jack. "That's a generous proposition, boys, but we couldn't impose on—"

"Orion," Dola called out, "I think it's a friendly offer, and the children need some rest. We will have to pitch our tent on someone's ground—it might as well be on the place of nice gentlemen like Mr. Gately and his friends."

O. T. Skinner hesitated and then took the folded paper back from Gately's hand. "Mama says it's okay, so I reckon we'll accept your gracious hospitality. Where can I find you in the mornin' to give this back to you?"

"Check at the Northern Saloon," Wasco replied. "I got a friend who runs the place. He'll know where we're stayin'."

"Where are you going to sleep tonight?" Tommy-Blue asked.

"We'll find a place," Charlie Fred replied.

Tommy-Blue lifted his arm and scratched. "You can come camp over at our tent."

"I imagine your tent is full," Lucky Jack laughed.

"Sometimes Daddy and me sleep outside," Tommy-Blue reported. "You could sleep outside with us."

"Son, don't pester these men. They need to check on their lease and make their plans." O. T. climbed back into the wagon. "I'll look you up tomorrow."

"Good night, Mr. Gately," Rita Ann called out.

The tall, blond-headed man tipped his bowler. "Good night, Rita Ann, darlin'."

O. T. waited for the men to wander out of sight before he started up the wagon. The street was crowded with freight wagons, horses, and men milling about as if waiting for something to happen.

"He calls everyone darlin', you know," Corrie pointed out.

"He didn't call me darlin'," Tommy-Blue proclaimed.

Columbia Street stretched east beyond the power of the electric street lights. Lot #124 was beyond the bladed dirt road, way beyond any semblance of a city. But not beyond the tents. Scattered like huge clumps of sagebrush in the desert night were tents of all shapes and sizes. There was enough light for the Skinners to drive on the street, but it was a struggle to keep from running into the crates, wagons, horses, and bedrolls littering the roadsides and cross streets. It looked as if half the population just camped out wherever people first hit town.

O. T. walked ahead, tugging the mule's bridle. Corrie clutched her daddy's arm and carried the small brass lantern. Mrs. Skinner held the lead lines while Rita Ann clutched Punky. Tommy-Blue sat beside them.

"Where you headed?" a man at a small campfire called out.

"Lot #124," O. T. answered.

The man's face in the flickering light looked like a goateed villain in a melodrama. "This is lot #94. Keep going. Cross the dry streambed and check out the numbers. They painted numbers on rocks, but some of the boundaries got moved."

The streambed was indiscernible from the rest of the desert. It was not deep nor rocky nor vegetation-lined—just flat, dry sand. About 100 feet from the previous numbered stone, O. T. stared at a foot-wide rock that had 124 scrawled on it in red paint.

Corrie held out the lantern in front of her. "The 4 is backwards, Daddy . . . and there's a tent already here!"

"What's the matter?" Dola called out from the wagon seat.

"There's someone camped on our lot, Mama," Corrie called out.

"What are we going to do, Orion?" Dola asked anxiously.

He pulled off his hat and ran his fingers through his hair. "Maybe this isn't the right place. Maybe we'll go on out to the hills and sleep under the wagon."

"Again?" Rita Ann grumbled.

"I promised the girls a tent tonight," Dola informed him.

Corrie laid her head on his arm. She didn't bother brushing her bangs out of her eyes. "I'm really tired, Daddy."

"I'm hungry," Tommy-Blue fussed.

A deep male voiced boomed from inside the shadowy tent set back thirty feet on lot #124. "Who's out there?"

O. T. strained to peer through the dark. "Didn't aim to disturb you, mister."

"This lot's occupied. Move along." The deep voice echoed out of the tent, but still there was no movement. "Say, do you have any whiskey?"

"No. We were just looking for lot #124," Rita Ann called out.

Suddenly a huge head poked out of one end of the tent. "You got kids with you?"

"My whole family," O. T. answered.

The man pointed back inside the tent. "Me too. Got them all bedded down for the night . . . I think. I jist got in myself."

O. T. stepped over toward the tent and lowered his voice. Corrie trailed after him, carrying the lantern. "We didn't mean to wake you up," he said, "but Rita Ann's right. We were just lookin' for lot #124."

"Why?" The word blasted out of the man's mouth as if to silence any response.

O. T. took the lantern and tried to see the man who was talking. "We've got the patent deed on lot #124 and—"

Suddenly a huge, unshaven man wearing long underwear cut off at the elbows and knees staggered out of the tent. He scratched his wild red hair and squinted at the lantern. His tone was more subdued. "Can I see the deed, mister?"

O. T. handed him the folded, wrinkled deed. The man bent low to hold it in the lantern light. His fat fingers spread out and made his hand seem wider.

He let out a deep sigh, shook his head, and handed the paper back to O. T. "I reckon you're right, mister. You've got the deed. I was told that them that held the deed was out of state, and I'd be able to squat here for a spell. Sorry about that. I ain't a claim jumper nor a lot stealer. The missus is feelin' poorly, but I'll wake her and the kids. We'll get moved as quick as we can."

"You'll do nothing of the kind," Dola called out from the wagon. "There's enough room for two tents on the lot, I presume."

The big man pointed behind his tent. "Yes, ma'am, it's a big lot—150 by 300 feet—so they say. I ain't stepped it off myself."

"We'll pitch our tent behind yours," O. T. told him. "You folks stay right where you are."

The big man reeked of alcohol. "We're broke. We can't pay you for the night," he mumbled.

"What do you mean, pay us?"

The man stared down at his feet. He was wearing red socks with holes in both toes. "They're charging a dollar a night to pitch a tent."

"A dollar?" O. T. rubbed the two-day stubble on his chin. "Why, in Oklahoma you can rent a big hotel room for a dollar!"

"Not in Goldfield, you cain't."

"Well, you certainly don't have to pay anything," O. T. offered. "Right now I just want to pitch our tent and put the children to bed."

"Did you mean what you said about lettin' us stay the night for free?" the man pressed.

Skinner held out his hand. "You got my word on it."

The men shook hands.

"My name's Rokker. Elias Rokker."

"O. T. Skinner."

"How many kids you got, Mr. Rokker?" Rita Ann asked.

"Five. No, I mean four. The oldest is about your size, missy."

"My name's Rita Ann," she called out. "What's her name?"

"Him. My oldest is a boy. Jared."

"Mr. Rokker, we'll do proper introducin' in the mornin'," O. T. interjected. "Right now I've got a family and two mules to bed down."

"Ain't no livery on this side of the riverbed," Rokker reported.

"Don't matter. I couldn't afford it anyway," O. T. replied. "I'll park the wagon and picket the mules out in the lot. They're too tired to do anything but sleep."

"Watch out for that old gal on the lot straight up the slope of the hill behind us. She sleeps in a wooden rocker with a gun across her lap."

Corrie stared off toward the back of the darkened lot. "Why?"

"She claims there's gold under that sandpile of hers. Wants $50,000 for that lot. Can you imagine that?" Rokker declared.

"$50,000!" O. T. gasped. "I know banks in Oklahoma that don't have that much money."

"The banks have it around here. Course, the banks is mostly all in Tonopah," Rokker explained.

"We'll watch out for the lady back there," O. T. assured him. "Maybe we'll get a chance to visit in the mornin'."

A boy with curly red hair stuck his head out of the tent.

"Can I come with you?" Rita Ann called.

"When?"

"When you visit the Rokkers tomorrow."

"I suppose so," O. T. replied. He and Corrie hiked back toward the wagon.

"Thanks, Skinner. It's real decent of you to let us stay," Rokker called out from his tent.

"Say," O. T. asked, "where can we get some water? We pretty much drank the barrel down comin' in from Tonopah."

"The mines have plenty of water, but they don't share with anyone. Mostly the drinkin' water comes from Rabbit Springs."

"Where's that?" Skinner asked.

Mr. Rokker pointed back down the dirt street in the direction they had traveled. "About two miles west, at the base of Malpais Mesa."

"I'll have to wait until morning to go fill my water kegs."

"You better take cash. I hear they're charging two dollars a cask, and they want silver or gold."

"They're really selling water?"

"Someone is. It's the desert, Skinner. Sometimes water is more valuable than gold."

"That ain't right," O. T. protested. "I just don't think children should be denied a drink of water or a bath."

The big man turned as he entered the tent. "Welcome to Goldfield."

Even in the dark everyone knew what to do. The routine was the same. O. T. and Tommy-Blue set the tent poles. Corrie held a lantern and Punky's hand. Rita Ann and Mrs. Skinner unpacked the wagon. Within fifteen minutes the tent lines were taut, and the worn pine-green carpet was rolled out across the dirt floor. The narrow single bed frame was bolted together. The feather mattress was stretched out on the sagging wooden planks. Three quilt pallets were neatly lined up opposite the bed. And the lantern was hung from the clothesline that stretched between the two poles.

The mules were fed and picketed.

The wagon was parked out near the edge of the street.

Faces and hands were wiped with a damp cloth.

They devoured cold white beans and chili peppers, with only stale bread to soothe the hot spice, since the water was gone.

The girls combed their hair.

Teeth were dry-brushed.

Prayers were said aloud by every family member, except the one dressed only in underpants and sound asleep in the middle of the feather mattress.

Rita Ann, Corrie, and Tommy-Blue crawled under the flannel sheets on the pallets. After the lantern was turned out, Dola hung up her dress and pulled on her cotton nightgown. O. T. lay on top of the covers, barefoot, wearing denim trousers and a torn undershirt.

Dola stretched out on her back, her head on the pillowcase stuffed with rags. "It's been a long day, Orion." Her right arm flopped down to the carpeted floor.

Punky slept on his stomach between them. O. T. laced his fingers under his pillowless head. "It's been a long year, darlin'."

"I'm not complainin'," she whispered.

He leaned his head toward hers, only inches away. "I know. You never complain."

"It's been tough for you, Orion. I know that. But we'll be in California in a few days. Everything will be better then. I hear the weather's so mild they sleep out on the veranda every night from May to October," she offered.

"A veranda sounds nice. Let's build us a house with a veranda," he said. "Of course . . ." His voice softened even more. "That's what I promised you about Oklahoma."

She reached over in the darkness and laid her hand on his stubbly cheek. "I liked Oklahoma."

She could feel his jaw move as he spoke. "But we were starvin' to death."

His rough, chapped lips kissed her fingers. "I didn't like that part," she admitted.

"You know, the only good thing about goin' to bed tired ever' night is that I don't have time to think about this miserable life I'm givin' you, Dola Mae Davis."

"Don't you start feelin' sorry for me, Orion Tower Skinner. I'd rather be in a tent with you than in a mansion anywhere else."

"I've moved you sixteen times in twelve years, and that's counting the last six months as one move."

"Eighteen times, if you count living with Granny those two summers," she corrected him.

"Twelve years, and we can put everything we own in a wagon and have room to tote strangers," he sighed.

"That's not what you said to Mr. Gately this mornin'."

"I know, and I meant it. You and the kids are everything I ever wanted. Now I just want to find our place and settle down and enjoy you all."

The tent was quiet for a moment. In the distance they heard a gunshot or the backfire of a motorcar. Dogs began barking. Somewhere an angry woman shouted.

"I think a vineyard sounds nice," she whispered.

"Do you think you can get along livin' next door to Pegasus, Pearl, and those dogs of theirs?" he asked.

"Do you?" she countered.

"I wish I knew the answer to that. All I know is that Goldfield is not the kind of place I want to live in and raise kids in. I haven't seen a tree for four days. Water's two miles away. I didn't see a rose-bush or a garden anywhere in town."

"It was dark," she replied.

"Did you see anything that looked like a garden?" he quizzed.

"No, and I haven't heard a bird sing in a week. Sometimes it feels like we've moved to the absolute edge of creation. Are you planning on us leaving early in the morning for California?"

"I need to get up early and go see about water. We can't leave until we have plenty of water. They say the trip to Lone Pine is bad."

She turned on her side and tried to scoot her head closer toward him. Her voice was no more than a soft whisper. "We could stay one day more and let the mules and the children rest. Did you notice how Ada and Ida are slowin' down? I trust they will make it to California. We could leave early the next day with plenty of water. I'd really like to wait until the Wilkins brothers bring me my olive crock. Besides my ring, it's about the only wedding present we have left."

Orion reached his hand across the sleeping toddler and clasped her fingers. Both hands felt chapped, rough, and callused. "Dola, dar-lin', wouldn't it be something to drive across the desert in one of those motorcars?"

"What would we do with Ida and Ada?" she cautioned.

"I didn't mean really doin' it." He squeezed her hand. "I was just supposin'."

"Those motorcars scare me," she admitted. "Have you noticed the way horses buck and shy when one rolls by?"

O. T. took a deep breath and let it out slowly. "Well, I hear they break down a lot too. But wouldn't it be something to just get in that rig and point it in any direction you want to go and then take off? 'Where are you headed?' someone would ask. 'I'm goin' to California.' . . . 'I'm goin' to Texas.' . . . 'I'm goin' to Idaho.' . . . Well, maybe not Idaho."

"You got to buy gasoline for it. Now where's a person going to buy gasoline out in this desert?"

"I know. It ain't practical," he agreed.

He continued to clutch her fingers. "I heard those tires explode if you hit something sharp."

"Not the solid ones."

"And they heat up in the desert. That's what happened to the Wilkinses, remember?"

"I know, I know," O. T. said. "I just let my mind run away with me for a while. May the Lord forgive me for covetin'."

He pulled her hand over to his lips and kissed her fingers. Punky fussed and rolled over. They separated their hands and rolled to the sides of the mattress.

"Orion?" Dola whispered.

"Yes?"

"I've never seen such hatred as between Mr. Gately and the Wilkinses. If it's a matter of law, they should go to the authorities."

O. T. put his hands back under his head. "Pride and vengeance are slave drivers, Dola Mae. I think they've hated each other so long they don't know any other solution but to shoot it out."

"Both sides treated us nice enough, but they were ready to kill each other on sight. I was scared, Orion," she whispered. "Very, very scared. I wish I could be like you, so peaceful and calm."

"I was calm 'cause I couldn't for the life of me figure out what to do . . . but peaceful? It was all I could do to keep from grabbin' up the kids and go runnin' out into the desert," he admitted.

"Yes, but it's not what a man feels like doing, but what he actually does that makes a man. You're my strength, Orion Tower Skinner."

"I reckon a place like Goldfield has lots of folks on the verge of violence. You mix gold and alcohol and jam them into a hot, barren sandpile, and there's bound to be trouble," he added.

"Maybe we should leave early tomorrow. But what about these folks, the Rokkers?"

"I'll ask Lucky Jack and the others to let them stay awhile. That's all we can do. What about your olive crock?"

"*Our* olive crock. I'm sure that motorcar has made it to Goldfield by now," she declared.

"Do you think the children will be rested enough?" he asked. "I don't know how they get along so well, always travelin', never settlin' down."

"It's about the only life they know anymore." There was no remorse in her voice—just resignation.

He turned back toward Dola and whispered, "If I dwelt on that, it would bring tears to my eyes."

Her hand fumbled across the mattress and began to rub the back of his neck. "I didn't mean that to judge you. It's just that I'd like to let them go to the same school for an entire year sometime."

"That's a promise," he answered. "This year we won't move them out of school."

He was silent so long she thought he had gone to sleep.

Then a deep-voiced question came: "When you were a young lady living in Lake Jackson, and you thought about married life . . . did you think of this?"

"I thought that someday I would find a man who absolutely adored me and treated me as the queen of his life. And I always thought I'd have healthy, happy children that I could raise in the nurture and admonition of the Lord."

"That's all you ever dreamed about?"

"And . . . and that we would live in a big, old house overlookin' Galveston Bay."

"See, I knew it!" The words spurted out like watermelon seeds.

"I was teasing you, Orion Skinner. Besides, two out of three isn't bad, and I got the best two."

"We aren't ever goin' to live in a big house overlookin' a bay."

"I am," she declared.

"Oh?"

"I've got a mansion in the sky, and so do you."

The voice was high but insistent. "Well, maybe you two could go to that mansion and visit a spell, because there are some people in this tent trying to get to sleep."

"Rita Ann, that is not a proper tone to address your parents," Dola lectured.

"I'm tired, Mama."

"I know, darlin'."

"And I can't get my mind to go to sleep."

"Why do you think that is?" O. T. asked.

"Because of him."

"Who?"

"Jared," Rita Ann declared.

"Who's Jared?" Mr. Skinner quizzed.

"The Rokkers' oldest," Dola answered.

"I didn't see any boy," he said.

"I did," Rita Ann replied.

"So did I," her mother added.

"Go to sleep, darlin'," he insisted. "You don't have to worry about those kinds of things for another six or seven years."

"Seven years!" Rita Ann moaned.

Even though she had tried to clean up, without any water, Dola could still feel dirt on the back of her neck. She closed her eyes and relaxed her shoulders. "Don't worry, darlin'," she shushed. "It's Daddy who's dreamin' now."

# THREE

The ground was soft, powdery beneath the mule's feet as O. T. drove the wagon west early the next morning. The muted sound of hoof-beats and a small cloud of fetlock dust fogged each step. As morning light blued the desert-gray sky, Goldfield's wide, mostly straight but uneven dirt streets looked more pronounced than they had the previous evening. Freight wagons groaned, teamsters shouted, boots scuffled along the boardwalks, and an occasional backfire from a motorcar could be heard, though none were on Columbia Street. The dust had settled from the day before, and Malpais Mesa peered down at Goldfield like a javelina surveying an invasion of ants. Behind the mesa the Montezuma Mountains loomed on the distant horizon, catching the morning's first light. A wave of sunlight was sliding down the mountain range's flank.

As O. T. reached the edge of Goldfield proper, he drove the wagon slowly, surveying each building and peering down every side street. Although the oldest structure in town was less than two years old, many of the unpainted buildings looked well worn.

*The Mint . . . the Peerless . . . the Louvre . . . the Oregon . . . the Monte Carlo . . . the Elite . . . the Hunter . . . the Eagle—takes a lot of money to run eight saloons to a block. And a lot of booze.*

*Never have I seen so many folks trying so frantically to ruin their entire lives. I know You love us all, Lord. And I'm glad . . . 'cause I'd like to pull out of this town as soon as I can. So I'm glad to know You'll stick it out with them.*

*I was right about one thing. There isn't a blade of grass, a flower, a bush, a shrub, or a tree anywhere. There's not a bird in the sky or a squirrel in the yard. It's just pure, old, desolate desert floor, rimmed by a mountain, some hills, and a mesa. Without gold it would be the kind of land folks would pass through in a hurry . . . or avoid completely.*

*Hard to believe that someone actually bothered to come out here and look for gold in the first place. And it's incredible that they actually found it.*

*Kind of like a joke, isn't it, Lord? In the most barren and worthless-looking land, You hid some of earth's most valuable treasures. Kind of like people, I reckon. Sometimes Your spiritual riches are discovered in the most unexpected, unspectacular lives. Makes a man wonder how many more treasures are waitin' to be found . . . in the soil . . . and in the souls of men.*

O. T. rubbed his freshly-shaved chin and then glanced down at his hands. There were calluses, scars, and two fingers that didn't heal straight after they had been broken. A memory of excruciating pain when the loaded wagon wheel dropped on his hand flashed through his mind. He could see Dola's tears at his pain. His mind jumped to having his hand laced in hers the previous night.

*Her hands are just like mine, Lord. They're battered, tough, and old-looking. She isn't thirty, and her hands look fifty. It wasn't that way when I married her. She had the sweetest spirit and the most disarming smile in Texas.*

*She still does.*

*She's lived a hard life, Lord. A real hard life.*

*She's suckled babies and planted corn. Baked pies and picked rocks. Chopped wood before daylight and scrubbed clothes till midnight. She's pushed wagons out of mud holes and scrubbed four children before Sunday school. She's been forced to go weeks without a hot bath and years without a new church dress. And all she does is kiss me and tell me she's the luckiest woman on earth.*

*It ain't right.*

*Lord, I don't deserve anything better than this. I've never been able to save a dollar to my name. I never can make a go of it, no matter how hard I work. But Dola deserves better. She's right . . . Rita Ann, Corrie, and Tommy-Blue need to be in a regular school. Children shouldn't have to sleep on the ground. Not ever' night anyway.*

O. T. stopped the wagon and stared over at the huge canvas banner draped across a twelve-foot-wide store. "Slaughter Clothing and Furnishings: Big Overstock Sale! $6 Dress or Work Shoes—only $3.50. $4 Hats—only $1.90. Lots of other big snaps!" He slapped the lead lines and started up the wagon.

*And ever' child ought to have a new pair of shoes once a year, not worn-out hand-me-downs. Children's shoes shouldn't be more than $2.50. If me and Mama got a new pair, it could cost $17 to shod all of us . . . $17! It might as well be $100.*

*I know it ain't Your fault, Lord; it's mine. I just don't know what to do anymore. How many times can I keep tellin' them it will be better next year?*

*We've been on the road for months, and we still aren't there. It's almost like I don't want to get there. I'm not sure I'll like livin' next to Pegasus and Pearl, but it's got to work out. We have to settle down.*

*I guess I'm askin' for that little vineyard in Dinuba to be our place. The Skinners of Dinuba—that's what we'll be. I reckon that will be all right, even when they ask, "Which Skinner?"*

Several two-story buildings squatted on the horizon as he arrived downtown. Almost every dwelling he passed was a small cabin or tent, scattered without pattern on a lot identified by painted stones.

Smoke curled up from cookstoves. Dogs ran in packs, darting down alleys and between rigs. The dry, stale taste of the air foretold another hot day. When O. T. reached the two-story buildings, he saw wagons and carriages parked alongside the eight-foot-wide covered wooden sidewalks. Electricity and telephone wires crisscrossed each other. Twenty-foot poles pierced the dirt streets at every corner.

When he reached the intersection of Main and Crook, he pulled over by the Northern Saloon. Even at the break of day, it looked busy inside.

*That's where Lucky Jack and the others were headed. I hope they come look us up, 'cause I'd hate to have to go in there lookin' for them to give the deed back.*

He surveyed the four corners of downtown Goldfield. *Well, I reckon this intersection tells it all—the Northern, the Hermitage, the Palace, and the Mohawk. The two principal occupations in this town must be miner and bartender.*

A man wearing ballooned wool britches tucked into his plaid socks just below his knees, plaid long-sleeved shirt, and a short-billed cap waved a sheaf of papers at him as he drove by. "You lookin' for a mining lease to work?" he shouted.

O. T. glanced over and tipped his hat but kept the mules at a steady plod. "No, sir." *If that's the style of clothes they wear around here, I'm in the wrong town . . . the wrong state!*

The man's black patent leather low-tops lapped halfway over the edge of the wooden sidewalk. "You lookin' for a job?"

Skinner pulled over toward the man and reined up the mules. "No, sir. I reckon I'm just travelin' through." He refused to look at the man for fear of laughing.

The man glanced east, then west, as if trying to locate someone. He stepped down from the sidewalk and lowered his voice. "Mister, are you lookin' for a gal?"

Any hint of a smile dropped off O. T. Skinner's face. "I'm lookin' for water for my family, mister," he snapped. "That's all—just drinkin' water."

The man tugged at the top button on his green and red shirt and then waved the papers at O. T. again. "You'll have an easier time findin' gold in one of these leases than findin' drinkin' water."

O. T. pointed west. "Will this street take me over to Rabbit Springs?"

The man pushed his dark brown felt hat to the back of his head and shoved the papers into the back pocket of his britches. "Yep.

Keep goin' west. It's right at the base of the Malpais, just south of the cemetery."

"Thanks, mister."

"My name's Bryant. Digger Bryant."

"I'm O. T. Skinner, but like I said, we ain't stayin' here long enough to have you remember it."

"Well, listen, Skinner, if you'll haul me some water, I'll pay you two dollars for each twenty-gallon keg, as many as you can haul."

O. T. glanced at the back of the wagon where his two twenty-gallon water casks were perched. "A man shouldn't have to pay for water from a public springs."

"I won't be paying for the water," Bryant hollered. "I'm payin' for haulin' the water. Even when the merchandise is free, a man has to pay freight to have it delivered."

"Sounds like a steep haulin' fee for only a mile or so."

"Gettin' water is expensive. There ain't no cheap way to do it. It takes time and tolls and taxes."

"What do you mean, tolls and taxes?"

"Depends on where you get your water. But you'll find out soon enough."

The man stepped back up on the boardwalk, bent low, and wiped the dust off his patent leather shoes.

Rabbit Springs proved to be as far west of downtown as lot #124 was east. O. T. watched the sunlight creep down the steep flanks of Malpais Mesa as he approached the base. Houses, cabins, tents, and lean-tos thinned out as he entered a small strip of undeveloped barren desert. No sage. No creosote bushes. No Joshua trees. No grass. Nothing but a twelve-by-twelve-foot red rock and mortar tollhouse perched next to a road barricade about 100 feet short of Rabbit Springs. The building looked seasoned and had long narrow gun slots on all four sides.

A man with a short-barreled saddle ring carbine draped casually over his arm stepped out of the tollhouse. "How many barrels you plan on fillin'?"

"Two twenty-gallon kegs," O. T. replied.

The round-faced man rubbed a five-day stubble of beard on his chin and flashed a yellow-toothed grin. "That will be two dollars cash toll fee."

Skinner could hear the water bubble out of the spring and could see tumbling water. "I thought Rabbit Springs was public water," he stated.

The smile dropped off the man's face. "Yep. The water's free." He glanced back toward town. "I ain't sellin' water. This is a toll road."

O. T. turned back. Two more wagons were headed their way. He rubbed the back of his neck. It felt dirty and sticky. He thought about how it would feel to dip his head in the gurgling springs. "Ain't much of a road. It's only 100 feet long."

"It's a short toll road. The road to the springs goes over my property. I got the papers filed on the land. You can go down to the courthouse and check it out. Like I said, that will be a two-dollar toll. Now that's a round trip. I could charge you for both ways. Make up your mind 'cause I've got other customers comin'."

Skinner studied the distance to the concrete pool that housed the springs. "How much if I walk over to the springs?"

The man peeked over the sideboards of the wagon. "It depends on the size of the container."

O. T. shot a glance at the two empty water barrels. "What difference does that make? You said you weren't selling the water."

"Compaction. That's what costs money. All that weight compacts the soil. I'll have a hard time puttin' in a garden if my dirt is hard as a rock. Carryin' them two kegs of water produces two dollars worth of compaction on my soil."

O. T. surveyed the land in all directions. "What if I go around to the north to get to the well that way?"

"I own that too. It's fenced off, and you'd have to come right back here." The man now cradled the carbine in the crook of his arm.

"And to the south?"

"Yep, that's mine too." The short man spat out a wad of tobacco juice and used the carbine like a pointer. "The only thing I don't own is the flank of the mesa, but not even a goat can climb around on that hill. Man will walk on the moon before anyone hikes across that wall."

O. T. studied the rocky cliff that dropped like a steep roof in snow country behind the concrete-lined springs. He pointed north. "Do you own the cemetery?"

"Of course not. Mister, you're wastin' my time. I've got two more rigs rollin' up here now. Are you going to pay the two-dollar toll or not?"

"I think I'll pass on that. It sounds too much like extortion." O. T. felt his right leg cramp. As he reached down to rub his jeans, the tollhouse man checked the lever on the carbine. "Don't you go pullin' no sneak gun! Extortion, is it? A man's got a right to recoup his expenses."

O. T. felt his face and neck flush. "Mister, I ain't got a gun, so I don't know what you're so excited about. You didn't have any expenses here to speak of. All you did was take over this rock cabin, install a barricade, and then string up some barbed wire. You didn't even drag a Fresno scraper down the road. You didn't spread gravel or plow a drain. You're makin' money because folks are too busy tryin' to find gold to worry about your intimidatin' them out of two bucks." O. T. turned the wagon around.

The man trotted after the wagon. "Where you goin'? Ain't no deal around here any better, so you might as well pay me."

"To the cemetery," O. T. mumbled as he slapped the lead lines on the mule's rump.

"What for?" the man shouted.

"To fetch water," Skinner mumbled. He wasn't sure if the man heard him.

The Goldfield Cemetery was as barren as the rest of the desert floor. No greenery. No landscaping. No singing birds, fluttering butterflies, or chirping crickets. The sagebrush had been cut down, and in its place concrete, stone, iron, brass, and wooden tombstones had been erected. Some of the sites had borders of rock or concrete—and a layer of broken glass covering the entire grave in hopes of dissuading coyotes from digging up a loved one's remains. Others had black iron fencing surrounding the individual site for the same reason. There was one Joshua tree and a rough wooden bench at the entrance.

O. T. parked the wagon at the back of the U-shaped loop drive and tied the lead lines to the brake handle of the wagon. He hiked to the back of the cemetery where the flank of Malpais Mesa met the desert dirt like a rough rock wall. The soles of Skinner's boots warmed from the earth's heat, and he felt his toes sweat in his often-mended socks.

A sagging barbed-wire fence stretched perpendicular to the mesa prevented anyone easy access to the springs in their concrete basin jutting out like a peninsula into toll land. The only sound he could hear was the faint whistle of the desert wind in the barbed-wire fence.

O. T. surveyed the rock wall. Out of the corner of his eye he could see the man at the tollbooth lean against the red rock building, watching his next move. There were at least two water wagons rolling up to the barricade. Another was already parked at the well.

*There's a game trail about ten feet up the slope in those rocks. But I don't know what kind of game. Maybe mountain lions . . . or wild goats. Most wouldn't even recognize it as a trail at all. Reminds me of that trail along Buford Crags down on the Cimarron . . . or was it the Republican? I never could see why folks shied away from that trail. I never had any trouble.*

*Course, I didn't have to carry a twenty-gallon cask of water neither.*

*If a man kept his balance, he could probably do it. Prop it right across his shoulders. Balance would be the key.*

*Provided a man was as strong as a mule.*

*And dumb enough to try.*

O. T. removed one empty water barrel from the wagon and propped it across his shoulders.

*Lord, my children, my wife, and me, and my mules need water. I don't see any other way. I don't have two dollars to my name. I'd rather not fall off this cliff and break my leg. And I'd rather not play the fool. But fool or not, I've got to get them some water.*

The jagged edge of descending rock provided shallow toeholds, and he leaned tight against the cliff. Five steps straight up against the mesa, he came to a ledge from two to five inches wide, meandering along the contour of the rock wall in the direction of the springs. In some places it had broken off, leaving a sizable gap.

He adjusted the wooden barrel across the back of his neck. It stretched from shoulder to shoulder, held there with both hands. As he began the trek, his elbows pointed straight out, looking like stubby wings. The thin leather soles of the worn work boots did little to protect his feet from the jagged edges of the rock ledge. His right elbow, which extended toward the mesa cliff, slammed into the rocks several times, shooting pain up his shoulder and tearing at his cotton shirt. He tucked the elbow in as close as he could. Sweat rolled down his neck and back as he inched closer to the springs one slow, careful step at a time.

*If this springs was hidden back in some trees someplace, I'd just crawl in it and take me a bath. I ought to have Dola wash these jeans, but I'm not sure they would stand up to another washing. She could mend them again, I suppose. A man ought to have a second pair of jeans.*

He avoided looking down at the fifteen-foot drop and pushed himself to ignore the pain. *It will be a lot worse than this comin' back, Skinner. You can't whine and complain now.*

The bullet struck rock ten feet to the south of O. T. at the same moment he heard the report from the carbine. Rock chips sprayed his face. He ducked down, though there was nothing to hide behind. His left foot slipped off the cliff as he threw himself against the rock wall to keep from tumbling to the rock pile below. The elbow of his shirt further ripped as he crashed into the rock. He felt blood trickle down his arm. He stared out toward the tollhouse. "What are you doin'?" he yelled.

The man at the tollhouse sauntered toward the mesa, the '73 Winchester still held tight to his shoulder. "I'm shooting snakes!"

O. T. regained his balance, shifted his wide-brimmed felt hat to the front of his head, and then continued toward his goal. "I don't see any snakes!"

"You can thank me for that," the man hollered.

Two wagons slowly drove across the toll road, keeping well behind the man with the gun. O. T. did not take his eyes off the narrow ledge in front of him.

"I'll take my chances. Don't shoot snakes while I'm out here."

"What do you think you're doin' up there?" the man bellowed.

"Getting water for my family. The water's free, and you said this rock wall is public land."

The man let the carbine sag down to his side. "I didn't reckon anyone was dumb enough to try hikin' over it."

"Well, I'm dumb enough . . . and desperate enough," O. T. yelled. The rock ledge widened to almost six inches, and Skinner hastened his pace. Another bullet blasted rock chips into O. T.'s face. Some of the grains stuck in his left eye, but he continued with only one eye open.

"Turn around, mister! It's too dangerous. You'll fall off there and break your neck. I'm just trying to save your life," the man screamed.

"Mister," O. T. hollered, "I'm not on your land, and I'm not doin' anything illegal. Go collect your tolls and leave me alone."

"You're a fool!"

"I won't argue that, but I'm gettin' water for my children."

"Not without payin' my toll. Turn around," he screamed, "or I'll put this bullet in your head!"

O. T. stopped and glanced toward the man. Balancing the wooden cask with one arm, he brushed rock and sand out of his eye with his finger. "You ain't got no reason to shoot me, and you know it. And now you have witnesses." O. T. pointed to the wagons. "You take care of your business, and I'll take care of my family." Skinner continued the final descent to the springs.

The man began to back step toward the tollhouse. "You'll never be able to carry a full keg of water out of there."

O. T. glanced back up the rocky cliff toward the cemetery. "That might very well be true, but it's mine to try."

"You're dumber than mud!" the man screamed. He turned around to face the incoming wagons.

When Skinner reached the springs, he refused to look back at the tollhouse man. Instead, he washed the blood off his elbow and then washed his face and hands. The water was cold on his face and neck. He felt it cascade down inside his shirt and streak across his back. He was surprised that there was little or no alkali taste.

The water surged out of the concrete basin and ran parallel along the base of the cliff about twenty-five feet. Then it sank completely out of sight in the jagged rocks.

He yanked the stopper out of the keg and rolled the wooden keg over to catch the flow streaming out of the concrete tank. He stared at the water that disappeared into the jagged rocks. *That must be the shortest creek known to man. But water goes somewhere. There must be an underground pool, and if there's a pool, then a well can be drilled and a tank installed and water piped right into every home and business. But ever'body knows that. It's as if everyone is in such a hurry to find a fortune that no one has time for ordinary things like water systems and cesspools and decent streets. Boomtowns is funny that way. Ever'body hopin' someone else will do the right thing.*

A lanky man in a tight suit drove up to the well and started to unload his water casks. "I cain't believe you walked that wall. Wouldn't have believed it without seein' it with my eyes. You don't mind if I stay and see if you can make it back?"

"You're free to watch. But I'm hopin' there's not much to see."

"I don't know which is more exciting—seeing you walk on that wall or seeing old Jug Cherry get his due."

"Jug Cherry?"

"The tollhouse man."

As he waited for the barrel to fill, O. T. surveyed the tollhouse. The gatekeeper seemed to be having a heated discussion with several men on horseback. When the keg began to overflow, he rammed the stopper back in and hoisted it to his shoulders.

Another wagon pulled up to the springs, and the two drivers conferred, pausing to point in his direction.

*Now, Orion Skinner . . . we'll find out how wise . . . or how foolish . . . you really were in trying this.*

The trip back up the slope was awkward. O. T. had found it had been easier to lean to his right as he hiked in on the trail. Now he had to lean to his left and try to keep from scraping his elbow on the rocks while toting the water.

His shoulder cramped.

His other sleeve ripped.

The soles of his feet felt red and raw.

Pain shot down his back and seemed to explode near his tailbone.

Someone shouted from the general vicinity of the springs, but O. T. couldn't chance looking back and throwing himself off balance.

*At least no one's shootin' at me this time.*

When he finally reached the cemetery on the desert floor, gunfire caused him to scurry toward the wagon. But this time the shots weren't directed at him. They were fired in the air in celebration by those standing next to the springs. After he set the barrel in the wagon, he waved to the men, and they returned the greeting with another round of gunfire.

The coolness of the water was only a memory as he wiped his soiled bandanna across his sweating face. He stretched the tight muscles on his arms and shoulders, then rubbed his back on the wagon wheel, putting pressure on his tailbone.

He stared for a minute at the second barrel. *Well, one more time. Course, I ought to haul a little for the neighbors. If I don't give out, that man on Main Street wanted to buy a couple barrels at two dollars each. Ain't that somethin', Lord? He's willing to pay two dollars for a twenty-gallon cask of water. A man could make a little money. Didn't take me much more than thirty minutes to go in and back. But that—that ain't right. We've been livin' on a dollar a day for so long, it seems almost sinful to be lustin' after more. It is sinful. Forgive me, Lord, for my greedy thoughts.*

Skinner plucked up the empty barrel and started back up the narrow, rocky trail. *Lord, thanks for a barrel of water for my family. I'd surely like to be able to take them one more.*

This time when he reached the springs, a steady line of wagons were parked at the tollhouse, proceeding to the springs one at a time. When he reached the concrete pool, a tall black man wearing a dark gray three-piece suit, no tie, and a black felt drover's hat was filling his barrels at the springs.

"That's quite a hike, partner," the man called out as O. T. let down the keg from his shoulder and waited his turn.

O. T. pulled off his hat and studied the sweat marks halfway out on the brim. "I didn't have the toll, and my children needed water." He ran his fingers through his short, thin, mostly gray hair.

The man's wide smile narrowed his full lips. "I didn't think anyone could hike that wall. That's incredible. Felt like I was watching the circus."

"I didn't have much choice. A man will do a lot when it comes to his family."

The black man stared at him for a moment, then nodded. "You're right about that. You're a hard-workin' man." He held out his hand. "I'm Lucian LaPorte."

"O. T. Skinner."

The man's black mustache was very narrow and neatly trimmed. "You need a job, Skinner?"

A faint, cool breeze bounced off the tumbling water. Suddenly O. T. felt very tired and very sleepy. "We're not staying in Goldfield. I'm on my way to California. Just needed a little water for the trip."

"You need work today for some grocery money?" LaPorte yanked a gold watch from his vest pocket and checked the time. "I'll hire you just for one day if that's all the time you have."

*I had a watch like that once. Traded it for ten pounds of beef and some croup medicine.* O. T. looked into the man's brown eyes. "What kind of work?"

"Just what you're doin' now—haulin' water."

"You mean hikin' the cliff?"

"Yep. I'll tell you what I'll do. I'll put my casks right over on the ground next to your wagon in the cemetery. You hike in here, fill the barrels, and hike out. I'll load them up and deliver them. I'll give you $1.50 per keg."

"What do you do with them?"

"I've got a water route that I supply water for. I'm tired of payin' Jug Cherry half my profit for sittin' on his backside."

O. T. looked back at the red rock building. "What's the story with him? Did you see him try to shoot me?"

"Yep. I hear he moved in last spring. He checked the county maps tryin' to find mis-surveyed parcels to mine, but all he found was the entrance to the springs. So he filed on it and turned the block-house into a tollhouse. Until then there were no restrictions. He ought to be booted out, but folks is either too scared or too busy makin' money to care. I'd rather pay you than him, and I can save time because my whole load will be filled when I come out here.

Even if it's just for one day. You could use the money, couldn't you?" He pointed toward O. T.'s worn boots.

"Yes, sir, we could use a few supplies before we leave town, but me makin' $1.50 a barrel for public water seems like cheatin' folks."

LaPorte stepped closer. He was several inches taller than Skinner. "They ain't goin' to get it cheaper if you turn me down. Who's to say Cherry won't go and up the price? Competition is good for the folks buyin'. You'll be doin' them all a favor."

"Lucian, you're quite a salesman. But I'm not sure how many loads I can actually take."

"That's up to you. Quit any time you think you should."

"We could use fifteen dollars."

"Maybe buy yourself a pair of boots."

O. T. stared down at his boots. *If I bring home fifteen dollars, we could purtneer all leave town with new shoes!* "Well, I was goin' to rest up the family until tomorrow anyway."

"Then you'll do it?" LaPorte pressed.

"I'll try."

"I'll meet you around at the cemetery."

"I'll need to go take some water back to my family first."

LaPorte plucked up the empty cask and put it back in his wagon. "Where are you staying? I'll deliver them for you when I go back for more empties."

"On east Columbia Street, lot #124."

"That's way across the riverbed, isn't it?"

"If that streak of sand is called a riverbed."

"Say, you haven't got a title deed to that lot, do you?"

Skinner hoisted the full keg and braced it across his shoulders. "Some friends lent us the deed for as long as we stay in town."

LaPorte climbed back into the buckboard harnessed to two black geldings. "Buy it from them," he suggested.

"I don't have money for that kind of thing. Besides, I told you, we're leavin' town. I don't want a lot."

"Well, there's a rumor that those places are sittin' on top of the next strike." Lucian LaPorte turned the rig around.

"I'm not interested in gold mines."

LaPorte's eyes twinkled. "Now there's a phrase a man don't often hear in Goldfield."

Dola Skinner sat on the edge of the bed and stared across the tent at the sleeping children. Next to Rita Ann on the worn pine-green carpet stretched over the desert floor were her neatly folded purple gingham dress and her black lace-up boots that had been Dola's cousin's discards only six months previous. Next to them were her tattered but beloved Shakespeare book and her spectacles. She slept on her back, her dark pigtails coiled on her head, the cotton sheet pulled to her chin and neatly folded back two inches.

*Lord, she is everything I always wanted to be at her age but never could—smart, self-disciplined, graceful. She's like Mama. Rita Ann, you should live in a big two-story house with a room for your own, in a shady part of town across the street from a Carnegie library.*

Dola could feel her shoulders and breasts sag under the thin gown. She straightened her back and stretched her arms. There was a sharp pain at the base of her tailbone, and she once again slumped forward.

Corrie lay sprawled across the faded quilt on the middle pallet on her stomach, her arms and legs extended. Her short, thick dark brown hair sprang out randomly in every direction. She wore a flannel shirt of her father's that had both sleeves cut off at the shoulders. When she stood up, it dropped to her knees, but in her tossing and turning, it was up around her waist. Her cotton pants had a small faded violet and yellow pansy embroidered on them. The bottoms of her feet were filthy.

*Corrie Lou, either you got up in the night and hiked around town, or you did not wash your feet last night as I asked.*

Dola glanced down at her own dusty feet.

*No one washed their feet last night. We ran out of water.*

She glanced back at the feather mattress where O. T. had slept. *Daddy's gone to fetch water. I trust he can do that without much trouble. I'd like to leave this town as soon as possible. I have an uneasy feeling about this place. It struck me as soon as we rolled in last evening.*

*It's not like Guthrie . . . or Bisbee . . . or Winslow . . . or even Tonopah. It's a prickly kind of feeling in my spirit, Lord. I don't think You want us here. I'm not sure You want anyone here.*

She stared at O. T.'s side of the small bed. *He left without waking me. He always does when we're short of food. He refuses to eat breakfast until the children are full.*

She gazed at the two-year-old. Punky slept, wearing only his undies, in the middle of the featherbed. He too lay on his stomach, his head and legs plastered to the patched white cotton sheet, his rounded rear end pointed at the top of the tent.

When she stood, Dola felt a raw place on the side of her right heel and thought about how the shoes rubbed her feet. *I will go barefoot today and wear both socks on my right foot tomorrow on the journey. We could be in California by tomorrow night.*

She heard Tommy-Blue's faint snore as he slept with a pillow on top of his head. Sometime in the night Rita Ann had made her pilgrimage to her bother's pallet, trying to muffle his snores. He too had the covers kicked off. He slept in his coveralls, his socks tossed on top of the ripped boots that were two sizes too big.

Dola knew there was a mirror in her carpetbag but refused to pull it out even as she combed her hair. A chipped enameled tin basin sat empty on the trunk at the foot of the bed. She parted her hair in the middle, then pulled it back tight and clipped it behind her ears as she stared at the empty basin.

*He'll be back pretty soon, and then we can all wash up. I will fix us some breakfast. We have a dozen hard-boiled eggs, but they must last until California. We shouldn't eat them all today. I wish we had fresh fruit. California is full of fresh fruit. We shall have oranges in California.*

She licked her lips, half expecting a citrus flavor, and was disappointed to taste alkaline dust. She pulled a quilt from the bed and hung it across the rope strung between the two tent poles, separating the three sleeping children from herself and Punky.

Slowly Dola dressed.

The same worn chemise.

The same dusty dress.

When she finished, she pulled down the quilt and neatly folded it on the edge of the feather mattress. Then she stepped over to the tent flap and slipped outside.

The sun had just broken over the mountains on the east, and long shadows raced toward downtown Goldfield to the west. She heard dogs barking. Someone shouted either at the dogs or at their children. To the north, the Rokkers' tent looked almost identical to theirs, but it had more of a red clay tint to it. Next to the Rokkers' tent was a large wooden chair with one arm missing. There were crates, tins, and sacks of goods. A barrel and a door served as a table. It was littered with dirty dishes and food scraps.

Next to her own tent, Dola looked over their own belongings. Each item was neatly packed in a crate and stacked like a protective fence around the front of the tent. The dirt next to the crates was shaded and felt almost cool to her bare feet.

Gritty.

Prickly.

But cool.

Dola opened the crate labeled "groceries." It was almost empty. She stared at the half loaf of bread.

*If we don't have wood for a fire, we'll have to have that bread later. Maybe we can buy some bread. A fresh loaf would be nice.*

A woman's angry voice caused her to snap her head up. A quick, sharp pain shot from her neck to her ear as she peered toward the back of the lot. A short woman in a tattered light blue dress stalked slowly toward her. Behind her was a small rock and mortar privy, and behind that a woman with a rifle was shouting.

The woman in blue seemed to ignore the other woman and kept coming straight toward Dola. The angry woman disappeared back into the huge tent with walls of both wood and canvas.

Stopping near Dola's crates, the woman shaded her deep-set eyes. "Are you Mrs. Skinner?"

Dola stepped closer, but a stack of crates still separated them. "Yes, ma'am."

Her visitor stood three inches shorter than Dola's five feet, four inches. The woman's cheeks were sunken. Her expression revealed no emotion at all. "I'm Mrs. Rokker. I believe you met my husband last night."

"Oh, yes, we did." Dola tried a gracious smile. *There is nothin' gracious looking about dimples!* "Very nice to meet you."

The woman brushed down the front of her dress as if it would bring back some of the faded color. "We appreciate you allowing us to stay on the lot."

Dola started to curl her toes back but stopped when she realized that Mrs. Rokker could not see them anyway. "We're only guests ourselves," she replied.

Mrs. Rokker's tired eyes widened. "I heard you held the title deed."

"Yes, we do. But we're merely holding it for friends we met in Tonopah. It really belongs to them."

The woman pointed toward her tent. "Mr. Rokker said he will be back this afternoon to move us."

"Don't move on account of us. We won't be here too long. I believe we'll be leaving tomorrow. I'll introduce you to our friends who own the lot. Perhaps they'll let you stay awhile." Dola glanced to the back of the lot. "What was that woman yelling about? Didn't she want you to use her outhouse?"

"That's Mrs. Marsh. She owns that back lot and won't let anyone on her property. Claims she's sitting on top of a gold mine. She resents the outhouse being placed on the back of this lot and makes dire threats when someone uses it."

Dola stared at the little building. "You mean that outhouse belongs to lot #124?"

"Yes, it does. Isn't that strange—a lot with nothing permanent on it but a privy?"

"I, for one, am happy to see it," Dola commented.

The pain in the woman's brown eyes faded a little. "I know what you mean. How many children?"

Dola looked at the tent flap. "We have four. And you?"

A sad resignation gripped the woman's face. "Just four . . . now. We lost our Richard last winter."

Dola's hand went to her mouth. "Oh, dear . . . I'm very sorry."

Mrs. Rokker stared off at Columbia Mountain, but it seemed as if she were looking far beyond it. "The Lord gives, and the Lord takes away," she mumbled.

"Yes . . . yes, I know that is true," Dola concurred. "Yet it is so difficult. I had several miscarriages before little Punky was born. Was your Richard ill?"

"He starved to death." The voice was so deep and emotionless it sent chills down Dola's back.

"He what?" she gasped.

"He was just six months old. I was breast-feeding him. One mornin' he was dead. Doc said it happens sometimes, but I knew he starved to death." The woman shook her head. "It don't seem right."

Dola's mind raced to try to find words to say. "Where were you living at the time?"

"Right there in that tent. Course, sometimes it gets cold in the winter around here. Real cold."

Dola could feel her hands begin to shake. She clenched her fists to try to keep them from showing.

Suddenly the woman's foreboding eyes seem to brighten. She

pointed back at the outhouse. "Tell your children to pay no atten-tion to Mrs. Marsh when they go to the privy. She'll threaten to shoot them, but she don't mean it."

"She what?"

"She threatens to shoot anyone who uses the privy, but you just have them go right ahead. What kind of woman would forbid a child the use of a privy? Say, I hate to ask, but do you have any spare water?"

"No, we shared ours with others yesterday. But Mr. Skinner went to fetch some. He should be back shortly, and we'll give some to you then."

"Did he have any cash?" Mrs. Rokker pressed.

"I don't think so. Why?"

Mrs. Rokker rubbed her nose on the back of her hand. "Water costs money around here."

"Orion will figure something out. In fact, I thought he would be back by now." Dola laced her fingers together and held her hand against her growling stomach.

"I know what you mean. Mr. Rokker takes off every morning to look for work, and he comes home drunk with hardly a penny in his pocket saying he can't find work. Now I ask you, where does he get the money to buy booze?"

"My Orion is a temperance man."

"That's good . . . that's good. But Goldfield is not the place to be. Many a sober man has lost his will in this town."

"Mrs. Rokker, is there any wood around here to build a small cooking fire? I didn't see a thing that looks like firewood."

Mrs. Rokker examined Dola's crates. "Do you have a cookstove?"

"Eh, no, I was just going to make an open fire."

"There's no regular wood, if that's what you mean. But I've been sending Jared downtown ever' mornin', and he cleans up around the new hotel they're building. They give him the scraps. If you want to send your boy along, they could bring back a couple of gunny sacks full."

Dola could feel her bony shoulder rub against the thin cotton dress. "I'll try to wake him. He's our best sleeper."

"I'll go, Mama!" The words shot out of the tent like a dart.

Mrs. Rokker stared toward the Skinner tent flap.

"That's our daughter, Rita Ann. Do you think Jared would mind if she tags along and scoops up a little scrap wood?"

"Well, it don't matter if he squeals or not, your girl can go. I'll send him over in a few minutes."

"I'm ready now!" came Rita Ann's reply. She was still hidden inside the tent.

The thin woman in the straight blue dress stared at the tent flap and raised her voice. "And I said, I'll send him over in a few minutes!"

Dola stayed out by the crates until Mrs. Rokker went back to her tent. When Dola stepped back inside, Rita Ann was dressed and her pallet neatly folded. She sat on the edge of the bed tugging on her lace-up shoes.

"I appreciate your eagerness to go fetch the wood," Mrs. Skinner mused. "But I'm not sure of your motivation."

Rita Ann stood up and unpinned her braids from the back of her head. "'Oh, that one might read the book of fate and see the revolution of the times.'"

"*Henry the Fifth?*" Mrs. Skinner prodded.

"No, *Henry the Fourth*," Rita Ann replied.

"Well, you be nice to Jared the First. Don't overwhelm him with all your quotes."

"Mother, I'll only be going to get firewood."

"Yes, and be careful. We don't know this town very well."

"I will come straight back. I will not talk to strangers . . . except Jared, of course. And I'll not run out in front of a horse or wagon."

"Mrs. Skinner?" It was a male voice, a rather high-pitched male voice.

Dola followed Rita Ann out of the tent. A redheaded boy, holding two gunny sacks over his shoulder, rocked on the heels of worn brown boots. His ducking britches were worn at the knees and pockets. His leather braces were obviously too large and had been cinched like a latigo on a saddle. He wore a shirt that had the tint of Goldfield dirt.

"I'm Jared." He blushed. His curly red hair jutted out from under the wide-brimmed felt hat.

"And this is Rita Ann," Dola introduced her.

"Pleased to meet you, Rita." He tipped his hat.

"My name is Rita Ann, not Rita," she snapped as she ran by him toward the street.

Dola watched the boy scurry to catch up and then stepped back inside the tent.

*Did my eyes ever dance like hers? Did my face blush with excitement over a boy?*

Dola went to the olive-green-and-black flowered carpetbag and tugged out a hand mirror. For several moments she stared at her face. *Dola Mae Davis Skinner, you are twenty-nine years old. Your hair is coarse, oily, and your blue eyes are dulled with dust and worry. The face is tanned, rough, and lined with years of hard work. Your lips are too full . . . your face is too thin.*

*You are plain, Dola Mae.*

*You have always looked plain.*

*You even looked plain on your wedding day.*

A smile broke across her face, and she stared at two dimples.

*Of course, Orion didn't think I looked plain on that day.*

*He still doesn't.*

She gazed down at her rough, chapped hands and thought about how it felt the night before when Orion's hand held hers. She quickly put the mirror back in the carpetbag.

*My-oh-my, Lord, how I love that man. Being next to him makes the whole world alive and purposeful.*

She stared at the three children still sleeping and thought about Mrs. Rokker's exhausted eyes. She thought about a husband who came home drunk and a baby who died at the breast. She knelt down on the carpet between Corrie and Tommy-Blue.

Dola gently tugged a patched cotton sheet up around each child, then stood, and gazed at their tent and belongings.

*Lord, I just might be the most fortunate and blessed woman on the face of this earth. You have been incredibly good to me.*

She wiped a tear on the sleeve of her dress and then stepped back outside. To the north, on the street on the other side of the Rokker tent, she heard a man call her name.

"Mrs. Skinner?"

She shaded the morning sun from her eyes with her hand. "Mr. Gately?" Dola scurried toward the wide dirt street and the tall man with the crisp black bowler who was holding the reins to a two-horse buckboard. Only when she reached the smiling man did she realize that he was staring at her bare feet.

# FOUR

Dola curled her toes into the dry desert dirt and tried to tuck them under her long, straight brown dress that hung only two inches from the ground. "Mr. Gately, please excuse the bare feet. I'm terribly embarrassed. I stepped out to fix breakfast and thought I'd give my feet a break from my ill-fitting shoes."

Lucky Jack Gately's blond hair looped out of his hat and across his forehead just above his gray eyes. "I reckon we all have toes, ma'am."

*He could be a handsome man if he had a few more pounds on him.* Dola Skinner looked down toward the ground to cover the blush. "But most have the decency not to expose them. I see you found yourself a buckboard."

"For the price I had to pay to rent it, I should have received an auto truck." When his suit coat pulled back, she could see the big knife still lashed to his belt. "Say, do you folks have two tents?" he questioned.

She glanced back at the two dust-covered tents and the piles of belongings scattered around them. The embarrassing trashiness of it made her breath shorter. "Oh, no. This first one belongs to the Rokker family."

Gately pulled off his hat and ran his strong fingers through his recently washed hair. "They friends of yours?"

Dola lowered her voice, knowing that Mrs. Rokker was just

inside the tent. "They are now. We just met them last night . . . and this morning."

Lucky Jack rubbed his hand across his clean-shaven chin. "Were they squattin' on our lot?"

*I need to wash my hair. It's much lighter when it's clean. The strands of gray do not show up nearly as much then. Of course, even clean it's not as light as Mr. Gately's. He's probably not too much older than I am.* "I believe they were just using the location until someone else needed it. It's quite impossible for a family to just spend a night in Goldfield without paying an exorbitant amount."

"Well, Mrs. Skinner, you just tell them to move. Or I can do it for you. You ought to be up here next to the street." Caught with the right light, Lucky Jack's square chin reflected a slight dimple right in the center of it.

Dola stepped close to the carriage. The soles of her feet were now prodded by sand and stabbed by gravel. She motioned for Lucky Jack to lean forward. She could smell the spice aroma of his shaving tonic. "Mr. Gately," she whispered, "the Rokkers are having a rather rough time of it. I don't mind them staying up here next to the street. We'll be gone in a day or so. Then you may deal with them as you must, but while we're here, would it be all right if they stay? Actually I like being further back on the lot. It's a good distance from the road dust and closer to the privy." Dola quickly stepped back as if stung by a bee.

Lucky Jack sat up and leaned against the back of the buckboard seat. "There's an outhouse on the lot?"

His dark tie seemed a little tight, and Dola fought back the urge to ask him to loosen it. "Yes," she replied. "It's at the back of the lot. The lady in the place behind us is quite sure her property is sitting on top of a great lead of gold."

Gately spun the lead line around the hand brake and swung down to the ground. "Is that so?" He began to hike out toward the middle of the lot.

Dola scurried to keep up. *I forgot how tall he was.* "Don't pay any mind to this clutter. We had to unload the wagon in the dark last night and . . ."

"Mrs. Skinner, your place don't look any different than most in town. Don't you go apologizing to me." Gately hiked halfway between the Skinner tent and the privy.

Dola almost stumbled into him when he abruptly stopped. She held her hand to the collar of her already tightly buttoned dress. "From what we hear, this might be a good lot to hold on to."

Gately squatted down on his haunches and ran his fingers through the barren, bone-dry soil. "Ever'body in town thinks they're sitting on a gold mine. This is river wash land. Sometime, ages ago, there must have been water rushing through here. If there's any traces of color here, it's been swept down here by some spring flood. But I reckon we'll keep the lot until we need the money. They can stay as long as you don't mind."

"Thank you, Mr. Gately."

He stood up and once again towered over Dola. The sky was now hot blue and clear. Only his shadow stood between her and the bright morning sun. "I got two reasons for stopping by." He cleared his throat and hiked back toward the crates and tents. "Wasco, Charlie Fred, and me are going to start developing our lease tomorrow. We think it's best to camp out there and protect it. Besides, rooms in this town are too expensive."

The desert dirt was burning into the soles of her feet. She followed two steps behind him. "That doesn't surprise me."

"And the meals in this town are way too expensive as well. You wouldn't believe what they charged us $2.50 for last night at the Klondike Klub. We had boiled beef, watery mashed potatoes, gravy that we could see plumb through, canned corn, tomatoes curled at the edges, and cold, crumbly, tasteless baking powder biscuits."

"It sounds rather flat the way you tell it," she said.

"So here's our deal, Mrs. Skinner," Lucky Jack proposed. "At least as long as you're in town, we want to hire you as our cook."

"Cook? My heavens, no one has ever asked me to cook before." *I must have gotten a little sunburned yesterday. My face feels flushed.*

He turned around to face her, pushed his hat back, and leaned against the crates. "Before you turn us down, hear me out. Me and the boys will buy the groceries—enough for us and for your whole family. We'll also set us up an outdoor table right over here. Then we want to have breakfast, a lunch bucket packed, and supper. You don't have to travel to the mine. Just cook up a big batch of food, and we'll buy all the groceries. The price of groceries isn't nearly as high as cafe food."

Dola suddenly wished she was wearing a hat and gloves. "Did I understand you to say that you want me to cook right here for you three, and you'll supply enough groceries for my family as well?"

He stared at her for a minute. "You got nice dimples, Mrs. Skinner, especially when you blush. Now if that deal ain't fair, we'll pay you on top of it."

Dola tried to stand up a little straighter and pulled her shoulders back. "Mr. Gately, are you aware of how much a hungry family of six eats?"

He glanced back at the tent. "I believe I am."

"I will not take a penny for cooking. But there might be a problem heating with firewood. There doesn't seem to be a stick of wood for a hundred miles." She glanced down at her interlaced fingers and noticed she had clutched them until they turned white.

"We'll get all you need from wood scraps over at the mine. We'll bring some by every evenin'." He pulled off his hat and held it in his hand. "What do you say?" His hair was neatly parted, every blond strand slicked down in place.

*Lord, are You tempting me or providing for me? Sometimes it's difficult to know the difference.* "You understand that we might not stick around more than a day or two?"

"Yep, we know." He jammed his new black hat back on.

"Well, then, yes, of course I'd be happy to cook while we're here."

"That's wonderful!" He reached his hand out as if to pat hers, then pulled it back. "Eh, you make me a list of supplies, say, three days' worth to start with. I'll buy them and deliver a table by noon."

"Mr. Gately, that's very kind of you, but I'm not sure we'll be staying three days."

"Don't worry, we'll haul the extras out to the mine if you leave early. As far as being kind, I reckon we're just lookin' out for ourselves. We get hungry and don't want to see our poke used up paying inflated prices. And don't you go skimpin' on meals. We're going to eat hearty, and we expect you to do the same." He walked back toward the street.

She followed behind. "Yes, sir, I'll do the best I can."

"We know you will, Mrs. Skinner. That's why we want you to be the cook. Now there's one other question I have for you. Have you or Mr. Skinner seen the Wilkins brothers in town yet? Have they returned that olive crock?"

The thought of three dust-covered men riding burros trudged through Dola's mind. "No," she offered. "But it's early. If they get the motorcar running, they should make it today, don't you think?"

Gately pulled himself up into the buckboard. "Well, that's what I'm thinkin'. Could you do me a favor, ma'am? Don't tell them that I'm lookin' for them, but let me know when they roll in. I'd like to keep an eye on them without them keeping an eye on me."

Dola felt her shoulders and neck stiffen. "Mr. Gately, do not ask me to be a part of anything nefarious."

A wide grin broke across his face. "Mrs. Skinner, ain't no one ever in my life called me nefarious. We don't aim to do anything but protect ourselves. I've got a couple more errands to run. Then I'll come back for that list."

Dola scooted toward her tent across the hot desert dirt.

Mrs. Rokker called out from inside the tent. "Did he want us to move?"

"No, he said it was fine for you to stay there for now, but they reserve the right to change their minds. That goes for my family as well as yours."

Corrie was barefoot but dressed when Dola returned to the shady ground just outside the tent.

"Well, good mornin', young lady."

Corrie's round cheeks, mouth, and lips always made Dola smile. "Mornin', Mama. Where's my daddy?" Her dark bangs flopped down to her eyes.

*From the day she was born, she's been Daddy's girl.* "He went to get some water. He'll be back soon . . . I think."

Corrie shifted her weight from one foot to the other, then back to the first. "Where's Rita Ann?"

Dola tried to brush down Corrie's hair with her fingers. "She went to fetch us some firewood from downtown."

Corrie was now bouncing on her heels. "By herself?"

Mrs. Skinner nodded toward the other tent. "Eh, no . . . Jared Rokker went with her."

"Why?"

"He needed some firewood for his family too."

A huge, dimpled smile broke across Corrie's round face. "Is that our privy?" She pointed toward the back of the lot.

"Yes, isn't that nice? I believe you need to go check it out."

"Yes, Mama, I surely do." Corrie trotted toward it.

"Corrie Lou, don't get in that woman's lot. She doesn't like company, and she's an angry woman. She might try to chase you off, but don't listen to her. That's our privy."

Corrie stopped near the middle of the lot. "Why is she so angry?" she called out.

"I think she's afraid someone will steal her lot."

"Why would anyone want to do that?"

"Gold makes people do very strange things, Corrie Lou. Now be careful."

"Yes, Mama."

"Are your brothers awake?"

"I don't think so."

Dola watched Corrie sprint to the rock privy and dart inside. Then she hefted the canvas flap and stepped into their tent. Stale, warm air hung lifeless, smelling of dust and sweat. Tommy-Blue and Punky slept as she sorted through the carpetbag by the bed and retrieved a torn scrap of brown paper and a stubby pencil not more than two inches long.

*Lord, this is an unusual opportunity You've provided for me to be of help to those three men and feed my family. I'm not sure what kind of meals they're accustomed to. But they will be working very hard and will certainly need their strength. Meat and eggs for breakfast. Meat and bread for lunch. Meat and potatoes for supper. Beans, rice, fresh vegetables and fruit, if available. And pie . . . I must find the Dutch oven and bake a cobbler. I've never met a man who wouldn't eat pie.*

Punky sat straight up on the bed. "Hi!" he grinned.

A wide smile broke across Dola's face. She felt her neck and shoulders relax. "Well, good mornin', little darlin'. Is Mama's boy ready to get up?"

He stood up on the feather mattress, balanced himself, and then dove into her pillow. He rolled on his back and tossed the pillow to the floor.

She scooted over and hugged him. "I assume that's a yes." He threw his chubby arms around her neck and kissed her on the lips.

"My mama's purdy," he squealed.

Punky wore only denim bib coveralls over his underwear as he toddled around the crates, watching his mother dig out some breakfast. Tommy-Blue appeared at the door, wearing identical garb. His hair stuck out in all directions.

"Comb your hair, young man."

"I'll just pull on my hat."

Dola rested her hands on her thin, almost nonexistent hips. "Comb your hair first."

"But it hurts," Tommy-Blue whined.

"That's because you don't comb it enough."

"Hey, you want to go dig for gold?" an unfamiliar croaky voice blurted out.

Dola looked up to see a very thin red-haired boy about Tommy-Blue's age holding a wooden bucket in one hand and a broken-handled shovel in the other.

With wide eyes, the toddler looked up at the boy. "I'm Punky," he announced.

"I'm Danny. I live up there in that tent." He wore ducking trousers more tattered than his brother's. His braces were cotton ropes, and the cuffs of his shirt were so frayed they looked like fringe.

Dola brushed a strand of dark brown hair out of her eyes. "Well, Danny, you met Punky, and this is Tommy-Blue Skinner."

The boy set the bucket and a tin plate on top of a crate. "What kind of name is Tommy-Blue? I ain't never heard of anyone named after a color."

Tommy-Blue gave his mother a blank stare.

"You never knew anyone called Red or Whitey?" Dola replied.

"Oh, I guess them is colors. Some folks call me Red, but I don't like it none." Danny turned to Tommy-Blue. "Anyway, do you want to help me look for gold? We'll split whatever we find fifty-fifty."

Tommy-Blue's eyes widened. "Where?" he probed.

Danny stood up straight and gazed across the lot. "Looks like pay dirt to me about halfway between here and the outhouse."

Tommy-Blue glanced up at his mother. "Can I?"

"We were going to have a bite of breakfast first," she replied.

"Mama said it was too hot to cook, so we just skipped breakfast today," Danny reported.

"I don't think I'll build a fire either. Would you like to eat with us?" Mrs. Skinner offered.

"I, eh . . ." Danny looked back at his tent.

Dola rubbed the back of her neck and could feel beads of perspiration forming. "Do you need to ask your mother?"

He stared down at the dirt and then licked his narrow, thin lips. "I reckon."

"Danny, why don't you tell her that I have six extra hard-boiled eggs that need to be eaten before they spoil. You and your family can have them if you'd like."

He looked her straight in the eyes. "We ain't got no money." His green eyes pleaded more than his words.

"I meant, I'll give them to you," she said.

Danny dropped the shovel and sprinted to his tent. Dola waited for Mrs. Rokker to step outside. She never did.

Danny came dashing back. "Mama said we could help you out and take them extra eggs off your hands."

Dola counted out half a dozen eggs into a small wicker basket, leaving six in the tin box.

"Can me and Tommy-Blue eat ours out at the pay dirt?" Danny asked as he waved toward the middle of the lot.

"Don't drop them in the dirt," she lectured. "It could be a long morning before we eat again."

"Yes, ma'am." Danny ran back to his tent with the eggs and reemerged with one in his hand.

The two barefoot boys laughed and whistled their way out to their intended gold mine.

Dola was peeling an egg for Punky when a heavy wagon rumbled up the street. A tall black man dressed in a dark gray suit and vest hopped down. "Would you be Mrs. Skinner?" he called out.

She set Punky on a crate and handed him the peeled egg. "Yes, sir. Can I help you?"

He glanced at her bare feet and at her dress. She felt unkempt. "I got two casks of water here for you from Mr. Skinner."

Dola stared west toward downtown. "Where is he?"

The man hiked toward her, a cask on his shoulder. She noticed his very thin, neatly trimmed mustache. "My name's Lucian LaPorte. I hired him to tote a few kegs of water for me, ma'am. He'll be tied up for a while, but he wanted you to have these."

The thin face and tired eyes of Mrs. Rokker peeked out from her tent flap just as they hiked by. Her voice was somewhere between a plea and a whine. "You have water?"

Dola stared into her sunken eyes. "One keg goes right here to the Rokkers' tent and one to ours," she instructed.

LaPorte plopped the keg down near the old broken chair.

"We ain't got no money," Mrs. Rokker whimpered.

"Mrs. Rokker, I don't believe I've ever heard that phrase more times than in the past few days. A thirsty person never has to buy water." She turned back to the black man. "Mr. LaPorte, would you tell Mr. Skinner that we'll be needing two more kegs?"

"Yes, ma'am, I'll tell him. I presume you want this other keg by the second tent." Sweat drops beaded on his forehead like rain drops on a pane of glass.

Once the cask of water was stacked next to their crates, Dola drew a small basin full, washed her feet, and pulled on her shoes and socks. She put two socks on her right foot and none on her left.

Then Dola scribbled on the brown paper: "sugar, maple syrup, baking soda, yeast . . ." Punky nibbled all the white off his egg and held the yoke carefully between his fingers. "Don't you drop that egg, young man!" she demanded.

Punky crammed the entire yolk into his mouth, chewed several bites, and began to cough, spraying yellow particles into the dirt.

"I didn't mean for you to hog down the whole thing at once." She plucked up a tin cup of water and squatted next to the two-year-old. Her arm around the smooth tan skin of his shoulder, she held the cup to his lips. "Take a little drink, darlin'."

"Mama!" a girl's voice hollered. The tone was somewhere between a shout and a giggle. "Here's the wood, Mama." Rita Ann pointed to the full gunny sack on the ground beside her.

"How about you pulling it out and stacking it beside that big square box? Daddy sent us some water, so when you're done, wash up."

Rita Ann rubbed her upturned nose with the palm of her hand, leaving a slight smudge. "Where is Daddy?"

Dola gathered up Punky and set him on top of the crate. "He landed a day job hauling water for a man. He'll be along later."

"Hi, Rita Ann!" the toddler grinned. "I had an egg!"

Rita Ann brushed yellow crumbs off his chin. "Good mornin', Punky, dear. Yes, it certainly looks like you had an egg." She toted the gunny sack next to the square box and squatted down, her long purple dress now draped in the dirt. She pulled wood scraps from the sack. "Mother, I had a very congenial time."

Dola washed Punky's face. "Is Jared nice?"

Rita Ann glanced back toward the Rokker tent and lowered her voice. "Yes, he is, Mama. You know, he wouldn't let me carry our wood home."

"You don't say."

"Yes, he toted both sacks. He looks thin, but he must be very strong. He only had to stop and rest a few times." Rita Ann emptied the gunny sack, folded it, and stood up. "I sort of wish we didn't have to leave tomorrow. Parting would be 'such sweet sorrow.'"

"My, that was quite a walk." Dola grinned as she took Punky off the crate and put him on the ground. "And what was Juliet's line before the parting reference?"

Rita Ann rolled her eyes toward the blue sky and rubbed her nose again. "Eh . . . 'Yet I should kill thee with much cherishing.' What does that mean?"

Dola slipped her arm around her daughter, who was only a few inches shorter. "It means enjoy yourself. You're twelve, not twenty. But, the truth is, we just might stay two or three days."

Rita Ann's blue eyes danced. "Really? I'll go tell Jared. He wanted to show me around town. Can I go for a walk with him?"

Dola nodded. "If you'll watch out for horses and wagons. Everyone in Goldfield seems to be in a hurry. Perhaps Corrie would like to go with you."

"Mama!"

Mrs. Skinner searched through a wood box and pulled out a two-foot-square cast-iron grill. "We'll see. No one can leave until we get a few things set up. Now you wash that smudge off your nose and eat your egg."

"A smudge?" Tears began to puddle up in the corners of Rita Ann's eyes. "I had a smudge on my nose all morning?"

"Only for the last two minutes."

A wide smile broke across Rita Ann's face. She picked up a wet rag and wiped her face. "How's that?"

"Not bad for a girl who hasn't had a hot bath in two weeks."

"Can we have a hot bath here in Goldfield?"

"Perhaps. It depends upon how much water Daddy is able to get." The thought of a hot, soapy bath caused her to close her eyes and sigh.

"I get to use the water first this time. After Tommy-Blue and Punky got through last time, it was all muddy looking." Rita Ann stood by her mother and glanced to the back of the lot. "What's Tommy-Blue and that boy doing?"

Dola snatched up her brown paper list and wrote "coffee." Then she glanced south. "He and Danny Rokker are out there digging for gold."

Rita Ann unpinned her black pigtails and let them drape her shoulders. "But there isn't any gold over there."

"Gold fever and common sense don't often accompany each

other." Dola glanced west toward downtown. "'Gold is a living god, and rules in scorn all earthly things but virtue.'"

Rita Ann stared at her mother. "Did Shakespeare say that?"

"No, it was Shelley. There are other writers, you know." Dola pointed toward the boys. "Besides, the vast majority of people who dig for gold never find any. So the real fun must be in the digging."

Rita Ann began peeling her hard-boiled egg. "Mother, may I have some bread and jam? Or do we need to save that for lunch?"

"Go ahead." Mrs. Skinner studied the brown paper list in her hands. "I'm not sure what we'll have for lunch, but for supper we're having ham, white beans with molasses, and cornbread to go along with peach cobbler."

Rita Ann studied her teeth marks in the egg white. "Cobbler?"

Dola glanced at her daughter. "And we're having guests."

"The Rokkers?"

Dola observed how the long cotton dress hung straight down on her daughter. *Apparently, young lady, you are going to have the same physique as your mama.* "Lucky Jack, Wasco, and Charlie Fred are going to take their meals with us as long as we stay here. They buy the groceries for all of us, and I cook for them. I'll need your help, of course."

Rita Ann pushed her shoulders back, but her dress still hung as if on a hanger. "This has been a day of very good news." She grinned.

Dola slipped her arm around her daughter's waist and gave her a hug. "Yes, I'll agree. Why do you think it is?"

"Maybe," Rita Ann bit her lip and raised her eyebrow, "the Lord wants us to stay awhile in Goldfield."

"Lard!" Mrs. Skinner blurted out.

"What?" Rita Ann questioned.

Mrs. Skinner released her daughter and swung over to the crate with the list. "I need to buy lard." She scribbled another word on the list and turned back to her daughter. "Now, Rita Ann, you know we are on our way to Dinuba."

"Yes, but what will a few more days . . . or weeks matter?" Rita Ann peered around her mother's shoulder at the grocery list.

"I want you three in school by September."

"I like it when you are our teacher. Kids make fun of me quoting Shakespeare in school," Rita Ann complained.

"That's only because you've never been in a school long enough for everyone to get to know you."

Rita Ann glanced back at the tent. "Can I go on a walk with Jared now?"

"First, I'll need you, Corrie, and Tommy-Blue to tote some of those river rocks over here. I want to build a fire pit."

Rita Ann stuck her head inside the tent flap and then quickly pulled it out. "Where is Corrie?"

"She's, eh . . ." Mrs. Skinner stared toward the back of the lot. "She went to the privy a long time ago. I'd better go check on that girl. Maybe she got herself locked in."

"I'll go, Mama," Rita Ann offered. "You'd better take care of Punky."

Dola spun around. The two-year-old had jam smeared across his cheek and stuck to his fingers. "Did you get into the strawberry preserves?" she scolded.

Punky shook his head. "No," he offered meekly.

"Young man, you are absolute proof of the sinfulness of mankind. Come on, I'll try to clean you up with cold water. Daddy sent the water just in time."

After scrubbing Punky's face, Dola heard Lucky Jack's voice from the road. When she walked past the Rokker tent, a young red-haired girl was washing out sheets on a washboard.

"And what's your name?" Dola stopped to ask her.

The girl dropped her gaze to the ground. "I'm Stella Rokker, and I'm ten years old."

"Well, Stella, it's nice of you to help your mother with the washing." Punky toddled up beside his mother.

"Daddy puked on the sheets, and I always have to do the washing," the girl mumbled. "What's your boy's name?"

"This is Punky."

"Not that one—the one out playing with Danny."

"His name is Tommy-Blue."

Stella's eyes were still focused on the dirty sheet. "Thank you for the eggs, Mrs. Skinner."

"You're quite welcome, Stella."

Lucky Jack and Wasco were struggling to unload an old cast-iron stove from the back of the wagon when Dola and Punky reached the street.

"Lucky Jack!" Punky hollered.

The men set the stove on the dirt and looked up. "Well, if it isn't Silas Paul Skinner!" Lucky Jack grinned.

"No . . . I'm Punky," the boy replied.

"A stove?" Dola chirped.

Wasco tipped his new round-crowned felt hat. "Yes, ma'am. We found a table for sale, and the folks was selling this stove as well. I know you told Lucky Jack you'd only be here a short while, but a stove beats cookin' on a campfire."

Dola folded her arms and hugged her waist. "But we don't have room in our tent for a stove."

"I reckon in this kind of weather you can just set it out in the open. Cain't hurt it much. We only paid four cash dollars for it," Wasco added as he and Lucky Jack toted it toward the back of the Skinner tent.

"If it gets rainy, maybe we can hang a canvas over it. But I don't think it rains four days of the year out here." Lucky Jack plopped the stove down in the dirt next to the crates. "They claim that table seats twelve, but it looks bigger than that. We'll have to make our own chairs or somethin' 'cause chairs are hard to come by."

Dola Skinner trailed after them. "This is wonderful. I can't believe I get to cook on a real stove."

Lucky Jack pulled off his hat and wiped his forehead. "Well, Dola . . . eh, Mrs. Skinner . . . I don't know how wonderful it is. The folks wanted to sell it and buy a new one. There might be something wrong with it."

Dola stayed by the stove and watched as they carried over the huge, slightly battered, sturdy oak table. Mrs. Rokker did not exit her tent, but the flap was thrown back, and Dola could see the thin-faced woman peering out.

Dola had the men set the stove so she would be facing the morning sun while she cooked breakfast. The table was placed a few feet away.

"Here's my list. If it's too expensive, cut back anywhere you want . . . and if you find something else you want me to cook for you, just buy it. I think we'll need to buy the meat fresh every day. In this heat it would spoil without ice. I'm not a professional cook, but I spent many an Oklahoma spring and fall roundup cooking for a bunkhouse full of cowboys. Of course, cowhands have never been accused of being discriminating eaters."

"Mrs. Skinner," Wasco grinned, "we're gettin' hungry just thinking about it. I know it's kind of late for supper, but we was thinkin' 6:30 P.M. would be a good time to aim for."

"That will be fine."

"It'll probably be a couple hours before one of us returns with the groceries," Lucky Jack added. Then he lowered his voice. "Sorry about that 'Dola' comment. That ain't proper, and I apologize."

She found herself brushing her hair back off her ears. "No apology needed, Mr. Gately. I doubt if there are many rules of polite society in a place like this."

"If there are, I reckon you will help set them." He tipped his hat and climbed back up into the buckboard.

*I will help set the rules of society? Hardly. I've never even known the rules of society, let alone taught them to others. I do believe Mr. Gately is a tease.*

She rubbed her hand across the smooth, clean surface of the table. *Lord, it's like a blessing falling out of the sky. I can't believe how good You are to me. A stove and a table. I'll do all my food preparation on the table and cook on the stove. No stooping or bending over the fire. I'm not complaining, Lord, but the change will be nice. Very nice. I like cooking for men. Why is that, Lord? Oh, I do hope it's not sinful.*

"Mrs. Skinner?"

Dola spun around. Jared Rokker stood next to the crates, hat in hand.

"Mrs. Skinner, can Rita Ann go for a walk with me around town?"

"Yes, I already told her that would be . . . Where is she?" Mrs. Skinner stared toward the back of the barren desert lot. "Oh, yes, she went after her sister. Let me go get them."

Punky sat by her feet pushing a block of wood with four empty green thread spools nailed to it through the light brown dirt. She reached her hand down to him. "Come on, darlin', let's go find your sisters."

"Carry me!" he squealed.

"You're too big a boy to carry."

"I'm not big, I'm medium," he insisted.

Dola laughed. "You're right. You're medium." She reached down and scooped him up, letting him settle on her thin hip. A sharp pain hit her low in the back. Then her right shoulder cramped. She shifted him to a better position and trudged across the nearly level lot. Her shoes rubbed her raw feet.

Tommy-Blue and Danny had dug a hole about two feet deep and were staring at the powdery dry dirt in the old pie pan when she reached them.

"How's it going?" Dola asked them.

Tommy-Blue looked up out of a dust-covered face. "It would be better if we had water to wash out the ore," he replied.

She glanced back toward the tent and the water barrel. "We

don't have any water to spare. But after a while, there might be some old dishwater you can use. She stared down into their shallow, sandy hole. "Besides, you might want to dig a little deeper before it gets too hot to play out here."

"If we strike pay dirt, I'm going to buy me a brand-new Winchester .03 automatic .22 to hunt mountain lions," Tommy-Blue announced as he grabbed up the broken shovel.

"How about you, Danny? What are you going to buy?" Dola asked.

Danny Rokker looked up with a dirty face under unkempt blond hair and bit his tongue. "I'm goin' to buy me a whole pan of biscuits and a bucket of beef stew and . . . and all the cold milk I can drink and . . ."

"Ain't you goin' to buy anything fun?" Tommy-Blue chided.

"Oh, yeah . . . and a motorcar," Danny grinned. "I bet them is fun."

Dola continued her hike toward the back of the lot. *Nine-year-old boys shouldn't have to dream about having a decent meal. Lord, the Rokkers trouble me. You put them in our path, yet there doesn't seem to be much we can do for them.* Dola stopped a few feet short of the rock and mortar outhouse.

"Corrie? Rita-Ann?" she called out.

There was no reply. About twenty feet behind the small building was the sprawling tent of Mrs. Marsh. All four corners of her lot were marked with piles of stones and crudely painted "Keep Out . . . For Sale . . . $50,000 cash" signs.

Dola could see a couple dozen more tents scattered on the gradual incline of the mountain stretching to the south. There seemed to be people and animals near every tent except the one in front of her. A few old empty tin cans and a rusted milk can full of sand was all she spied.

"Rita Ann?" she shouted.

A round head with black pigtails drooping and blue eyes peering through wire-framed glasses appeared at the tent flap. "Hi, Mama."

"What are you doing over there?" Dola asked.

"Getting Corrie, like you asked me to."

"Go away or I'll shoot you!" a woman screamed from inside the tent.

Dola held her breath and stepped back.

Rita Ann pulled her head back inside the tent. "It's okay, Mrs. Marsh. It's our mama."

Dola took a deep breath, let it out slowly, and tried to relax. "Girls," she said evenly, "I need you to come home."

Corrie popped out of the tent, followed by her older sister. Dola expected Mrs. Marsh to follow. When she didn't, Dola waited for the girls to cross the property line and then turned back toward their tent.

"What were you girls doing over there?" she quizzed.

"Just bein' neighborly, Mama," Corrie replied.

"Perhaps Mrs. Marsh doesn't want to be neighborly."

Rita Ann reached up and took Punky out of her mother's arms. "She doesn't mean it when she yells."

Corrie slipped her slightly sticky hand into her mother's. "She's just tired and hungry, Mama."

With her free hand, Dola rubbed her shoulder. "She's tired and hungry?"

"Look, Mama." Corrie dug into the pocket of her torn dress. "She gave me five dollars."

Mrs. Skinner stopped and glared at her daughter. "You take it back right now, young lady. You don't take money from strangers, Corrie Lou. You know better—"

"Mama," Rita Ann interrupted as she bounced Punky in front of her, "Mrs. Marsh didn't give that to Corrie to keep. She wanted her to go buy her some groceries."

Corrie handed her a very neat list written in pencil with almost perfect penmanship. "She's afraid if she goes to the store, someone will steal her land. She ran out of food and wants me to buy these things."

"You're too young to buy groceries for someone."

"Jared and I will go with her," Rita Ann offered.

"She said she'd pay me fifty cents if I brought her groceries."

Dola looked down the list—beans, canned meat, fruit, crackers. "Fifty cents is too much to pay a ten-year-old. You shouldn't take more than two bits. A person shouldn't get rich on another's need."

"That's what I told her," Rita Ann added. "'Thou bear'st thy heavy riches but a journey, and death unloads thee.' *Measure for Measure*, Act 3, Scene 1."

"Fifty cents isn't all that heavy," Corrie grumbled.

"You tell Mrs. Marsh that you only need twenty-five cents, and then if she insists on giving you fifty cents, that will be a bonus," Mrs. Skinner instructed.

Corrie's blue eyes lit up, and dimples framed her smile. "Then you'll let me do it?"

"If Rita Ann goes with you."

"And Jared?" Rita Ann added.

"Yes, and young Mr. Rokker." She turned to Corrie. "You'll need to wash your face and hands, eat your boiled egg, and comb your hair." They continued to walk toward the tent. "Now, young lady, tell me how you came to be in Mrs. Marsh's tent in the first place."

"When I came out of the privy, she was staring at me and holding her gun. She said if I came on her property, she'd shoot me."

"And what did you say?" Dola quizzed.

Punky squirmed in his sister's arms. "I want to play with Tommy-Blue!"

Rita Ann plopped Punky down. All four stopped to study the boys' hole.

"Punky throws dirt, Mama," Tommy-Blue protested.

"Then you will have to stay with me," she told the toddler, grabbing his hand. They continued the trek to the tent. "Now, Corrie Lou, what did you say to Mrs. Marsh when she threatened you?"

"I said she looked sleepy. I told her I always get cranky if I don't have enough sleep. I told her she'd probably feel better if she had a nap."

"What did she say?"

Corrie skipped along ahead of her mother. "She cried."

"She did?"

"She said she's very tired." Corrie turned around and walked backward across the flat lot. "She said she can't sleep much at night because they try to sneak up on her at night."

"Who does?" Mrs. Skinner asked.

"Claim jumpers," Corrie replied. "I didn't hear anyone sneaking around last night, did you, Rita Ann?"

"'Sleep, O gentle sleep . . . nature's soft nurse.'" She turned to her younger sister. "*You* never hear anything at all when you go to sleep."

"I hear trains," Corrie declared. "They always wake me up. Especially when we're camped down next to the tracks."

"Why does she think there's gold on her place?" Mrs. Skinner queried.

Corrie reached down and plucked up a pebble of cloudy quartz about the size of a dime and shoved it into her dress pocket. "She said her husband told her there was gold, and she should never sell the land for less than $50,000."

"Did Mr. Marsh die?" Mrs. Skinner quizzed.

"Yep." Corrie put her hands on top of her head. "He's there in the tent."

Dola Skinner felt the hair on the back of her neck stand up. "What?"

"Not *in* the tent," Rita Ann scolded her sister. "He's *under* the tent."

"They were here two years ago when the town was still called

Gran Pah," Corrie explained. "There wasn't any cemetery then, so she buried him next to the gold mine shaft and moved the tent over the top of it so the coyotes wouldn't paw at the grave."

"She dug the grave and buried him all by herself," Rita Ann added.

Dola looked back. "She told you all this?"

"I think she's lonesome, Mama," Corrie declared. "She doesn't have anyone to talk to. Ever'body needs someone to talk to. Maybe I can visit with her while we're staying here."

"Corrie, darlin', I think that would be a good idea. Now you get your breakfast and clean up. You have some grocery shopping to do."

It took less than ten minutes for the trio to get ready and start down the dirt street toward the main part of town. Dola watched them skip, giggle, and laugh as they went. Standing by her own tent, Stella Rokker also watched them depart. She turned back to Mrs. Skinner.

"Stella, I'm going to build a small fire and warm some water just to try out this old stove. Would you and your mother like to come over for some tea in a bit?"

The girl popped into the tent, and Dola could hear a heated discussion. Finally Stella reappeared. "Mama's feelin' poorly and needs to stay in the tent. She ain't well, you know. But she said I could come have tea if I brought her some."

"Certainly."

"Are we goin' to have crackers with our tea? I like crackers."

Dola glanced over at the nearly empty food box. "I'm sorry, honey, but we don't have any crackers. I'll hunt around. Perhaps I can find something else."

Dola Skinner took the cotton rag that had been immersed in boiling water and washed her face and neck. Then she scrubbed her hands. *Well, Lord, they are clean finally. But they still look old and battered.* She glanced down into the nearly empty tin. *I've been saving this last spoonful of tea leaves for a special occasion. Perhaps this is it. Mr. Gately will bring me a new tin when he comes back with the groceries.*

When the open pan of water began to boil, Dola scooted it to the side of the stove. The heat from the firebox and the desert sun caused sweat to pop out all over her face. She lined up four tin cups of boiling water and tried to stir tea leaves into each to a similar darkness. Then she rattled a small square tin box and opened it, pulling out a one-inch section of sugar cane stalk. She swirled it in each cup and then put it back in the tin.

"Stella," she called out, "tea is ready."

The girl, in sagging oversized beige dress, darted out of the tent and over to the big oak table.

"Take that one on the end to your mother," Dola instructed. "I'm going to take this one up to Mrs. Marsh. When I get back, you and I will try to find a little bread to smear strawberry jam on."

Within half an hour all four empty cups sat lined up on the oak table. Stella returned to her tent, red jam stuck to her fingers and cheeks.

Punky was playing with a bucket of empty wooden spools on the middle of the featherbed. Danny and Tommy-Blue had toted two empty crates, a broom, and a piece of canvas out to their hole to create shade. They also had a dishpan full of dirty water to work with.

Dola sat on an old black trunk at the opening of the tent. She had pulled the flaps back at both ends to allow some movement of air. The collar of her dress was ringing wet with sweat. She fanned herself with a faded circular fan that at one time had proclaimed, "Chicago World's Fair."

*Lord, there are some days when I look at our predicament and shake my head. On those days I can't figure out how or why we ended up in a situation like this. This isn't one of those days.*

*There seem to be people who need my friendship and encouragement all around us. The Rokkers . . . Mrs. Marsh . . . Lucky Jack and his friends . . . the Wilkins brothers . . .*

*Well, perhaps not the Wilkins brothers.*

# FIVE

When Lucian LaPorte returned to the cemetery, he had five more empty kegs and two pair of used boots.

O. T. tried to wipe his forehead on his shirt, but the thin cloth was soaking wet already. Every piece of clothing he wore was sweat-drenched. *Lord, I can't even remember being clean. We had pictures taken right after Punky was born. I know I was scrubbed up then. There's just too many people out West anymore to live this dirty.*

LaPorte's hat was pushed back and the top button on his white shirt unfastened as he climbed down from the wagon. His vest still flashed a gold watch chain. "Skinner, I can't hardly believe you got them other kegs filled already."

"The trail wasn't gettin' any easier, so I kept pushin' harder just to get done," O. T. reported. "I don't reckon I'd want to spend the rest of my life doin' this." He tried rubbing his shoulder, but it felt too raw to touch.

"The city's takin' over the water business pretty soon anyway. They're diggin' three new wells. They claim they'll put in a big cistern up on the ridge. That ought to supply all of town. But they don't figure it will be done until November." LaPorte poured a wooden bucket half full of water and toted it up to his team. "There's a lot of talk around town that since you are hikin' in after free water, others will do it too."

Skinner stared across the cemetery to the north. "Maybe that's what makes the man in the tollhouse so edgy."

"Edgy? He plumb tried to kill you! Some are just mean that way," LaPorte called back. "Did you ever see a place that was as hot and dry as this desert?"

"Kind of like workin' in a furnace, isn't it?"

LaPorte finished watering his team and wandered back to the wagon. The braided leather stamped string of his felt hat drooped down his back. "They say them that makes it rich in Goldfield all go build them a big ol' place along the California coast."

"Is that what you're goin' to do?" O. T. pressed.

"Yep, Skinner, I reckon I will." LaPorte's white teeth glistened when he talked. "I got my eye on a stretch of beach just south of Santa Barbara called Carpenteria. How about you? What are you goin' to do when you get that big gold strike?"

O. T. splashed water on his face and let it slide down his neck and chest. It plowed a cold path clear to his waist. "No gold for us. We're not goin' to stay here, you know. But I do want a place in California. I want a quiet little vineyard next to my brother's in a town called Dinuba."

LaPorte brushed his pencil-thin mustache with the tips of his fingers. "I've been there."

"You have?"

"Got a cousin who works for the Yagers on the Proud Quail Ranch just east of there on the slope of Stokes Mountain. They have a daughter, Miranda Yager, that rides buckin' horses in one of those Wild West shows. Maybe you've heard of her?"

"I don't reckon I know anyone in California, except my brother and his family. Is it nice country around Dinuba?"

"If you like flat irrigated land that can grow any crop on the face of the earth."

O. T. paced around the empty casks to keep his side from cramping up. "Sounds nice to me."

"But you don't get an ocean view." LaPorte reached into the back of his wagon. "I brought you these two pair of boots. Didn't know which one you'd like more. You can have them both." He handed them to O. T.

Skinner stared at the boots. "I couldn't afford to buy two pair."

"They ain't new—just polished up nice. And I ain't sellin' them; I'm givin' them to you. I got them for free. One of these places I deliver water to is like a . . . like a hotel. Sometimes folks leave their shoes or boots. So there's a box of extras in the back room. They told me to help myself."

O. T. turned them over and rubbed his hand across the soles. His fingers were so calloused he could hardly feel the thick leather. "These are in nice shape. Men just ride off and leave a good pair of boots at a hotel?"

LaPorte's round brown eyes studied him. "Something like that."

O. T. stood a little straighter, and the pain in his shoulder lessened. He stopped pacing. "Don't that beat all?"

LaPorte waved a huge, long finger at Skinner. "Those brown ones have a dry pair of socks in them. They're clean too. I checked them out."

"I feel like the first hog to the trough. I'm not usually that excited about a pair of boots, but the soles on mine are wearing out quick," O. T. laughed. "I patched them up last time with some calf rawhide. It wasn't the toughest thing in the world." He sat down on a water keg and tugged off his old boots. Then he slowly pulled on the clean socks and the plain dark brown boots with fifteen-inch shafts and stovetops. He carefully tucked his denim trousers inside the boots. *These boots are worth showin' off.*

He stood up and tramped around the cemetery driveway. "These are nice feelin'. Tell that hotel I appreciate their generosity. In fact, I could stop by after I'm through and thank them myself." He handed the black pair back to the man.

"I'll . . . see that they're thanked. You don't want to . . . It's not the kind of place that . . ." LaPorte rubbed his hand across his mouth. "Anyway, keep this other pair too. They didn't cost me a penny."

He tried again to hand them back, but Skinner shook his head. "I can't do that, Lucian. It ain't that I'm not grateful. But my kids have one pair of shoes. My wife has one pair of shoes to her name, and they don't even fit her good. It just wouldn't be right for me to have two pair. No, sir, I couldn't do that even if they're free."

LaPorte tossed the black boots back into his wagon and shook his head. "O. T., I ain't never known a man, black or white, who's tryin' to stay poor as much as you."

"I'm not tryin' any such thing. It's just that a man has to be fair to his family, that's all. I can't ask them to do somethin' I ain't doin'." *I never knew a clean pair of socks could feel so good. I do believe I could dance all night in these boots. Of course, I've never danced in my life.*

The tall man pulled off his dark felt hat and ran his fingers across his short, curly black hair. "I took the two kegs of water to your wife like you asked," he reported.

"I surely appreciate it." O. T. continued to walk around, testing the boots. "Did you tell her I'd be busy for a while?"

"Yep." LaPorte began to load the wooden water casks into his wagon. "She said she wanted two more kegs of water. She was sharin' the others with the neighbors in that front tent."

Skinner helped LaPorte load the barrels. "Then I'd better get back to work." He smiled. "By the time I get home, Dola will be supplying water to half the town."

When the kegs were all loaded, Lucian LaPorte swung back up in his wagon. "You might want to crawl under that rig of yours and get a little siesta in the shade this afternoon. It ain't healthy workin' too long out in this desert heat."

"I think I'll tote a couple more loads and then do just that. How soon will you be back?"

"It'll be midafternoon. You got something to eat for lunch?"

O. T. sucked in his stomach. *Lord, I surely hope Dola and the kids have something to eat. At least they have a dozen boiled eggs. That ought to last awhile.* "I'm too tired to eat," he sighed. "I'll make it up at suppertime."

LaPorte shook his head. "Skinner, a lot of people in this town are making money hand over fist. And I've been feelin' like the poorest man in Goldfield for weeks. You folks make me seem like a rich man. I feel ashamed that I've been complainin'."

"We're not poor. We just don't have much, that's all."

The big black man began to laugh. "Some folks call that the definition of being poor. O. T., I'm serious. Don't get too much heat. You take care of yourself. You've got a nice-lookin' family that's countin' on you."

O. T. nodded and watched the wagon roll out of the cemetery.

*Lord, I'm not sure whether it was LaPorte—or You—talkin' to me. Nobody should have to work in this heat, and there's thousands camped out here lookin' for gold. It's like You play a joke on folks. It's like You said, "I wonder if they'll be foolish enough to wade around in a cold California stream and hunt gold. . . . I wonder if they'd climb to the top of a Colorado mountain for gold. . . . How about the frozen wasteland of the Yukon? . . . I know, I'll send them out into the middle of the Mojave Desert." People fall for it ever' time, don't they, Lord? Well, they can have it. I'm movin' on.*

*But we're not poor. Two mules, a wagon, a lovin' wife, healthy kids, and a strong back . . . well, before today it was strong.*

*We ain't poor.*

*We jist don't have much more than that . . . that's all.*

After two more treks into the springs, O. T. found the temperature even more stifling. Heat radiated out of the ground like when a bedroll has been stretched out over buried campfire coals. There was no wind. The ground was hard-packed from lack of rain and the weight of heavily laden wagons. O. T.'s shirt was torn and his elbows raw from bouncing off the rocks of Malpais Mesa. From his new socks to his hat, every stitch was soaked in sweat. His upper arms ached as if prodded with hot branding irons. His shoulders and back were cramped with sharp pains.

But there was shade under the wagon. He rolled completely under the middle and lay on his back. Instantly he was asleep.

"Hey, are you dead or just takin' a nap?"

O. T. sat straight up, slamming his head on the bottom of the wagon bed. The impact caused him to fall back down. The dozing mules bolted forward about ten feet, leaving him lying out in the open dirt. A dirty, grinning man gazed down at him.

"Skinner? I thought this wagon looked familiar. But I ain't never known a man who came out from under a wagon in that particular fashion."

O. T. gingerly sat up. He rubbed his forehead as he stared at the man covered from head to foot with light gray alkali dust. His wide-brimmed hat flopped down over squinting eyes. His mustache was caked. His lips had cracked open, bled, and then dried to form hideous streaks. His holster, revolver, and bullet belt hung around his neck.

"Mr. Wilkins! You look even dustier than last time," O. T. grinned.

Wilkins held out his hand to pull O. T. to his feet. "Ain't no mister about it. Call me Ace. And I ain't been clean for so long I'm afraid to wash up 'cause I don't even know if I have any skin left under there." He glanced at the wooden barrels lined up in the cemetery drive. "You reckon I can get a drink? You got some water in those barrels, don't you?"

O. T. jammed on his hat and walked up to quiet the jittery mules. "Help yourself. I been usin' the one on the back of the wagon. I'm just gettin' ready to fill some more of them."

Wilkins took a ladle of water, wet his finger, and splashed a few drops on his cracked and bleeding lips. Then he took a small sip, swished it around in his mouth, and spat it out. Finally he took a long drink. He surveyed the cemetery. "Where's the water well?"

"There's a public spring over there to the north, but the man makes ever'one pay a toll to get to it." Skinner rolled the keg so that it would pour out into Wilkins's cupped hands. "I didn't have the money, so I hike into the springs and tote them out along the canyon wall."

Wilkins splashed water on his face and dried it off with a red bandanna, reddened even more with red dirt. He shook out his hair and reset his hat. "That just might be the best drink of water I've had in ten years. Alkali seems to suck ever' last drop of moisture out of a man." His lips were still severely chapped but no longer covered with dirt and dried blood. He walked down the line of water kegs and plopped down on the end one. "I don't see a trail up there."

"It's kind of like a rock ledge."

"Totin' these kegs looks like a lot of work. How much water does your family need?"

"I'm helpin' out another guy and earnin' a little grocery money." O. T. tried to roll up the sleeves of his shirt to protect his raw elbows.

Ace Wilkins looked east toward Goldfield and Columbia Mountain. Scattered behind the town were the rugged headworks of several mines with names like Sandstorm, Jumbo, and January. "You seen Lucky Jack and them?" he asked.

"Not today. I came out here early and haven't been back to town." Skinner leaned on one sideboard of the wagon, Wilkins on the opposite. "Where are your brothers?" O. T. probed. "And that motorcar?"

With alkali dirt partially washed from the lines and wrinkles of Wilkins's face, O. T. guessed Ace's age to be about forty-five. Ace pulled off his hat and used it as a fan. His mostly bald head was caked with dirt and sweat. "Your water got us another five miles, and then that Thomas motorcar gave out completely. I think the motor's busted. We turned them burros loose when we got her runnin'. So by then we didn't have no conveyance but our feet."

O. T. stretched his neck and took a deep breath that smelled like hot desert dirt. "So you got the job of hikin' into town?"

"Well, Deuce was crankin' on that gasoline engine. Then it blew up like a stick of dynamite and jumped back on him. That crank handle snapped his arm like a wishbone. He's hurtin' bad. I left Trey out there to take care of him and hoofed it into town. I started hikin' about dark last night, but I must have got confused, 'cause when mornin' came, I was still a long ways away."

O. T. gazed at the alkali flats to the north. "You hiked all night and all day in that stuff?"

Wilkins fogged the air as he brushed his denim trousers with his hands. "Some hard things just got to be done, especially when it involves kin."

"I know exactly what you mean. A man who don't look after his family ain't much of a man." O. T. scanned Wilkins's face for any trace of insincerity. *Lord, I'm not sure why Lucky Jack hates this man so. A man who looks after his younger brothers, well, Your image in him isn't totally destroyed.*

"O. T., I'll come right out with it. I need some help." Ace jammed his hat back on and stared Skinner in the eyes. "Can I hire you and your rig to go out with me and pick up my brothers? Maybe even tow that motorcar into town?"

Skinner looked away. His voice lowered and was so soft it was barely audible. "I cain't hire out to help someone in need. That ain't Christian. I'll do that for free."

Wilkins pulled the heavy bullet belt and holster off and draped them on the wagon. Then he rubbed his neck. "O. T., I cain't figure you out. You're wearin' rags and refusin' money. I don't know if you're noble or jist dumb."

O. T. laughed despite the pain in his elbows. "Ain't this shirt somethin'? I keep rippin' it on that rock mesa wall. But I don't reckon

I'm noble," he continued to chuckle, "so that should answer your question. Ace, I'll help you, but I have a problem. I'm workin' for a man right now. I've got to finish filling these barrels with water before I can go with you."

Wilkins moseyed to the back of the wagon and gulped down a couple of swigs of water. "How long will that take?"

Skinner eyed the rocky trail. "Well, if I get busy and quit nap- pin', about two more hours. Sorry, I cain't do it any quicker."

Wilkins studied the rocky cliff. "I'm amazed you can do that at all. You must be part mountain goat."

"It's a tough hike, especially coming back with a full cask. My shoulders are rubbed raw, and my legs are startin' to cramp up. That's the best I can do. I promised I'd finish the job, and if a man's word don't stand, he might as well crawl in a hole and die. But if you'd like, I'll give you a quick ride into town. Maybe you can find some- one else to help you sooner."

Wilkins stepped over to the holster of his gun hanging on the side of the buckboard and fingered the dusty trigger. "I'm not goin' into Goldfield alone until I see how Gately plays his hand."

"I sure don't understand why you and Lucky Jack seem ready to shoot each other."

"He told you, didn't he?"

"He told us about that woman gettin' shot in Mexico."

"Did he tell you about the bombin' death of Pete Phillips?"

"Bomb?"

"What else would you call six sticks of dynamite?"

"I didn't hear about that. Was that during that there railroad has- sle north of Telluride?"

"Hassle? It was the Rocky Mountain Railroad War, that's what it was. Two armed camps tryin' to kill each other. Pete Phillips was a railroad superintendent that we worked for. He hated violence. Refused to pack a gun."

"Yet he hired you men to do his shootin' for him?"

"Nope, we were hired by the owners. Pete got stuck with the job of bossin' us. He was a family man. Had his wife and kids livin' with him. They say he'd turn down any job that required him to be away from the family. Anyway, someone on the other side called him out of the house and tossed six sticks of dynamite under his porch. Blew him to pieces while his wife and kids were at the kitchen table."

"Are you sayin' Lucky Jack and them did it?" O. T. pressed.

"Lucky Jack used to set off explosives in the Wild West Show. What do you think?"

"He don't seem like the type to me."

"Well, that's only the first chapter. We got a score to settle, but not by myself. So I'll wait for you to finish up."

Skinner tried to study Ace Wilkins's eyes, but they were still too red from the blast of desert sand to read any emotion. "I'll try to hurry it up. I reckon Deuce is sufferin' fierce, all busted up and out in the heat of the day."

"Hopefully, they got enough sense to stay in the shade of that motorcar." Ace squatted down beside the wagon. "I ain't slept in two days. Maybe I should jist crawl under here and catch some sleep myself."

O. T. shoved an empty wooden keg onto his aching shoulders and started up the narrow, rocky trail. Every square inch of his back felt raw. His new boots softened each step, but his feet were blistered and hurting from the old ones.

*Lord, I never know when to back away, do I? I should have just hiked in here, got my two kegs of water, and went home. I piled my family out on a borrowed lot and took off. I should be home and getting us ready to pull out tomorrow. Must be a mighty borin' life, sittin' on a crate waitin' for Daddy to come home.*

When he got to the springs, a well-dressed man in a pressed wool suit was struggling to shove a full water cask back into his carriage. The man's crisp black bowler tumbled to the dirt.

O. T. set his empty keg down next to the springs and let it begin to fill. "You need some help, mister?"

"Thanks, partner. I don't normally wrestle these casks, but I was taking an assay report to the Little Combination Mine and thought I'd bring some water back to the office on the way back. I'll be glad when those city wells are finished and piped into every building in town."

"You run an assay office?"

"Me and a partner. I'm Daniel Tolavitch."

"O. T. Skinner."

The men shook hands and then shoved the heavy wooden cask into the back of the black leather one-horse carriage.

Tolavitch pulled out a white linen handkerchief and wiped his forehead. "Thanks for the help. To be honest, the main reason I'm here is that I wanted to take a look at you."

"What do you mean, take a look at me?" Skinner retreated to his barrel at the springs.

The man strolled over, soaked the handkerchief, and dabbed the back of his neck. "I wanted to watch you walk that wall. You're gettin' to be famous in town," he declared.

"You got me confused with someone else, mister. I hardly know anyone in this town. We just pulled in last night."

"That might be, but the chaw in every shop and saloon, on every street corner and telephone call is that there is a crazy man hiking the mesa wall and fetching free water. Ever since Goldfield began, folks said it couldn't be done. Even the Paiute Indians won't try that stunt."

O. T. scratched the back of his neck and shook his head. "It's a sad commentary on a town if they don't have nothin' better to discuss than a man carryin' water," he chuckled. "Anyway, Mr. Tolavitch, I ain't doin' it much longer. I think one day is about it." Skinner pounded the wooden peg back into the keg and rolled it away from the springs overflow.

The man wrung out his handkerchief and then folded it neatly. "Did you know you're puttin' Jug Cherry out of business?"

Skinner glanced across at the tollhouse and the man who stood there, allowing entry to a long string of wagons and carriages. "A dozen barrels or so ain't goin' to put no one out of business."

"He already cut his price in half because of you."

"He did?"

"Yep. The boys have been threatening to follow your lead and bypass him entirely."

"They're welcome to it. A man can get tired of that wall mighty quick."

"There's even a plan bantered around in town for some of the miners to bring explosives over here on Sunday afternoon. They aim to set charges in the wall and open up a real trail that everyone can follow."

"Maybe I came here a week too early. That would surely be easier."

"They never would have tried it without your example, Skinner. By next week Cherry will be out of business, and he knows it."

"I had no intention of that happening. I just didn't have any choice."

"The truth is, Jug Cherry would like to run you out of town. If he can encourage you with a gun, he will. Watch out for him. Have you told him where you're stayin'?"

"No, sir."

"Don't. He's the type that'll show up in the middle of the night with torches, tar, and feathers." The man looked past O. T. to the north. "Looks like your partner's headin' out." The man pointed toward the cemetery.

O. T. glanced up in time to see Ace Wilkins gallop his mule and wagon out of the cemetery. "Partner? I don't have a . . ." *No! Don't take my wagon! Lord, I'm exhausted and achin' all over. I don't need this! A man ought to ask before he borrows a wagon.*

O. T. quickly hefted the full barrel onto his shoulders and scooted up the rocky trail toward the cemetery. "I've got to go!" he called back.

*Lord, I need that wagon. I can't leave Goldfield without it. I don't know why he'd take it without askin'. If he pushes Ada at that speed, she'll be dead before he reaches his brothers. Lord, I don't have nothin' but a wagon and two mules.*

Skinner was surprised when Wilkins didn't turn the wagon toward the alkali desert but rather toward Goldfield.

*Maybe he's just borrowin' it to go get someone else to help him.* O. T. continued the trek, his thighs cramping at each step. *Lord, forgive me. I condemned the man as a thief on no evidence at all. I started condemnin' him before I even knew what his intentions were. I need to be more like Dola. She has the delightful ability to ignore a man's failures and be thrilled with his virtues. What else accounts for her puttin' up with me all these years? Ace's brother's hurtin'. He's got to go find help. Me bein' sore and tired ain't no excuse to think poorly of a man.*

When O. T. looked back again, the wagon had veered off to the north. *He's goin' to the tollhouse? Maybe he's buyin' some water for his brothers. Maybe he saw someone he recognized in that line. I surely hope it wasn't Lucky Jack and them.*

It became impossible to look back at the rolling wagon and continue making his way to the cemetery, so O. T. tucked his head down and focused on the rock ledge. When he reached the row of barrels on the cemetery drive, he plopped the full one down and sat on it. He pulled off his hat, wiped his brow, and watched a commotion at the tollhouse.

From the distance of half a mile, all he could tell was that the wagons waiting in line at the gate suddenly surged across the toll land for the springs all at the same time, while a lone horseback rider galloped toward town. Ada, pulling his wagon, thundered back toward him. A cloud of alkali dust followed the wagon, which didn't slow down when it entered the cemetery. Wilkins roared up next to the barrels, reined the mule to a sliding stop, and jumped down.

"Let's load up these empties. We can drive in there and fill them all at once," Wilkins announced.

Skinner began loading water kegs into the back of the wagon. "What about Cherry and his tollbooth?"

Wilkins joined in loading the barrels. "Cherry retired."

"Retired? You mean, quit for good? Ace, what did you do to him?" O. T. pressed.

Ace Wilkins pulled a little leather pouch out of his vest pocket, took out a pinch of tobacco leaves, and shoved it down in his mouth between his cheek and gum. "I merely suggested that perhaps he had made enough money off the folks of Goldfield." He offered the tobacco pouch to Skinner, who declined. "I told him this might be the perfect time to look for some other line of work."

"What did he say?"

"Said he was plannin' on retirin' this weekend. I suggested he would enjoy his retirement more if he started a few days early."

O. T. glanced down at Wilkins's revolver and holster, now strapped to his hip and no longer dust-covered. "I got a feelin' there was more to it than that."

Ace Wilkins guffawed. "O. T., you got your ways; I've got mine. It was strictly by mutual consent. I made a proposition, and all them in line mutually agreed they wouldn't pay him another penny. Now you can drive in with the others and get all the water you want."

"I don't feel like arguing," O. T. remarked as he quickly pulled himself up into the wagon.

It didn't take him long to fill and load all the water kegs at the springs. Wilkins scrubbed himself up and helped him load the full casks. Then Skinner drove back to the cemetery entrance to wait for Lucian LaPorte.

While O. T. lounged against the wagon wheel, Ace Wilkins

paced in front of the mule. "Maybe you ought to take these kegs on into town and find your man," he suggested.

"I wouldn't know where to look." O. T. scrunched around so the pressure from the wagon wheel helped relieve the pain in his lower back. "I could wander all over and never find him. Besides, he should be back soon."

Wilkins circled the wagon. "Well, in that case, I think I'm goin' to finish that nap now. There's a little bit of a breeze. If I remember not to sit straight up, I can use the shade of your wagon."

Ace slept on his back, his hands folded on his stomach, his revolver holstered at his side. O. T. unharnessed Ada and brushed her down. He was watering her and checking her hooves when Lucian LaPorte's wagon pulled toward the cemetery. The mule was rehitched by the time the big man rolled in.

LaPorte pointed toward the man under the wagon. "Did you run over him?"

O. T. grinned and glanced at Ace Wilkins, who now held his revolver in his right hand. His eyes were still closed. "He's just sleepin'." Skinner transferred the barrels into LaPorte's wagon.

"I heard Jug Cherry up and retired." LaPorte raised his thick eyebrows and helped stack the barrels.

Skinner paused and scratched his stubby three-day beard. "I'm not sure why."

LaPorte's voice dropped to a whisper as he scooted over next to O. T. "Do you have any idea who's sleeping under your wagon?"

O. T. glanced down. "That's Ace Wilkins."

LaPorte put his hand over his mouth as if to mute the words. "You've heard of the Gately/Wilkins feud, haven't you?"

"Not until just recently."

"How big a reward do you think there is out for him?"

"I don't know anything about that." Skinner continued to lift kegs into the other wagon. "Besides, I couldn't turn a man in for a reward. Don't seem right to make money off another man's sin. If it's a legal matter, I reckon the law will deal with it."

When they finished, both men climbed down and strolled to the front of the wagons.

"You're a trusting soul, Mr. O. T. Skinner. Some folks don't want to be in the same county as the Wilkins brothers, let alone the same wagon. But that's your business, not mine. All I care about is that you got me my casks of water." He reached in his vest pocket and pulled out a thin wad of bills. He counted out three five-dollar bills and handed them to O. T. "Here's your fifteen dollars. You earned it. But with Cherry retiring and the toll road abandoned, the price of water just dropped to zero. I reckon we both might have to look for some other line of work."

O. T. stared at the money a moment. Then he shoved it deep into his right front jeans pocket. His left front pocket had ripped off in Nebraska, and Dola had just sewn it shut. "I hope that isn't a hardship for you, Mr. LaPorte. Personally, one day on that mesa wall is about all I want. My shirt's ripped up pretty bad as it is."

"That reminds me . . ." LaPorte strolled back to his wagon and pulled out a bundle wrapped in brown paper. "I brought somethin' else for you and somethin' for the wife," LaPorte announced. He handed Skinner the bundle.

O. T. tugged the sisal twine back and unfolded the paper. He let out a long whistle. "Now that is a handsome white shirt."

"It's silk," LaPorte informed him. "Cool in the summertime, warm in the wintertime."

"I don't reckon I ever had anythin' this nobby before," O. T. chuckled. He handed it back. "But I can't accept so generous a gift."

Lucian LaPorte shoved it forward. "We've gone through this before. These were given to me free. Someone went off and left them. It don't fit me, so either toss it in the rag barrel, or you can wear it. Those alligator boots are for Mrs. Skinner. I know they look fancy all polished up, but the reason I wanted her to have them is that they are so comfortable. I found a pair that fit my wife, and she won't ever take them off. It looked like your wife's feet was hurtin' her, so this might help. They didn't cost me a dime either. So don't go thankin' me. Just have her wear and enjoy them." When he finished, his entire face was beaded with sweat.

Skinner stood holding the boots and shirt and sporting a wide grin. "You're starting to sound like a Baptist preacher, Mr. LaPorte."

"Methodist. My daddy is a Methodist preacher in Omaha, and he's the only one who deserves to be called Mr. LaPorte."

Skinner reached out his hand. "Lucian, I do appreciate you givin' me a job today."

LaPorte roared, "Skinner, I don't think I've ever been thanked for makin' a man work so hard. I'm not sure what kind of work I'll be doin' tomorrow, but if I need help, I hope to see you around."

Lucian LaPorte's loaded wagon had just coiled to the bottom of the draw between the cemetery and town when Ace Wilkins rolled out from under the wagon and stood up, revolver in his hand. "I thought that black man would never leave."

"You were awake?"

"I never could sleep good when others are whisperin' about me." Wilkins holstered his revolver. "You don't believe all that about me having a reward on my head, do you? I ain't a wanted man. Neither are my brothers."

"Whatever happened in the past is between you, the law, and the Lord. A man's mistakes don't excuse me from treatin' him in a Christian way."

Wilkins stared down the mesa slope toward town. "You know what, Skinner? A man like you in Goldfield stands out like a punkin in a snow patch. What in the world are you doin' in a place like this?"

"Jist passin' through. And this punkin is ready for supper before we go out after your brothers. I haven't had anything to eat all day. Did you eat anything?"

"Not since yesterday."

"Well, I reckon Dola's puttin' some kind of supper on the fire. How about you and me going across to the other side of town to our camp to eat?"

Wilkins rubbed his chapped lips. "I'm serious about stayin' out of sight until my brothers can make it to town. Contrary to what you might have heard, I don't look for trouble."

"Why don't you hunker down by those two water kegs, and I'll roll right across town. Not many folks over on that side of town."

Ace Wilkins pulled himself up into the wagon. "We need to eat somethin', that's for sure. Just steer me away from Gately and that bunch."

O. T. climbed up into the wagon and untied the lead lines. "Last I heard they're taking their meals at the Northern. I won't even slow down when we go by."

"Well then, let's go," Wilkins agreed. "A quiet meal will do me good."

O. T. drove the wagon down the cemetery slope. For the first time since morning he felt his muscles begin to relax. He circled around downtown Goldfield and turned east on Columbia Street. There seemed to be new buildings going up since that morning. Certainly there were more tents.

He parked the wagon at the edge of lot #124. O. T. and Ace Wilkins hiked past the first tent toward his own.

"Didn't know you folks was packin' a stove," Wilkins said.

O. T. gazed in astonishment at Dola, who was busy cooking on a cast-iron outdoor stove. "Eh, I didn't . . . I . . . ."

Punky toddled out from behind some crates squealing, "Daddy! Carry me, Daddy!"

Dola spun around with a wide, dimpled smile, then froze when she spied Ace Wilkins. "Well," she finally replied, "it's nice to have Daddy home, isn't it? Hello, Mr. Wilkins."

Ace tipped his hat. "Mrs. Skinner, sorry for the intrusion at suppertime. I had to hike to town, so I don't have your olive crock with me."

O. T. stared at the long oak table, fully set, perched out on the desert dirt like a strange dream of the Last Supper. "Ace's brothers are stuck in that motorcar out in the desert. I've got to tow them in."

Dola gaped at O. T.'s torn shirt and bloody elbows. "Tonight?" *Orion, you look like you wrestled a bobcat. And you drag home one of the Wilkins brothers? I've never known another man who could see good in even a rascal.*

"Darlin', Deuce busted his arm, so I reckon he'll need a doctor to set it. We can't leave an injured man out on the desert. I figured we ought to grab some supper before we go. I knew you wouldn't mind."

Dola wiped her hands on her green apron, then hoisted it and wiped her sweating face. *I know I should be more like O. T. But this time, Orion Tower Skinner, you've got a real challenge.* "Mr. Wilkins, no person has ever been turned away from our table. Not now, not ever. Of course you're welcome."

"Thank you, Mrs. Skinner. Our mama was always that way too. Wasn't a person so rough or ornery that she wouldn't feed him. It's jist unusual to find a younger woman who acts that way."

"Mr. Wilkins, it's been ten years since anyone called me a younger woman. You aren't tryin' to flatter me and borrow another olive crock, are you?" This time the dimples were back in her smile.

"The only thing I need to borrow is your privy back there." Ace pointed at the little stone building.

Dola nodded. "The lady in that back lot may threaten to shoot you, but just ignore her."

"Friendly neighborhood," Wilkins muttered.

"She thinks anyone totin' a gun is trying to steal her claim," Dola explained.

Ace loosened his holster. "Then I'll just leave this with you, Mrs.

Skinner." He tossed his gun and holster on a crate and hiked toward the back of the lot.

O. T. turned to his apron-clad wife. "The lady back there really threatened to shoot you?"

"Yes, but she's not all that gruff. The girls have befriended her."

"Where did the stove and table come from?"

"I see you noticed."

"Of course I noticed."

"And you have new boots," she observed.

"LaPorte had some extras and gave me a pair. What about the stove and table?"

"Lucky Jack, Wasco, and Charlie Fred found them somewhere and brought them over."

"Hi, Daddy!" Tommy-Blue called out from the middle of the lot. "Come see our gold mine!"

"I'll be there in a minute, son. Did you find pay dirt?"

"Yes, sir. I reckon it will run $200 to the ton."

"That's good. Have you dug a ton yet?" O. T. hollered.

"Daddy! I'm just playin' make-believe," Tommy-Blue admitted. Then he disappeared back into the hole.

O. T. turned back to Dola. "Are these groceries ours too?"

"Yes, they are."

"Good thing I made fifteen dollars today. I'll be able to pay the grocer."

"How did you rip your shirt and bloody your elbows?" she asked.

"Bouncing off the rock wall on the cliff carrying those water kegs. I've got some new boots for you too. Well, they're not new, but they're quite nobby-looking."

Dola lowered her voice. "I can't believe you brought Ace Wilkins to our place." She glanced back toward the outhouse. "I do believe the Lord has given us an unusual assignment tonight."

"Looks like you're already expecting company."

"Lucky Jack, Wasco, and Charlie Fred should be here any moment." With a wet rag she gently dabbed the blood off his elbows.

"What?"

"That's what I've been tryin' to tell you, Orion. They brought us all these groceries because they hired me to cook for them for a couple days."

"Daddy!" Corrie ran up from the street and threw her arms around Mr. Skinner's neck. He squatted down and balanced Corrie on one knee and Punky on the other.

"Where have you been, darlin'?" he asked.

"All over town. I bought groceries for Mrs. Marsh 'cause she's afraid to leave her property, and she paid me fifty cents, but Mama said that was too much, so I only kept twenty-five cents, but Mrs. Marsh made me take the rest, so then we went down to the store, and I bought myself two pairs of socks and a peppermint for me, Rita Ann, and Jared Rokker."

"Where is your sister?"

Corrie leaned her cheek against his. "With Jared, of course."

He looked up at Dola. "How long have I been gone?"

She raised her eyebrows. "Too long, obviously."

"You kids will have to stand up. My legs are crampin' up from carryin' water today." He stepped over by the oven and peeked into the pots on the stove. "Now, what is this about you being hired to cook?"

"I wouldn't take pay, of course. It's more like a partnership. They provide food for themselves and for us. I do the cooking. Two hot meals and a cold lunch."

"Isn't that nice, Daddy!"

O. T. glanced up to see Rita Ann, her pigtails pinned to the back of her head, stroll up to the tent.

"Lucky Jack is going to be eating all his meals with us!" Rita Ann announced. "I believe he's quite handsome . . . for an older gentleman."

"Older gentleman? He's as young as . . . as . . . your mother," O. T. sputtered.

"Well, Mother said I could sit next to him."

"This is one meal where we'll have to be careful who sits next to each other," O. T. mumbled as he picked up Ace Wilkins's revolver and holster.

"Perhaps you and Mr. Wilkins could hurry and eat and leave before . . ."

"Look," Rita shouted, "here they come!"

A buckboard rumbled up east Columbia Street.

"Are we going to have a repeat of what happened out on the desert?" Dola whispered.

"Not if I can help it," O. T. replied.

While he stared down the street, a redheaded boy came out of the Rokker tent and timidly approached. "Mr. Skinner?"

"Who are you?"

"That's Jared, of course. Remember, you saw him last night?" Rita Ann explained.

"Rita Ann, you help me serve up the food," Dola instructed. "Corrie, you and Punky go call Tommy-Blue to wash up for supper."

O. T. walked over to Jared. "You need something, son?"

"You didn't see my daddy today, did you?" The boy's red hair had recently been slicked down.

"I don't think so. Course, I don't know what he looks like in daylight. But I was clear over on the other side of town all day," O. T. explained.

Jared focused on the dirt beside his boots. "He didn't come home, and Mama's worried sick."

O. T. studied the boy's thin face. "Maybe your daddy's workin' late."

"He don't have a job—anyway, nothin' regular that I know of." Jared chewed on his tongue and then blurted out, "Could you drive me around town and help me look for him?"

"Skinner! You're the talk of the town," Lucky Jack Gately hollered out as he, Wasco, and Charlie Fred hiked toward them. All three wore dirty denim trousers and soiled, collarless, long-sleeved white shirts.

"Howdy, Mrs. Skinner." Wasco tipped his dusty felt hat. "Standin' over that stove, you're sweatin' like a fat hog in July. Surely is hot today, ain't it?"

"It's going to get hotter," she mumbled. *Thank you for that encouraging barnyard comparison.*

Jared Rokker grew persistent. "What about it, Mr. Skinner? Could you give me a ride after supper?"

"I got to help another man first, but we'll see. Your daddy might be home by then."

"I hope so." Jared hung his head. "He was supposed to bring home groceries. We ain't got nothin' to eat, you know."

"Well, goodness, why did you wait so late?" Dola interjected. "Let me send a few things home with you, and tell your mama you can replace them when Mr. Rokker comes home with the groceries."

She grabbed a canned chicken, three huge yams, a loaf of sweet bread, and a bag of dried apricots. "Tell your mother I've got extra tea in those little bags if she'd like them."

She thought she saw a tear in the boy's eyes, but he turned away. With his arms loaded down, he scurried back to his tent.

Dola walked over to Lucky Jack and spoke softly. "Did you ever see skinnier, hungrier children?"

"Once. In the mirror. When I was ten," he mumbled.

"Lucky Jack!" Punky squealed as he led Corrie and Tommy-Blue back to the tent.

Gately reached down and picked up the toddler. "You been a good boy today?"

"Maybe." Punky answered.

"I like that . . . sort of like all of us. If the truth is known, 'maybe' is about the best anyone can answer," Lucky Jack said.

"Orion," Dola blurted out, "could you take Punky to the privy before supper, please?"

Lucky Jack held the toddler straight out in front of him as if suddenly discovering poison oak rash on the boy.

"I don't have to go," Punky protested.

O. T. grabbed the two-year-old. "That's the best time to go. Before there's an accident." *I need to warn Wilkins.*

"Maybe I'll hike over and take a look at Tommy-Blue's pay dirt." Lucky Jack took a step toward the back of the lot.

Dola grabbed his arm. "Mr. Gately, what is this you mentioned about Orion being the talk of the town?"

Lucky Jack spun back around and smiled. "They're callin' him the Wall-Walker down at the Northern Saloon."

She returned to the outdoor stove. He followed her. "The Wall-Walker?"

"He traipsed back and forth on a ledge everyone said could not be hiked to get free water," Gately explained.

"The tollhouse man just up and quit," Wasco added. "Said he was abandoning his claim. Now ever'one gets free water jist because of your husband."

"I bet O. T. could get free drinks in ever' saloon in town," Charlie Fred grinned.

"O. T. is temperance," she snapped.

"Yes, ma'am." Charlie Fred rolled up his sleeves to wash his hands. "I was joshin'."

Wasco and Charlie Fred toted crates around the table to serve as chairs. When O. T. and Punky returned from the privy, all the Skinners and the three men seated themselves at the big table. After O. T. prayed, the food was passed—potatoes, ham, beef chops, corn, biscuits, cucumbers, and deep-dish apple pie.

Lucky Jack finished chewing a big bite of potato and wiped his mouth on the back of his hand. "I told you boys that Mrs. Skinner would be a good cook."

"You ain't goin' to get no argument from this table," Wasco mumbled through a slice of ham that he had folded and crammed into his mouth.

"Thank you, but I agreed to cook for you whether you flatter me or not."

To the west the sun slipped down behind the mesa. A few lanterns flickered around the tent houses of Goldfield. Downtown the electric lights had not yet been turned on. A slight east wind began to swirl across the dry desert.

"Say," Wasco blurted out, swallowing a huge knifeful of apple pie, "did you start packin' a gun, O. T.?"

"No. Not unless you count that old shotgun under the wagon seat. I figure them days is over, boys."

"They aren't over for everyone," Lucky Jack mumbled through a big bite of boiled potato and molasses. "There's still a few of us ol' leaves hangin' on the tree."

"We heard you faced down that tollhouse man with a pistol," Charlie Fred added.

"Did you really, Daddy?" Corrie blurted out, spraying cucumber bits on Rita Ann.

"I don't carry a gun. You children know that."

"Someone's packin' one." Wasco pointed toward the tent. "I put it inside the tent when I moved the crate. It's a single-action Colt .45."

"Oh, that gun . . ." O. T. took a deep breath. "Belongs to a friend of mine. He didn't want to wear it around just anywhere, so he left it here."

"I wish you'd put it someplace where the children won't play with it. You know how I—" Dola began.

"He's in the privy!" Punky interrupted.

"Who's in the privy, Silas Paul?" Lucky Jack questioned.

"Punky, don't interrupt your mama," Dola scolded. "I really don't like—"

"Who's in the privy, Punky?" Rita Ann probed.

"Children, I don't think this is appropriate conversation during mealtime," O. T. lectured.

"Daddy's friend is in the privy," Punky declared with an air of triumph. "Me and Daddy talked to him."

"He's surely been in there a long time," Tommy-Blue laughed. "Which friend is it, Daddy?"

O. T. crammed a huge bite of ham into his mouth and chewed slowly as everyone waited for his response. *Lord, all I want is for no one to get injured or hurt.*

"Well, he's a serious gunman," Wasco added. "He's got a double row of cartridges on his bullet belt just like—"

"Like Ace Wilkins!" Lucky Jack jumped to his feet and yanked a pistol out of his belt.

Wasco and Charlie Fred drew guns and started across the lot.

"Keep the kids back," O. T. hollered to Dola as he sprinted after them.

"Skinner, I don't know why you'd betrey us like this," Gately groused.

"I didn't know you were coming to dinner. Ace isn't lookin' for trouble." O. T.'s voice was firm. "His brother broke his arm, and so naturally I need to help . . ."

"That's goin' to be the least of Ace's worries." Lucky Jack slowly approached the outhouse.

"He's an unarmed man," O. T. insisted. "You can't just—"

"I cain't believe Ace Wilkins is ever unarmed. Throw open the door, Wasco. Let's catch ol' Ace at his finest!" Charlie Fred demanded.

"Wait!" Skinner called out.

But Wasco shoved it open and stepped forward. Suddenly he dropped the gun to the dirt and backed away, as a shotgun barrel was shoved in his face. "Sorry, ma'am . . . I didn't . . . I thought . . . ," Wasco mumbled as a fully dressed older woman with a pompadour and a fringe bang stalked out of the privy. The barrel of her shotgun was only inches away from Wasco's head.

"Do any of you think a jury in this town would convict me of murder for shooting an armed claim jumper who broke into a privy when I was about to do my business?" she growled.

Lucky Jack howled. "No, ma'am. I believe you're in the right." He jammed his gun into his holster and continued to chuckle.

"What are you laughin' about?" Wasco shouted.

"It just seems funny that we stalked a stone outhouse and let a woman with a shotgun get the drop on us," Lucky Jack explained.

"Well, do somethin'," Wasco pleaded.

"Mrs. Marsh, I'm O. T. Skinner."

"Are you Corrie Lou's daddy?"

"Yes, ma'am, and these are my friends."

She lowered the shotgun. "Well, why didn't you say so. How was I to know you weren't all claim jumpers. Next time you men want to use the privy, just knock. Don't go bargin' in."

# SIX

O. T. hung a lantern on the back of the wagon, shoved Wilkins's gun
under a folded piece of canvas, and climbed up into the seat. Jared
Rokker pulled up into the seat beside him. The last shade of evening
gray was slipping into black as he watched Lucky Jack Gately and
friends drive away in their buckboard toward their leased claim.
There was not enough wind to cool down the evening, but just
enough to drift the sounds of downtown to the outskirts. His three
oldest children stood barefoot in the dark beside the wagon.

"Your new shirt glows in the lantern light," Corrie declared.
Even in the twilight, he spotted her mother's dimples in his daughter's cheeks.

"Too nobby for a man like me, darlin'. But at least it ain't
ripped," O. T. replied.

"It makes you look very handsome," Corrie replied.

"Thank you, Miss Skinner. You make an old man feel young
again."

Rita Ann's braids were neatly coiled on the side of her head, her
glasses perched halfway down her nose, and her hands folded around
a very thick volume. "Who are you going to look for first, Daddy? Mr.
Rokker or Mr. Wilkins?"

"Well, sweet Rita Ann, since I don't know where either man
might be, I reckon I'll search for Jared's daddy. I have a feelin' Mr.
Wilkins will come lookin' for me. I've still got his holster and
revolver." The silk shirt felt cool on his recently scrubbed neck.

Corrie rocked up on her bare toes, holding onto the iron railing at the side of the wagon seat. "It's gettin' dark. It's hard to find people at night, Daddy."

Rita Ann looked up at the stars that randomly decorated the desert sky. "'Deep night, dark night, the silent of the night, the time of night when Troy was set on fire; the time when screech owls—'"

"Darlin'," O. T. interrupted, "maybe *Henry V* could wait until—"

"*Henry VI*," she corrected. "And I have very good vision at night. I don't know why you won't let me go with you."

O. T. could see the fire in her blue eyes even at twilight. *The man that captures that girl won't know what hit him.* "You have very good hands too. So use them to help your mama wash the dishes and give everyone a scrubbin'."

With his hat off, Tommy-Blue's hair seemed to be trying to escape in all directions. "You're comin' back tonight, aren't you, Daddy?" he quizzed.

O. T.'s calves began to cramp from the day's hiking along the canyon wall. He pounded on them with clenched fists through the thick leather shanks of his boots. "I told you all, that depends. I need to give Mr. Wilkins a ride out to his brothers. If I find him or he finds me, I won't be back until around noon tomorrow."

Tommy-Blue rubbed his eyes with short, stubby fingers. "Will you assay my ore samples then?" he requested. "It's a paying claim. It could be runnin' $300 a ton."

Mr. Skinner sat up and brushed a speck of dirt off his shirt sleeve. "I thought you said $200 a ton."

"It looks better in the dark," his son replied.

Mr. Skinner laughed and pushed his hat back. "I reckon ever' claim looks better in the dark, son."

Bare electric lightbulbs powered by lines all the way from Inyo County, California, drooped down from tilted pine-and-pitch power poles. O. T. could see everyone on the street, but no one clearly. The air felt slightly warmer as the permanent buildings closed in on each side of Columbia Street. "People-noise" tumbled out of every open door and window. But not all the voices were joyous and happy.

O. T. could still taste the apple pie, but his back ached. His feet felt much better, but his thighs and calves seemed to have progressed beyond the cramping stage.

When they reached the first open business, a saloon called The Goldfield Spade, he pulled the wagon over to the raised boardwalk.

"Son, I'm not judgin' your daddy, but is this the kind of place you would expect to find him?"

The boy hung his head. His pointed chin rested on his thin chest. The shadowy silhouette did not reveal the gaunt eyes and sunken cheeks. His voice was surprisingly strong. "Yes, sir, I reckon it is."

O. T. took a deep breath. *Lord, there just ain't no good way to do this.* "Jared, I don't like you peekin' in these kinds of places, but this a serious matter. We do want to find your daddy. I won't recognize him, havin' seen him only once in the dark. So you walk along and look in the windows or peek in the door. If you see anyone who looks at all like him, I'll hop down and go investigate. But I don't want you goin' into any saloons, you hear?"

Jared raised his head. "Yes, sir."

Elias Rokker was not in The Goldfield Spade.

Nor the Esmeralda Palace.

Nor the Twice-a-Night Casino.

Nor Sandy's Colorado Club.

Nor The-End-of-All-Hope Saloon.

There was a big man with curly dark hair passed out under the faro table at Pinky's Card Room and Used Mining Supply, but O. T. discovered that he was Professor Horatio Chapman, formally of Winston-Salem, North Carolina.

When they had covered four blocks of saloons and chop houses, Jared crawled back up into the wagon. Most had been crowded with men in high boots and wide felt hats, guns strapped in holsters, and braggadocio in their voices. Here and there a flash of bright color testified to feminine clientele.

"Maybe your daddy's working a night shift at one of the mines," O. T. probed. "We could be lookin' in all the wrong places. I heard that some mines are hirin' shift miners."

Jared chewed on his tongue and then leaned his head back and closed his eyes. In the shadows his red hair looked dark brown. "Daddy don't like tunnel work. Says he got stuck one time, and he ain't ever goin' back."

Skinner leaned toward the boy. "You gettin' tired, son?"

Jared's eyes shot open. "No, sir."

There were no windows at the Hawthorne Club, and the ten-foot-tall doors swung closed behind each customer that ventured in and out. "I can't see in there," Jared called.

"Come hold the reins. I'll take a gander," O. T. offered.

Inside, O. T. found a twelve-foot ceiling with a huge electric chandelier that glowed like the sun. Ninety percent of the customers were men, and most of them wore suits, vests, and ties, and had cigars in their mouths. The long walnut bar sported carved lions and a brass rail. The poker games seemed to draw as many spectators as participants. The few women present were all attached to a man's arm.

On a tiny stage with a black velvet-looking curtain stood a large, florid woman with a big pompadour and wasp waist. She was finishing the last strains of "Wouldn't You Like to See a Little More of Me?"

She had barely concluded when a hatless gray-haired man called out as Skinner inched his way across the crowded room, "There he is, boys!"

O. T. spun around and stared at the man's relaxed steel-gray eyes. "You talkin' about me?"

"You're the Wall-Walker, aren't you?" The man flashed a wide grin and stuck out his hand.

O. T. felt the tension in his shoulders and neck relax. He shook the man's hand. "I reckon some seem to think so. My name's O. T. Skinner, and I'm lookin' for—"

"This is him, boys!" the man shouted. "The man who brought free water to Goldfield!"

A roar went up from the crowd, and several men huddled so close to O. T. that he couldn't proceed.

"You showed old Jug Cherry a thing or two," one man declared.

A big man in a gray wool suit threw his arm around O. T.'s shoulder. "I'm Montana Mike. Let me buy you a drink."

A man with black silk garters on his ruffled white shirt sleeves and an untied black tie draped around his neck grabbed O. T.'s arm. "Did you know Cherry's lookin' for you?"

"Better watch your back—he's a mean sucker," a bald man with an empty beer mug hollered from the bar.

O. T. scratched the back of his clean neck. His hair felt oily and dirty still. "Look, boys, I didn't do nothin' but get a little water for my family and earn some grocery money. I wasn't tryin' to harm his business. I was just too broke to pay the toll—that's all. There isn't anything heroic about bein' poor."

"That ain't the way he tells it," another shouted.

A tall man wearing a white denim apron scooted in beside him and shoved a small glass into his hand. "Here's a taste of pure Tennessee whiskey, Skinner. You earned it, partner."

O. T. shoved the glass back. "Thanks, mister, but I'm a temperance man."

"Then what are you doin' in the Hawthorne Club?" the big man with his arm still on O. T.'s shoulder hooted.

"Just helpin' a neighbor boy look for his daddy. Maybe some of you can help." O. T. crept out from under the man's heavy arm on his raw shoulder. "He's a big redheaded man named Elias Rokker. Have any of you seen him?"

"You might try the Red Top Bar. I thought I saw a big, old redheaded boy down there about an hour ago." The spokesman wore a mustache that drooped to his chin and sported a scar almost as long.

O. T. glanced back at the closed front door. "Yes, sir. I'll try that."

A man in a long tattered black silk coat that had the sleeves torn off wormed his way up to Skinner. "I heard you run with Lucky Jack Gately and them. Is that right?"

O. T. scooted toward the door. "I don't run with anyone. Me and my family are just friends with them."

A man with a diamond collar pin in his purple silk brocade tie stepped closer. His accent was British. "My word, that's not at all what I heard. I was told by reliable authorities that Skinner here and the Wilkins brothers grew up together in Kansas."

"The Wilkins brothers?" a blond-bearded man gasped, exhaling whiskey breath.

"I grew up in Arkansas, Texas, and Oklahoma—not Kansas," O. T. protested as he continued to jostle his way toward the front door. "They must have me mixed up with someone else."

"One thing's for sure, you're either on one side or the other," the man in the cut-off silk coat declared. "You kin be friends of the mongoose or friends of the snake, but not friends of both at the same time. Ever'body picks a side in the Gately/Wilkins feud."

"I'm really not on either side." O. T. found his way completely blocked by a cluster of men, most of whom held whiskey or beer glasses.

A bartender in crisp white apron pushed his way through and again shoved a glass mug into his hand.

"I told you I—" O. T. began to protest.

"It's soda water. Ain't a drop of alcohol in it."

O. T. stared down at the mug. "I reckon I'd better avoid the appearance of evil. But thanks." He handed it back to the bartender.

"I was hopin' you'd say that." The bartender took a big swig of the soda water. "Be careful. The boys are right. I heard Jug Cherry say he was goin' to run you out of town. He was mean and nasty and wavin' a big ol' Bowie knife."

The crowd pulled back when he reached the front door. "That would be a waste of his time," O. T. said. "We're just passin' through. I'll be gone before he finds me."

"You might want to start packin' a pistol, just in case," the bartender cautioned. Then he doffed the rest of the soda water.

"A man could get hurt doin' somethin' like that. Those days are over. This is the twentieth century." O. T. searched the faces for the man with the drooping mustache. "What saloon did you say we ought to look for Rokker in?" he questioned.

"The Red Top Bar."

"And where is that?"

"Down on lower Main Street, but it ain't no ordinary saloon, of course."

"I've got to hurry, boys. Thanks for your help."

"Skinner, you got free drinks in here anytime you want," the bartender called out as O. T. pushed open the tall, narrow doors.

"Do you always make that offer to temperance men?" O. T. laughed.

"Shoot, no," the bartender hooted. "Only the ones I know are going to keep their pledge!"

The air was still hot when he made it outside, but it tasted clean and almost fresh compared to the smoky interior of the Hawthorne Club.

"Was he in there?" Jared called out.

"Nope." O. T. climbed up in the wagon next to the boy.

"It surely took you a long time in there, Mr. Skinner."

"It was a friendly bunch. They said they might have seen your daddy at a place called the Red Top Bar or Red Roof Bar—something like that."

"A redheaded man at the Red Top Bar? Where's that?" Jared asked.

"On the lower end of Main Street. You ever been down there?" The boy gazed out into the desert night. "No, sir, I ain't."

"Well, neither have I. I reckon it won't hurt to check out another saloon." *Lord, it seems strange for me to be visitin' ever' booze joint in town. These places are melancholy in the daylight. At night they are downright morose. I've only been in town a little over twenty-four hours, and I surely haven't had much time for myself or my family. This is the most tumultuous place I've ever been. If I get home by noon tomorrow, I believe we'll load up and pull out at sunset. I'd rather camp on the desert than stay any longer in a place like Goldfield.*

They drove the wagon farther west, then turned north on Main Street toward the lower end of town. After several blocks the street became increasingly narrow and rutted. Lining both sides were small, single-story, wood-framed cabins, each sharing a common wall with the next, each with a small window and a dim red electric bulb hanging above the unpainted solid-wood door.

"This must be Chinatown," Jared offered. "I heard Chinatowns always like them colored lights."

"I don't think Goldfield has a Chinatown, but somebody likes red bulbs. Don't know why your daddy would look for a saloon down here when there's plenty of them uptown."

"There it is!" Jared hollered and pointed through the dark. "The Red Top Bar."

The building leaned to the west, as if built on the side of a hill that had now disappeared. The double doors were propped open with battered brass spittoons. The tinkle of a piano and shouting filtered out into the street. The shattered remains of a red electric bulb dangled in the dark above the door.

"I'll take a look inside," Jared offered.

O. T. put his hand on young Rokker's shoulder. "It surely looks like a small building for a saloon. They must not do much business."

Jared pointed on down the street. "I think it's attached to them little cabins with the colored lights. Maybe it's a miner's hotel."

"Hey, nice shirt, mister."

O. T. glanced over and saw a woman standing at the door of the Red Top. She was decked out in fluffy pink organdy, hair parted in the middle and coiled softly at the back of her head. A deep pink silk rose was tucked behind her ear.

"Thank you, ma'am. It's a silk shirt."

She lounged against the door. "Are you two lost, or are you comin' in?"

Skinner glanced back. A black carriage rumbled toward them about a block away. It was the only rig on the street that looked to be in a hurry. "We're, eh, lookin' for someone," O. T. told the woman.

"Well, here I am," she replied with a wide, easy grin. "The name's Gracie Lil."

O. T. tipped his hat. "No offense, Miss Lil, but we're lookin' for the boy's father."

"His name is Elias Rokker, and he likes to drink whiskey," Jared blurted out.

"Ever'body in this town likes to drink whiskey." Her voice was hoarse, as if she had spent the day shouting.

"I'm temperance myself," O. T. admitted.

She studied him in a way that made him feel uneasy. Finally she took a step forward and motioned toward the open doorway. "Why don't you come in and look around? The boy can hold the mules."

Skinner handed the reins to Jared. "Your daddy is about as big as this entire saloon. I can't imagine what would bring him way down here." He had just climbed down to the dirt street when an old black leather one-horse hack dashed up beside him, coming to a sliding stop.

"Skinner?" a man called out from the shadowy recesses of the carriage.

O. T. peeked in at the driver, who wore a three-piece dark suit and a bowler. "Is that you, Lucian?"

"O. T., what are you doin' here?" LaPorte questioned.

"I didn't know you owned a hack."

"You didn't answer me, Skinner. Where do you think you're goin'?"

O. T. pointed toward the boy. "We're tryin' to find Jared's daddy. I was goin' to look in that saloon. The lady in the pink dress was goin' to show me . . ." When he glanced back, the woman was no longer standing at the doorway.

"Show you? Yeah, I bet she was." LaPorte leaned forward and pointed a massive hand at Skinner. "O. T., who told you that was a saloon? Get in your rig and follow me. You shouldn't be down here. It's full of—uh, sneak thieves and footpads."

O. T. swung up into the wagon and followed LaPorte's hack back up Main Street several blocks. The black man parked under a street lamp, and Skinner pulled up alongside him.

Lucian LaPorte gazed out from under the brim of his bowler. "Now, Mr. Wall-Walker, just who are you two lookin' for?"

O. T. gawked down the street at the crowds of men milling around every open business. "It's a funny town, ain't it, Lucian? I've only been here one day, and they give me a nickname." He glanced over at Jared. "The boy's daddy is a big, red-haired man named Elias Rokker. We thought he might be in a saloon."

LaPorte loosened his tie and unfastened the top button on his shirt. "Does he wear red long johns cut off at the elbows and knees?"

Jared sat straight up. "Yes!"

LaPorte shook his head in resignation. "I saw him walking down the middle of Second Street."

"When?" Skinner questioned.

"About ten minutes ago."

"How did you know he was wearin' cut-off red handles?" Jared asked.

The man's strong, round head sat like a pumpkin on a post. "'Cause that's all he had on, boy!"

"Daddy's plum naked?" Jared gasped.

"Almost, son. He was headin' barefoot in his long johns toward the east side of town."

"Maybe he's headed home. We'll go try to find him," O. T. said.

"What happened to his clothes?" Jared demanded.

"Well, that's somethin' you're goin' to have to ask your daddy," LaPorte replied. He glanced up at O. T. "And don't you go pokin' around the lower end of town again. It's dangerous to your health, your pocketbook, and your soul."

Skinner's eyes narrowed. "My soul?"

"Man, that's the crib district. You don't want to be down there, ever."

O. T. craned his neck and stared back several blocks at the lower end of Main Street. "What do you mean, crib?"

"You're livin' in a different world, Skinner." Lucian pulled off his hat and wiped his forehead. "You must have grown up on the moon. Either that or you're stringin' me along to see me squirm. You just pay attention to me. Don't go down there again."

O. T. leaned back on the wagon seat. The light layer of sweat stung the raw places on his back, but the silk shirt felt cool, almost therapeutic. "If it's so bad, what are you doin' down here?"

"I leased this hack and plan to ferry folks from the hotels all over town. So I have to pick some Chicago chemists up in a few minutes. But I was mainly lookin' for you."

"Why were you lookin' for me?"

"Did you know that tollhouse man, Jug Cherry, is on a drunk and threatenin' to shoot you or stab you or both?" LaPorte announced.

O. T. leaned against the worn wooden backrest of the wagon seat. "I heard something like that, but I don't think he means it. Just too much booze."

"Listen, Skinner, many a man with too much booze has pulled a trigger on a gun. The Good Book says, 'Behold, I send you forth as sheep in the midst of wolves; be ye therefore wise as serpents, and harmless as doves.' Now it seems like you got the sheep and the dove parts down purdy good, brother, but you need some practice on being as wise as a snake."

"Lucian, you got a lot of your daddy in you."

"Not to mention my mama and my grandma, bless their souls." LaPorte tugged a gold-chained watch out of his vest pocket, glanced at it, and dropped it back. "There's somebody else lookin' for you."

"Oh?"

"Your ol' saddle pal, Ace Wilkins."

"Where is he?" Skinner quizzed.

"When I saw him, he was hightailin' it down the alley behind The Louvre Saloon. He said for you to meet him at the cemetery."

"Me and Jared will see that his daddy is home safe, and then I'll go help Ace."

"You do plan on sleepin' sometime, don't you?" LaPorte chided.

"I caught me a little nap under the wagon, remember?"

"Well, you cain't spend your whole life helpin' others. You got to take care of yourself too. I cain't believe I found you wanderin' around down in the tenderloin," LaPorte lectured.

"Do you mean that was the . . . That woman was a . . . All of them little houses are . . . I—I almost went in there," O. T. stammered.

"I feel like a Kentuckian watchin' his hound pup sniff out his first raccoon. I like you a lot, Skinner, but this definitely ain't the town for you."

"I reckon you're right about that."

"Maybe I'll check on you tomorrow."

"Bring the missus by. My Dola would be pleased to visit with her."

LaPorte leaned across the carriage toward Skinner. "You do realize we're black folks, don't you?"

"What's that got to do with it?"

Lucian LaPorte sat straight up. "Well, it makes a difference to some folks."

"I'm kind of a simple man, I know. I hope my invitation don't offend your wife. If she'd rather not associate with us, I'll understand."

LaPorte laughed so deeply, his whole carriage swayed. "I don't know if you're makin' it all up, Skinner, but you're the best show in town. Don't ever stop bein' you. You'll captivate the world with that simple-man routine. My wife will be with me if I come by," LaPorte assured him. "We'll plan to sit and visit a spell."

"Good. That's good. Dola will be pleased."

LaPorte leaned against the back of the seat. "Good luck on finding Rokker. Say, that's a nice shirt you're wearin'."

"You know that's just what that—that—" Skinner rubbed his unshaven face. "—lady in the doorway said."

LaPorte pulled away from the boardwalk. A pack of dogs darted into the alley before Skinner's wagon rumbled on up Main Street. Several more coaches and hacks passed them as they made it to Columbia Street.

"I'm wonderin' what he meant by my 'routine'? Does that mean I do ever'thing accordin' to habit? Maybe it means I'm dull and boring," O. T. said.

"I was wondering what he meant by the 'tenderloin' district," young Rokker blurted out.

"That's a very good question, Jared. You should ask your daddy about that."

"Daddy ain't ever home when he's sober and awake," Jared reported.

"Never?"

"Not since we pulled into Goldfield."

"Well, he might be home tonight. Let's go see." O. T. slapped the lead lines on Ada's rump, and the mules broke into a trot.

At the sound of the rumbling wagon pulling up to lot #124,

Danny Rokker and Tommy-Blue ran through the dark to meet them. Both tents glowed with lantern light.

"Kind of late for you two to be up," O. T. declared as he swung to the ground.

"We were helpin' Mr. Rokker get to bed," Tommy-Blue reported.

"Daddy's home?" Jared called out as he jumped to the ground.

"Yep," Danny reported. "He's drunk, and he ain't got no groceries and no money."

"Does he have any clothes?" Jared probed.

"Only his red flannels," Danny said.

Jared glanced at Mr. Skinner and then back at his brother. "Where's his clothes?"

"He don't remember," Danny reported.

The two boys scooted off toward the first tent.

O. T. handed the lead lines to his son. "Tommy-Blue, as long as you're up, grain the mules and give them a drink. They might have a long haul tonight. I need to go talk to Mama."

Dola met him outside the tent flap and slipped her arm in his. She led him out into the darkness at the far end of the huge table.

"Where are we goin'?" he asked.

"Where the children can't hear," she whispered. "Orion, I'm worried about the Rokkers."

He stooped until his mouth was just above her ear. "Was he mean when he came in?"

"No, he just passed out on the floor. It took all of us to get him into bed. But Mrs. Rokker is beside herself. She hasn't been feeling well. Had some sort of stomachache. And now she just doesn't know what to do. He doesn't have any other clothes or boots. We certainly don't have a thing that will fit him."

O. T. reached into his pocket and pulled out the three five-dollar bills. "In the mornin' take this down and buy him somethin' to wear. If you got some left over, buy our kids some shoes."

"I'll need to replace the groceries I gave the Rokkers. I can't expect Lucky Jack and crew to feed them as well," she replied.

"Well, stretch it out as far as it will go." He kissed her ear. "Am I stoopin' more, or are you growin'?"

"I'm wearin' my new boots. I've never had a pair that fits so nice and looks so stylish. I feel rather guilty. I can't believe some woman isn't looking for them." She laid her head on his chest and slipped her hands around his waist.

In the dark of the desert night, he ran his callused fingers through her hair. "Rich folks is that way, you know. Losin' boots don't bother them none. Your hair smells nice."

"I finally got it washed. One good thing about the desert, it doesn't take long to dry your hair." She stepped back and let her hands slip down into his. "Orion, Mrs. Rokker doesn't look good. She says she has a side ache and can't eat."

"Maybe havin' Mr. Rokker home will quiet her stomach a tad." *I surely wish I could see Dola's dancin' blue eyes, the way they tickle and tease.*

"Orion, you have to talk to Mr. Rokker when he sobers up. His family is going to waste away, and he doesn't seem to know or care." *Lord, why is it me and Orion never have any time to ourselves anymore? We need a home with our own bedroom all to ourselves. Course it would be the first time we ever had such a thing.*

"Could be that's the reason he's never sober," O. T. pondered. "Maybe he's too bewildered to know what to do."

She pulled his hand up to her mouth and brushed a kiss across his rough, leathery, sweaty-smelling fingers. "Somethin' has to be done," Dola murmured.

"I'll agree with you there." This time he tugged her hand to his lips. The kiss was so soft and warm, Dola felt a tingle in her throat. "Now I've got to go help the Wilkins brothers," he added. "Are you and the kids doin' all right?"

"We've got a box full of food and a daddy that doesn't drink."

She slipped her fingers lightly back and forth in his. "Tonight we feel mighty blessed. But we'll feel a lot better tomorrow when you get back."

"I hope to make it by noon."

He gripped her fingers tightly. She thought she felt her heart skip. "Take care of yourself, Orion Tower Skinner . . . and bring me back my olive crock."

"Yes, ma'am."

Dola slipped her arm around his neck and the collar of his cool-feeling silk shirt. He winced at the pain but quickly brought his lips down to hers.

His lips were a little chapped and dusty-tasting, but tender and warm. His arm slipped around her waist and hugged her tight.

Real tight.

For a moment Dola forgot about Goldfield, sick neighbors, California, and children. It was as if she were sixteen, and he was twenty-seven, and they were standing in the dark on Mama's porch in Lake Jackson, and he smelled like barber's tonic, and his lips were the sweetest thing she had ever tasted in her life.

"What are you two doin' out there?" The voice was shrill, aggressive.

O. T. pulled his head back. "Hello, Rita Ann. Me and Mama are visitin'."

"Visitin'? You two are out there in the dark kissing. I could hear!" Rita Ann fussed.

"You want us to come over there and kiss where you can see better?" he jibed.

"Orion!" Dola whispered.

"Don't you dare!" Rita Ann called out.

O. T. continued to hold Dola at the waist. "How are you goin' to learn to kiss good like your mama?"

"Daddy, you're embarrassing me!" Rita Ann squealed. "People can hear us."

Dola tugged his arms away from her waist and slipped her callused hand into his.

"You and Mama can come kiss, and I'll watch," a younger voice called out.

"Corrie, you're supposed to be in bed," Dola chided.

"I was reading Rita Ann's book: 'Her lips, two pushing pill grams, ready stand to smooch that rough torch with a tender kick!'" Corrie giggled.

"You hush up!" Rita Ann snapped at her sister. "If you can't quote Romeo right, you shouldn't say it at all! 'My lips, two blushing pilgrims, ready stand to smooth that rough touch with a tender kiss.'"

"I like my way better." Corrie smirked.

Dola and O. T. strolled arm in arm to where the girls huddled at the tent flap.

"I like that part about a tender kick." O. T. grinned. He reached down and hugged Rita Ann, kissing her cheek. When he hugged Corrie, she spun her head around, and his kiss landed on her lips.

O. T. kept his arms around both girls. "Now you two help Mama out tomorrow. She'll have to do a little shoppin', and you'll have to watch Punky. Is he asleep?"

"He went to bed right after you and Jared left," Rita Ann announced.

"He was that naughty?"

"It's the only way I could keep him clean after his bath."

"Can I go with you, Daddy?" Corrie whined and clutched his arm.

"Not this time, darlin'. It's dark and dirty. We'll all be back on the road again in a day or two. If things go well and the mules hold up, we ought to be in Dinuba within the week."

"Can we stay here for the weekend?" Corrie pleaded. "Tommy-Blue heard there will be fireworks."

He looked into Dola's eyes as she watched the girls. *Now, Lord, those are just about the kindest eyes on the face of this earth.* He glanced back down at Corrie. "Why are they havin' fireworks?"

"Someone had an apex litigation case mitigate in their favor," Rita Ann announced.

"What kind of case?" he asked.

"Oh, you know—apex litigation. Establishing legal ownership of an underground mining site. When veins of ore appear on the sur- face as wide strips of metal-permeated rock, they usually bisect the ground on a slant. The person who finds the vein on top has a claim on the vein until it 'faults.'"

"Faults?" O. T. muttered.

"You know, until it breaks off or changes direction," Rita Ann explained. "You can imagine the lawsuits over who has claim to which vein."

"That's why there's fireworks, Daddy. They ruled in favor of the Taylor/Anderson Lease, and they've shipped in fireworks from San Francisco," Corrie announced. "Can we stay?"

"I'm still stunned by apex litigation. Have you been sneakin' off to law school?"

"Daddy," Rita Ann prodded with a grin, "quit teasing me. Everyone knows about apex litigation."

"Can we stay, Daddy?" Corrie repeated.

"Darlin', you know I won't give you a promise that I cain't keep. Some folks would like us to leave town a whole lot sooner than that," he admitted.

"Who?" Dola asked, as she tried brushing down Corrie's wild, clean hair with her hand.

"I heard that tollhouse man out at Rabbit Springs, Jug Cherry, is agitated at me." O. T. tucked his silk shirt back into his denim britches.

"Why, Daddy?" Corrie asked. "Why is he agitated?"

"Don't worry—he don't mean it."

"Doesn't mean what?" Dola pressed.

"Nothin', darlin'." He gave her a quick hug and started toward the street. "I'll see you all around noon tomorrow."

Dola followed him halfway to the dark street. "Orion Skinner, you be careful. You have no idea how important you are to this brood."

"Don't worry about me. I'll be out of town. Nothin' is goin' to happen out on the desert, except we might get hot and thirsty."

When O. T. climbed up into the wagon, Tommy-Blue handed him the lead lines. "You look after your mama and sisters," he instructed the ten-year-old.

"Remember, you promised to assay my ore," Tommy-Blue reminded him.

"Yep. I met a man today who has an assay office. Seems like a good, honest man. I'll hire him." O. T. reached under the seat of the wagon and pulled back a rolled-up canvas tarp. His fingers clutched the cold steel receiver of the shotgun. He handed it down to Tommy-Blue. "Tell your mama to keep this in the tent or in one of the crates."

The boy's voice was high pitched. "You expect we'll have trouble?"

"Nope. But there ain't no reason for it to fill up with more desert dust."

"Daddy, you think I ought to dig down to bedrock to get a better sample?"

"Sounds like a reasonable idea." O. T. stared down at the eager boy in the shadows. "Just remember, son, you'll have to shovel all the dirt back into the hole when we're ready to leave."

"You mean, if we don't find pay dirt, we'll have to shovel it back," Tommy-Blue corrected.

"Yep, that's what I meant. Now go on. Get back to Mama."

"Do you think I should stand guard outside the claim all night? There might be claim jumpers, you know."

"Now you're soundin' like Mrs. Marsh. I want you to go to bed, young man, and don't get carried away with make-believe. Say, did you hear me talkin' to Rita Ann a minute ago?"

"No, sir. Was I suppose to?"

"Nope. Tommy-Blue . . . have you ever heard of apex litigation?"

"You mean, where they go to court to prove who owns the particular vein and whether it's 'faulted' or not? And sometimes the judge—"

"Never mind, son. I don't want to keep Ace Wilkins waitin'."

By the time O. T. reached the cemetery, the three-quarter moon had risen high enough to provide a dull glow off the desert dirt. A shadowy figure waited for him at the entrance.

"Ace?"

The man swung up into the wagon beside him. "You took long enough, O. T."

"I didn't find out where you were until a little while ago. Which way are we headin'?"

"North on the Tonopah road, then out toward the Weepah Hills."

"Can we find the trail at night?"

"At least out to Alkali Springs."

Except for one keg of water the back of the wagon was empty, and the floorboards rattled like the stack pile at a sawmill.

"How did you get out of that outhouse?" O. T. asked.

"Your neighbor rescued me," Ace replied.

"Mrs. Marsh?"

"She came over while you were all bowed sayin' grace, and I explained my problem. She said you Skinners were good folks, and it looked like I was in a jam. So she hustled me over to her tent, and she waited in the privy."

O. T. could still feel the soft touch of Dola's lips on his. "Mrs. Marsh is a resourceful woman." *I trust I'm doin' what You want me to do, Lord. Because I surely ain't doin' what I want to be doin'.*

"She's a good ol' gal," Ace declared. "If she was twenty years younger and not as homely as a heifer, I would have kissed her. Anyway, I ducked out the back of her place when I got a chance. I sort of stuck to the alleys. That's when I saw your black compadre." Wilkins leaned forward and groped under the wagon seat. "You have my revolver, I trust."

"It's in the back under the canvas with some food. Dola packed the leftovers for you and your brothers."

Wilkins crawled into the back, and the wagon rumbled along. Even in the dim moonlight, O. T. could see Ace strap on his holster. "I almost laughed out loud to see Lucky Jack and the others stalking the woman in the outhouse."

"You saw that?"

"Yep." Ace pulled himself back into the wagon seat, a beef chop in his hand. "Did you know Mrs. Marsh's tent is right over the top of a mine shaft?"

"I heard something like that."

Ace smacked his lips and mumbled, "This is a tasty piece of meat. Be sure and thank the missus for me."

"And you can thank Lucky Jack. He paid for it."

Ace roared. "I reckon he'd pitch a fit if he knew that. Well, don't matter. The die is cast. Me and my brothers will have to confront them three sooner or later. But next time it will be a place of my choosin', and the sides will be even."

"What's that goin' to gain you?" O. T. challenged.

"It's a matter of principle now," Wilkins declared.

"Murderin' is a matter of principle?"

"Ain't no murder when both sides is armed and tryin' to kill the other. That's war, not murder."

"Those lawless days are over, Ace. It's 1905. Things are different."

"Well, some of us ain't ready to close the books on them days jist yet. I don't expect you'd understand. There comes a time to pull the trigger and send a man off to his heavenly reward."

O. T.'s voice was low and soft. "What kind of heavenly reward you got waitin' for you, Ace?"

"I reckon I'll get what I deserve, jist like ever'one else. But don't you go preachin' at me, Skinner."

"I don't need to."

Wilkins's voice was agitated. "What do you mean, you don't need to?"

"I've found that most folks who say, 'Don't go preachin' at me,' already have their conscience preachin' at them, and that's why they protest. You won't need no preachin' from me."

"Skinner, you're preachin' at me even when you ain't preachin' at me. Now that subject is done with."

"Whatever you say."

"That's what I say. And I'll say somethin' else. You don't know me nearly as well as you think you do. How do you know I won't just plug you out here on the desert and steal your rig?"

"Because you could have stole my rig this afternoon, if you were that type. You could have shot me the other day, if that's in your mind."

"You could be wrong about me," Wilkins insisted.

"Yep, I reckon I could. But I'd rather die tryin' to help a man than hide all day because I feared him."

There was silence for a moment. "Well, Skinner," Ace began slowly, "you're right about one thing. I've never shot a man without a good reason. And I won't shoot you. But you ought to be careful about who you call friends."

O. T. slapped his knee and snickered. "Them is the exact words that Lucky Jack Gately told me jist a few hours ago."

Wilkins joined in the laughter. "Well, I'm glad to see the two of us agree on somethin'."

The land between the Montezuma Range and Lone Mountain, northwest of Goldfield, sloped gently like a giant lakebed.

A long, dry lakebed.

A grayish-white powdery alkali dust layered the ground like sugar sprinkled thick on top of a cake. But the bitter, stinging, choking effect of the dust was evident, even on a night when there was very little wind.

Both men tied bandannas over their noses and mouths. The moonlight on the alkali gave the ground an almost glowing, snow-covered appearance. But the heat of the desert floor and the sweat rolling down his forehead reminded O. T. that they were still on the upper levels of Dante's Inferno.

Once they turned west off the Tonopah road, they ceased to see any traffic or any sign of vegetation. The small, scrubby sagebrush and greasewood disappeared completely. Mile after mile of dry alkali lakebed stretched out in front of them, burning the eyes and chafing the skin.

There was no road, no trail, no path to follow. Sometime in the middle of the night they turned north as they reached Paymaster Canyon. A slightly rutted wagon road meandered to the northeast. O. T. stopped the team at the bottom of a draw.

"What's the matter?" Wilkins asked.

"I'm going to fetch the mules a drink and wash their eyes out. They must be as miserable as we are."

"I don't think it's too much further. What time do you think it is?" Wilkins queried.

O. T. glanced up at the night sky as he climbed down out of the wagon. "Two hours till daylight."

"How can you tell?"

Skinner poured water into the wooden bucket. "By the position of the moon. It was hanging about twenty degrees above the horizon yesterday at daylight."

"We must be gettin' close to them. Keep followin' this trail. We pushed the motorcar up one of these arroyos to the west."

O. T. held the bucket for Ada. "Why didn't you leave the motor-car out in the open so it could be spotted more quickly?"

"There was a little protection out of the wind and dust up there. Besides, we didn't want to attract ever'one's attention," Ace explained.

"Well, you hid it good, all right." Skinner watered Ida. "If these mules can tow that motorcar at all, we should pull it straight out to the Tonopah road and down to Goldfield. It's an easier pull."

"No!" Wilkins insisted. "I don't want to be out in the open like that."

"For a man who's got nothin' to hide, you surely are cat-footin' around."

"Cautious. A man should be cautious."

"I ain't goin' to break down my mules pullin' that motorcar. I'll get you and your brothers to town, but if it's too heavy a pull, we'll just unhitch and abandon it where she sits."

"That's fair enough."

They rumbled north, the descending moon over their left shoulders. At the next dry arroyo, O. T. stopped the wagon. "How are we going to tell which of these is the one you pushed the motorcar into? I can't see wheel tracks in the dark."

"I reckon Trey will signal us," Ace replied. "It's a quiet night. He's got to hear this squeakin' wagon."

"What kind of signal do you—"

The report of a carbine up the arroyo sounded in unison with the splintering of wood in the wagon bed behind the men. Ada and Ida lurched forward. O. T. grabbed the hand brake. Ace Wilkins dove off the wagon, his gun drawn.

"That ain't exactly the signal I was thinkin' of," O. T. grumbled and held a tight rein on the team and the brake.

"Trey!" Wilkins shouted. "Trey, it's me, Ace. . . ."

A second shot scattered splinters off the tailgate of the wagon. O. T. jumped down and sprinted to the mules' heads and hung onto their headstalls. "Get him to quit shootin'. These mules are ready to bolt!" Skinner hollered.

"Trey!" Ace screamed. "For pete's sake, stop shootin'. It's me, Ace. . . . I've got Skinner and his wagon here to haul us to town."

There was a long pause.

"Trey, do you hear me?" Ace shouted.

Finally a deep voice replied, "I hear you. Is that the Wall-Walker?"

"You ain't my brother," Ace called out.

"And you are not my brother," the voice replied. "Do you have the Wall-Walker with you?"

"Yep."

"You have any water?"

"A little," O. T. hollered back. "You need a drink?"

"Yes."

"Come on down, but quit shootin'." O. T. hiked to the back of the wagon and dragged the water keg to the tailgate.

A short man carrying a sawed-off Trapdoor 45-70 rifle hiked out of the shadows of the arroyo. He wore a dark-colored, untucked shirt and a wide black felt hat, and his moccasins came up over the pant legs of his white ducking trousers.

"He's an Indian!" Wilkins called out, still gripping his revolver.

Even in the dim glow of the moon, O. T. could see the furrowed, leathery outlines of the old man's face and the gray hair curling out from under his hat. The Indian ignored Ace Wilkins and hiked straight at Skinner. "You are the Wall-Walker?"

"Yes. My name is O. T. Skinner."

"I'm Fergus."

Wilkins came over and stood next to Skinner. "What kind of name is Fergus for a digger Indian?"

"I'm Paiute. I was named after a cow," the old man announced.

Wilkins hooted.

"It was my mother's favorite cow," Fergus explained.

O. T. handed him a tin cup of water.

"Your kindness will be remembered," the old man said. "I was on my way to Fisherman Springs, but I am a slow, old man and had to make a dry camp in the Weepah Hills tonight."

"Why did you try to shoot us?" Wilkins pressed.

"I only shot at the wagon. I thought you were following me."

"Have you seen any men out here?" Wilkins asked.

"I have seen no one since I left Alkali Wells."

"We are lookin' for Ace's brothers."

The old Paiute turned toward Wilkins. "You are named after a card?"

"What's wrong with that?" Ace huffed.

"Was it your mother's favorite card?" The old Indian grinned.

"I asked you if you saw my brothers!" Wilkins shouted.

Fergus's reply was quite soft. "And I told you I have seen no one." He took another slow drink. "Did you ever hear the legend of the Wall-Walker?"

"Legend? What are you talking about?" O. T. quizzed.

"Wovoka's vision."

"The legend about the Ghost Dance? I thought all of that disappeared at Wounded Knee," Wilkins interjected.

"There were no Paiutes at Wounded Knee Creek. But this story is not about the Ghost Dance. Wovoka is a man who sees dreams as if they are real. In one such dream, a man appeared who walked on the wall of a cliff, and when he struck the rock, water gushed forth, and Paiutes would never again be thirsty. I was in Goldfield yesterday and heard there was a Wall-Walker making water free for all people."

"That's a nice story, Mr. Fergus, but it ain't me. I didn't strike no rock. Moses is the only one I know who ever done that. I'm just a man totin' a little water out for his family and to earn some grocery money. Nothin' miraculous about that," O. T. insisted.

"Mr. Skinner, I have lived so long I have seen my people die from bullets, from disease, and from a broken spirit. We will survive only by holding onto the hope that somehow we are in a divine plan. The fulfillment of Wovoka's words gives me hope. I choose to believe you are the Wall-Walker he spoke of."

"But in that medicine man's vision, what does the Wall-Walker do after the water comes out of the cliff?" O. T. asked.

"He travels deep into the bowels of the earth and sends forth golden poppies to mark his journey."

"Sounds like a grave to me, Skinner." Wilkins shoved his revolver back into the holster.

"Oh, no, the Wall-Walker will never die but will live eternally with the Creator."

"It's a nice story, Mr. Fergus, but I'll put my faith in Jesus." Skinner stared out into the night. "Now you haven't seen the Wilkins brothers or their motorcar?"

Fergus waved his arm toward the north. "There is a large automobile in the next arroyo."

"That's them!" Ace blurted out.

"It is a 1904 Thomas four-cylinder touring car. The engine has been run hot, and the block is cracked. Quite inoperable, I would suppose. There are no supplies in it. It is covered with dust, but there are no dents. With a rebuilt engine, it could be a real hummer. But, once again, I have seen no one."

Wilkins and Skinner stared at each other.

"How do you know so much about motorcars?" Wilkins questioned.

"I own a 1904 Oldsmobile Curved Dash and an eight-horsepower 1903 De Dion-Bouton," the old Indian announced.

"Wait a minute! You expect me to believe a blanket Indian that has to beg for a drink of water owns two motorcars, one an expensive model imported from France?" Wilkins barked.

"I couldn't care less if you believe me or not," Fergus replied.

"I have no idea what motorcars he's talkin' about, but I don't have any reason not to believe him," Skinner put in.

"If you've got two motorcars, why are you walkin' across this desert at night?" Ace Wilkins challenged.

"Night is the best time to walk the desert. That is common knowledge. And I walk because, like the Thomas, both of my motorcars were driven until they broke down. Many autos have been abandoned in the desert. I merely drag them to my cabin. My yard looks very impressive," the old Indian teased.

"Fergus, I like you," Skinner chuckled. "Hop in the wagon and show us where Mr. Wilkins's motorcar is."

They rumbled through the desert night about a hundred yards and then turned west into a shallow arroyo that ran water only in a rare desert downpour. About a quarter of a mile up the arroyo, they discovered the dust-covered Thomas.

"Trey? Deuce?" Wilkins hollered.

Only a heavy, oppressive silence followed.

# SEVEN

The sun was bright yellow but not too hot. Dola had no idea why it didn't burn her eyes when she stared up at it. A light breeze drifted across the young vineyard. It was the kind of breeze that lifts the spirit and makes a woman feel sixteen, with the whole world laid out in front of her like a flowered path through an enchanted land.

Each grapevine symmetrically wound itself around the taut wires that stretched from post to post. The leaves were a light green, not pastel, but a distinct light shade of forest green with crisp scalloped edges fluttering against a sky-blue backdrop.

She could see no one at all in the vineyard, but that didn't bother her. Dola knew that the vineyard belonged to her, and there shouldn't be another soul there unless she had invited them, and she couldn't remember inviting anyone.

The air tasted clean, refreshing, like a clear mountain brook bouncing over round rocks . . . only drier, unused. Her new alligator boots rested easy on her feet, almost as if she were wearing no shoes at all. Her feet felt clean and warm but were not sweating. There was no dirt between the toes. No hard callus on the heel. No corn on the little toe.

Her lightweight, white cotton dress had delicate purple and yellow violets embroidered beside the row of mother-of-pearl buttons and around the cuffs and hem. The dress was as soft as a well-worn bed sheet, and yet it held its shape as if starched at a Chinese laundry. As she walked along, she liked the way the long skirt fluttered in unison with the young grape leaves.

Dola stopped to examine a thick cluster of grapes, still in the immature green stage. She spotted a very wide gold band on her finger. A large diamond was in the middle, framed by two heart-shaped rubies on each side. *It's exactly like Orion promised. "Someday, darlin' . . ." he would promise. And I can't even remember when he gave it to me!*

Then she stared for a long time at her hands. *They look . . . they look so young, so smooth, so dainty . . . but they aren't my hands!*

The sound of sobbing brought her out of the dream.

She reached across the bed to Punky. He slept quietly on top of the covers with his rear end poked in the air. Dola closed her eyes and rolled over. She tried to think of the peaceful vineyard, but the sobbing continued. This time she propped herself up on her elbow. She heard Tommy-Blue snoring. She opened her eyes, but the tent was dark and stuffy, and only a few shadows were outlined by the moonlight striking the top of the canvas.

Dola sat on the edge of the mattress and fumbled on the crate for a sulfur match. It flared brightly enough to spot Rita Ann asleep on her back, covers pulled to her chest, arms neatly folded across her stomach. Corrie was on her stomach, one foot stuck out from under the covers and draped over Rita Ann's quilt. Her mouth was wide open on her pillow, her breathing peaceful.

Dola blew out the match and flopped back down on the feather mattress.

The crying continued.

*I'm not sure what's a dream and what's real. Am I dreaming that someone's crying? Am I lying in a tent dreaming about a vineyard, or walking in a vineyard dreaming about a tent?*

She reached up and brushed her long, flowing hair back behind her ears. She took a deep breath and let it out slowly. She began to relax.

But her eyes were wide open.

As were her ears.

When she heard footsteps outside the tent, she sat straight up.

"Mrs. Skinner?" a young voice called out. "Mrs. Skinner, I saw a match. Are you awake? Oh, please be awake. Mama's hurtin' bad, and she won't stop cryin'."

Dola swung to her feet and stepped outside the tent flap in the dark desert night. "Stella?"

"Mama's hurtin' real bad, and Jared and Danny can't get Daddy awake to look after her. What are we going to do?" she sobbed.

"I'll come take a look," Dola offered.

Barefoot and wearing a faded long cotton gown, Dola scooted around the crates and tent pegs to the front of the Rokker tent. Inside, one fat vanilla candle sent shadows flickering against everything in the room.

Elias Rokker lay sprawled across a sagging wood-framed cot. Danny Rokker was trying to wake him. "Jared ran to get a doctor!" he reported.

On a pile of old quilts scattered on top of a filthy piece of red carpet, Mrs. Rokker lay in her tattered blue dress, clutching her side and sobbing. Her knees were pulled up to her waist.

"Oh, Lord Jesus," Dola murmured as she knelt down beside the moaning woman. "Stella, light a lantern."

The ten-year-old sniffled and smeared the back of her hand across her nose. "We ain't got no more kerosene."

"Danny, run over to our tent and get one of our lanterns." The boy, barefoot and wearing only his rope-held duckings, hurried out of the tent.

"Stella, bring that candle over here so I can see your mama better."

The thin girl held the candle with one hand and scooted through the wadded bedding to Dola's side. "She's bleedin' at the mouth," Stella sobbed.

"I think she just bit her lip, darlin'." *Oh, please, Lord . . . not internal bleeding.* "Get me your cleanest rag and a bowl of fresh water. We'll try to wash her face and cool her down."

Dola cradled the woman's head on her lap. "We're going to get you a doctor."

The pain-afflicted woman tried to shake her head. "No," she whispered. "No money. No doctor."

Dola took the rag from Stella and dipped it in the chipped porcelain basin. She dabbed the woman's dirty forehead.

"It hurts so bad," Mrs. Rokker sobbed. "Oh, Lord, it hurts so bad."

Dola washed the woman's lips and then let her suck on a clean place in the wet rag. "Where does it hurt, honey?"

"My—my—my side. . . . My right side. Oh, how I wish I could just die."

"Mama!" Stella cried.

Dola reached up and patted the young girl on the back. "She didn't mean it, darlin'."

Stella kept sobbing. The tent echoed with moaning and wailing.

Dola leaned down near Mrs. Rokker's ear. "Does it hurt like a knife wound? Like you've been stabbed?"

The woman bit her lip and nodded her head.

Dola wiped the mouth clean once more. *Her appendix. Just like Mama. Lord, Mama died in my arms, and there was nothin' I could do. Not again. I can't do that again. I can't sit by and be so helpless. Worthless. They've made advancements. They can operate now. The doctors can do something.* "It's all right, honey. . . . We'll get you to the doctor. We'll worry about money tomorrow. We just want to get you fixed up."

Danny and a barefoot, robe-clad Rita Ann burst into the tent carrying a lit lantern.

"How's my mama?" Danny called out.

"She's hurtin' bad," Dola reported. "But we'll get her to a doctor as quick as we can. He'll know what to do."

The extra light revealed a layer of desert dirt on every object in the room. There were boxes, crates, tin cans, and dusty linens scattered from one side to the other. In the background Dola heard more sobbing. She searched each person's face. "Who's crying?" she finally asked.

"It's Caitlynn." Stella pointed to the back of the tent.

"Caitlynn? Who's Caitlynn?"

"My little sister."

*Little sister? How can I live in a tent thirty feet away and not know there was a little sister?* Dola laid Mrs. Rokker's head on the blanket and left the wet rag for her to chew on. She stood and held the lantern high enough to spot a small, paper-thin girl who looked about five years old squatted down on her heels. She faced the corner of the tent, rocking back and forth, clutching her knees and crying.

Dola stared at the girl's dirty, matted blonde hair. "Doesn't she have any clothes?"

Stella shook her head. "She caught her dress on a wire and ripped it up real bad. Mama said she would just have to go naked until she felt like mendin' it."

Dola put the lantern back down near Mrs. Rokker so that the sobbing girl would be hidden in the shadows. *Lord, my girls should have more than one dress so they can share with those in need! A naked child, and we have nothing to give her!*

She leaned her head back and closed her eyes. She did not see a vision of a vineyard. Or clusters of purple grapes. But she did see purple.

Dola opened her eyes. "Rita Ann, go get my pillowcase. . . . No, go get Grandma Davis's lavender silk pillowcase out of the cedar chest."

Rita Ann's dark braids hung down across her flat chest. "You said you weren't goin' to use it until we got to Dinuba."

"Yes, well . . . I've changed my mind. Bring my mending scissors also. Danny, go out and see if Jared's coming. Stella, help me wash your mama's face."

The children scurried.

Caitlynn rocked and sobbed.

Mrs. Rokker moaned and clutched her side.

Mr. Rokker remained unconscious.

Dola Skinner prayed.

*Lord, You simply can't let this woman die. There are too many young lives that depend upon her.* Dola chewed her tongue and tried to pray further. *Oh, gracious Jesus, not my will but Thine be done.*

When Rita Ann returned, she was fully dressed and carried the lavender pillowcase and a pair of scissors. Dola cut a scooped hole in the sewn end of the pillowcase and a small hole on both sides, right next to the top seam.

"You ruined it, Mama!" Rita Ann whispered.

Dola handed the pillowcase to Stella. "Help Caitlynn put on her pretty new sleeveless silk dress."

The minute the naked little girl pulled the case down over her body, she stopped crying and scooted over near her mother. She dropped down on her hands and knees.

"You look very pretty, darlin'," Dola encouraged her. The girl nodded her head and rubbed her hand across her runny nose. "Stella, come help Caitlynn wash her face."

"Someone's comin'!" Danny shouted from the street.

Rita Ann ran outside.

Dola cradled Mrs. Rokker's head. "You see? Your Jared found a doctor. It will be all right."

"I don't . . . have . . . any money," Mrs. Rokker moaned.

"Don't say that anymore!" Dola scolded. "I told you, we'll figure that out later."

The man who poked his head into the tent was well dressed. And black.

"Mr. LaPorte!" Dola gasped.

He tipped his bowler. "Mrs. Skinner."

Dola brushed some loose strands of hair out of her eyes. "Where's the doctor?" She suddenly realized that she was still barefoot and wearing her cotton nightgown.

Jared pushed his way into the tent. "There ain't no doctor. I couldn't find one, but Mr. LaPorte said he'd take Mama to the hospital."

Dola continued to rock the sobbing woman in her lap. "Goldfield has a hospital?"

LaPorte nodded. "Above the doctor's office. It ain't much I hear, but the new one won't be finished until January."

"Thank you, Mr. LaPorte. I will hurry and get dressed and accompany you."

The black man stooped down and inched his way across the clutter of the tent. "I'll go ahead and carry her out to my carriage."

"What about us?" Stella called out as she knelt down next to Caitlynn. "What are we to do?"

"I need you and Danny to stay here and take care of Caitlynn. And you'll need to keep tryin' to wake up your father and tell him what happened. When he awakes, he'll take care of things. Jared can go with us now to look after your mother," Dola instructed.

LaPorte dropped down on his knees and shoved his massive arms under Mrs. Rokker's blanket.

"No," Mrs. Rokker gasped. "No," she sobbed.

Dola brushed her hand through the woman's matted hair. "It's all right, honey. We'll take care of everything. Let's get you to a doctor."

"Don't let him touch me!" Mrs. Rokker screamed in panic. "That man . . . that black man . . . Don't let him touch me."

Still on his knees, LaPorte pulled his hands back.

Dola could feel the hair stand up on the back of her neck. *I can't believe this, Lord.* She ground her teeth and tried to talk slowly. "Mrs. Rokker, we are all trying to save your life. Your children need you desperately to pull through. So don't you lay there in agonizing pain and play the bigot on me!" she snapped.

"No!" The woman bit her lip and turned her head to the back of the tent toward her husband. "I can't. . . . Mr. Rokker would pitch a fit."

Lucian moved back to the pain-racked woman. "Mrs. Rokker, I want you to close your eyes and look over at the fat drunk who's passed out on that cot. What color is he with your eyes closed? He's black, isn't he? Now look at me with your eyes closed. What color am I? So me and him is the same if you keep your eyes closed."

"But there is a great deal of difference," Dola added. "Mr. LaPorte is going to help you find a doctor so that you will live to enjoy these beautiful children of yours. Mr. Rokker? Well, he isn't of any help whatsoever to any person in the world. So that's why you'll let Mr. LaPorte carry you out to the carriage, won't you?"

Mrs. Rokker closed her eyes and nodded her head.

Dola struggled to her feet. She had a sudden urge to grab one of the quilts and wrap it over her gown. "Danny, Rita Ann, help Mr. LaPorte while I run get dressed. Then come to our tent."

Dola abandoned any hope of pinning her hair up. She was pulling on her new boots when Rita Ann burst into the tent.

Dola looked into the twelve-year-old's eyes. "Darlin', I need you to stay and watch the children."

Rita Ann clutched her hands in front of her neat bowed ribbon belt. "They are all asleep. Why can't I go with you and Jared?"

"Because if we have complications, I might not make it back before breakfast." Dola slipped her arm around her daughter's shoulder. *Two more years, Lord, and she will be as tall as me. How can that be?* "If I'm not here, you will have to cook for Lucky Jack and the others."

Rita Ann's small, round mouth dropped open. "Me?"

"I'm countin' on you, honey." Dola gave her a squeeze. *Has it been that long since I was her age? That was the year Mother died.*

"But, Mama, I can't—"

"Yes, you can. You're a good cook. Start a fire in the stove, warm up the ham, scramble a dozen eggs, fry some pan biscuits, and slice some of those green apples and boil them with molasses and raisins. Tell Lucky Jack what happened and that we will deliver their lunch buckets to the mine site. Have them draw a little map to their lease."

"But, Mother, I can't. I'm just twelve!" she whimpered.

"Rita Ann, I really need your help just now. You're the only one I can turn to. I know you're only twelve, but I need you to be twenty just for one morning. Can you do that, darlin'?"

The twelve-year-old stood tall and threw her shoulders back. "I don't look twenty, Mama, but I'll do it for you. 'This day she was both pantler, butler, cook, both dame and servant . . . welcomed all, served all.'"

"My, where did you find that one?"

"*The Winter's Tale.*"

"Ask Corrie and Tommy-Blue to help you. They can set the table and slice the apples. Perhaps I'll be home in time. If not, I'll try to send word back. You stay in our tent until daylight."

"I wish Daddy were here," Rita Ann murmured.

"I know, honey. So do I. But he needed to help the Wilkins brothers."

"I hope that's as important as being here."

"Now don't you go fussin'. The Lord gave Daddy one assignment and us another. That's all."

Dola ducked out of the tent into the dark night. *I wish he was here too! Oh, my, how I wish he was here.*

Mrs. Rokker was blanket-wrapped and lying in the backseat of Mr. LaPorte's carriage. Jared sat next to her holding Caitlynn in his lap.

Dola pointed to the five-year-old clutching her big brother. "She'll have to stay with Tommy-Blue and Stella."

Jared continued to rock his sister. "She can't. She's never been away from Mama."

Dola glanced at Lucian LaPorte. He shrugged. "What do you mean?" she asked.

Jared patted Caitlynn's matted blonde hair. "In her whole life Caitlynn has never been away from Mama. She'll scream all night long if we don't take her."

LaPorte shook his head. "We've got room. Come on up, Mrs. Skinner. We better get Mrs. Rokker to the hospital."

The downstairs of the two-story, unpainted wood-frame building at 33 Carson Street served as an office and residence of Dr. Hershel Silvermeyer. The upstairs was the temporary location of the Esmeralda County Hospital.

They hiked up the wide wooden stairs along the outside of the building and pushed open the wide opaque-glass doors into the lobby. A nurse sat at a desk that separated the entrance from doubled rows of curtained beds. Her eyes reflected shock, as if seeing a dream, when the entire troupe trudged through the front door.

A well-dressed black man carried a pained, emaciated white woman in a tattered, dirty dress. Next came a barefoot twelve-year-old boy in duckings and a dingy white cotton shirt. His red hair flopped down to his eyes. Holding his hand was a small barefoot girl dressed in what looked like a lavender silk pillowcase. A woman wearing an old but clean plain dress and no makeup, whose hair tumbled down her thin shoulders, led the procession. Her eyes were narrowed with intensity, and the lines across her forehead told of a hard life.

The uniformed nurse stood, pushed back a strand of unruly blonde hair, and looked straight at Dola. "My heavens!" she gasped. "Was there an accident?"

Dola crossed the unpolished wood floor. "There was no accident. My friend, Mrs. Rokker, has a severe side ache. She needs to see a doctor."

The nurse glanced at the others behind Dola. "Then only one of you needs the doctor?"

"Yes, just Mrs. Rokker, but she's in dire need," Dola insisted.

"She has a stomachache?" The nurse glanced down at the open medical journal on her desk. "It's the middle of the night. Perhaps you could bring her back when—"

Dola marched up to the woman until her head was only inches away. "I sat and held my mother's hand when she agonizingly died from a ruptured appendix. I will not repeat that event. I want the doctor to look at her, and I want him to look at her right now!"

The nurse sucked in a deep breath and flushed red. "I schedule the appointments around here, and we'll leave the diagnosis to the doctor."

Dola's shoulders slumped. "I'm sorry if I offended you. I'm very worried, that's all." She lowered her voice so those behind her couldn't hear. "I'm scared she won't last through the night. Could you please summon the doctor?"

"Where do you want me to put Mrs. Rokker?" LaPorte called out. "She's hurtin' bad and needs to lie down."

The slender woman pulled off her glasses and rubbed the bridge of her nose with graceful hands. She glanced at the darkened room behind her. Her voice was librarian-soft, and she spoke through straight white teeth. "I suppose we can put her in bed #4 until the doctor makes his rounds in the morning, and then—"

Dola replied in a tone reminiscent of a barker at the county fair. "Perhaps I did not make myself clear. She needs a doctor right now."

The nurse crossed her arms and glared. "I'm afraid that's . . ."

Jared and Caitlynn scooted up beside Dola. "Mama's really in bad shape," Jared pleaded.

The nurse tossed her arms up in seeming resignation. "I said, I will watch her tonight, and then the doctor can . . ."

Dola spun back toward the big black man. "Mr. LaPorte, please put Mrs. Rokker in bed #4." She glanced back at the nurse. "You did say that was permissible, didn't you?"

"Yes, but I need you to fill out a form and pay three dollars for a twenty-four-hour stay."

Dola ignored the nurse. "Jared, you and Caitlynn wait out here in the lobby in that Morris chair and—"

Jared's eyes widened. "But, Mrs. Skinner, you know how Caitlynn will . . ."

Dola held up her hand to quiet the boy. "Yes, I do. I'm counting on her."

The minute LaPorte took Mrs. Rokker out of the room, the five-year-old began to scream and sob. Jared held her in his arms, but she kicked and fought to get down.

"My word!" the nurse gasped. "What is wrong with that child? You must keep her quiet. She'll wake up the other patients."

Dola stepped closer to the nurse. "The only one we want to wake up is the doctor."

The nurse grimaced and leaned forward. "What?"

"Get the doctor now, and I'll see if I can quiet her."

"But I can't—"

Dola stepped back. "It's up to you."

"She'll have to leave. This is horrid. She simply must stop. I can't have this." Then, with a deep sigh, the nurse trudged over to the wall and pushed an electric buzzer.

Dola called to the boy and his sister. "Let's all go sit by your mama's bed."

Mrs. Rokker writhed on the clean white sheets of the hospital bed. Caitlynn reached out and took her hand.

Lucian LaPorte pulled Dola aside. "Mrs. Skinner, I have some customers down in the lower end of town that need a ride back to their hotels. I have to leave now."

"You go on, Mr. LaPorte." She reached out and patted his big black hand. "Your assistance has been immeasurable. I can never thank you enough."

"Are you goin' to be all right?"

"Certainly. It's Mrs. Rokker that is in pain."

"I'll try to stop back by later and see if you need a ride home," he offered.

She walked with him back out to the lobby. "That would be nice, but we can walk home. You must take care of your own family."

He tipped his bowler. "Yes, ma'am. My Omega will be wonderin' where I've been."

"Your wife's name is Omega?"

"Yep. She was the last of fourteen children. Her mama thought Omega was a good name."

LaPorte had just left the room when a middle-aged, balding man with some white hair scurried in. He did not wear a suit coat. His charcoal-gray wool vest was unbuttoned, and his black tie hung limp around the collar of his white shirt.

"Miss Greer, what is this all about?" he demanded. "Is it Mr. Mills again?"

The nurse wrung her hands. "Oh, no . . . they brought in a woman with a stomachache and—"

He ignored everyone but the nurse. "The clinic is downstairs and will not open until 9:00 A.M. This is a hospital. Don't confuse the . . ."

Dola stepped over to the man. "It's her appendix, Doctor. She might not last until morning. Her children need her."

Startled, he glanced up. "Who are you?"

"A neighbor. I brought her here."

He turned back to the nurse. "Miss Greer, please explain to her the necessity of waiting until morning." He looked Dola up and down. "A hospital visit is quite expensive. I'm sure your money could be better spent elsewhere."

Dola tried to keep the tears back. She grabbed the doctor's arm. "In the name of Christian charity, Doctor, please look at her."

The doctor rubbed his chin. His eyes softened. "That's not a real convincing argument," he murmured. "I'm Jewish."

"So is Jesus," Dola countered.

"Yes . . . well . . ." He ran his fingers through his hair. "I am up. Miss Greer, get my instruments. I will examine her."

Dola walked with him to bed #4. It was isolated from the other beds by white curtains. A small lightbulb in the ceiling illuminated the area.

"You'll have to have these children sit out in the lobby," he instructed.

"The little one cries and pitches a fit when she's not by her mother's side," Dola explained.

The doctor dismissed them with his hand. "Then we will just let her pitch."

When Jared led Caitlynn out of the big room, the five-year-old began to yell and scream. He looked up at Dola. "I cain't keep her quiet, Mrs. Skinner."

Dola swooped the girl off her feet. The silk pillowcase dress felt cool. *This poor child is skin and bones. Lil' darlin' . . . oh, Lord . . . she's livin' next door to me and starvin' to death.* Dola hugged Caitlynn tight. The girl quit kicking and screaming.

"There you go, honey. . . . Ever'thing's going to be all right," Dola crooned.

Caitlynn laid her head on Dola's shoulder and began to suck her thumb.

*Normally I wouldn't tolerate a five-year-old sucking her thumb. But, sweetheart, that's the least of your problems today.*

Dola sat in the worn Morris chair in the lobby. Caitlynn slept in her arms. Jared paced the middle of the room under the single lightbulb.

Twenty minutes later the doctor returned. Dola gently laid the five-year-old down and joined Jared at the doctor's side.

Dr. Silvermeyer spoke in hushed tones. "You were right about your neighbor. I believe it's her appendix. I'll have to operate right now. Miss Greer can assist me. I think it's already ruptured."

"Is Mama goin' to die?" Jared asked.

"Son, that's a question we'll leave with the Almighty. I too believe we are in His hands. Mrs. Rokker is very weak. If she were stronger, she'd have a better chance. But it's my educated opinion that she will die if we don't operate soon. Now if you two will fill out the forms with Miss Greer, I'll prepare for surgery."

There were very few questions that needed to be asked. The nurse emphasized the last one. "How will you be paying for this?"

Jared looked panicked. "We ain't got no—"

Dola's hand silenced his reply. "How much will it be?" she asked.

The nurse pointed to the typewritten list on her desk. "Without any further complications, appendix surgery is twenty-five dollars."

"I, eh . . ." Dola reached into her dress pocket and pulled out the three five-dollar bills. "I can give you fifteen dollars now, and I'll . . . I'll work to pay off the rest."

"This is a private hospital, not a county clinic. We cannot operate for free," Miss Greer snapped.

Dola clenched her fist so tight that she wadded the bills. "I didn't ask for anything free. I said, I'd give you fifteen dollars now and the rest as soon—"

"I heard what you said," Miss Greer interrupted. "Perhaps you could go to a friend and borrow the balance."

Dola rubbed her temples. *Lord, what will we do? Mr. Rokker, you should be here taking care of your wife!* "We're new in town. . . . The Rokkers are about the only ones we know."

Dr. Silvermeyer scurried into the lobby. "Miss Greer, we must hurry. I will need your assistance now."

The nurse crossed her arms. "They don't have the money. They only have fifteen dollars."

Dola held up the three crumpled bills. "Doctor, I'd be happy to work off the balance. I could come in the evenings and scrub floors or whatever."

"I really don't have time to discuss it. I suppose now that water is going to be free, thanks to that Wall-Walker, we could scrub floors every night instead of twice a week. I'll pay you three dollars a night until your bill is settled. And for your Jesus' sake, I hope you are a woman who keeps her word."

Dola let out a long, slow breath. "Thank you, Doctor. You can count on me keeping my word. And that Wall-Walker, as you called him, is my husband."

The doctor spun around. "Your husband?"

"He's O. T. Skinner. I'm Mrs. Skinner."

The doctor stared at her and then glanced over at the nurse. "Miss Greer, fifteen dollars is sufficient for this operation. We all owe Mr. Skinner a vote of thanks."

Dola settled into the old Morris chair next to the sleeping Caitlynn. Jared pulled a straight-backed oak chair up next to them. The trio dozed and waited while hushed voices filtered out from the operating room.

Dola closed her eyes, but her heart pounded too strongly to sleep. *The ten-dollar debt was forgiven because of Orion? He's still taking care of us even when he isn't here.*

While Ace Wilkins scurried in the shadows, shouting for his brothers, O. T. lit the lantern he had in the back of the wagon and set it on the dirt beside the Thomas touring car. Then O. T. and Fergus studied the desert for tracks.

Ace yanked off his hat and stalked across the dusty, barren

arroyo. "I don't know why they ain't here. They were suppose to wait for me. All they had to do is wait one day."

O. T. pushed his hat back and rubbed his neck. "Maybe they thought you got lost."

"A man can't get lost. There are too many people around."

"That is good." Fergus continued to study the tracks. "If a person cannot get lost, then your brothers are not lost either."

Ace ignored the old Indian and strolled up to O. T. "Deuce was hurtin' bad. He should have known better than wander around in the desert heat. 'Stay by the motorcar,' I said. 'Be smart.'"

"Perhaps they were surprised by wolves," Fergus suggested without looking up.

Ace waved his hands and shouted. "That's outrageous! There ain't no wolves out here in the Mojave Desert."

The old Indian continued to study the ground, but a wide smile broke across his face. "Then they would have been very surprised."

"Go on. Get out of here. . . . We don't need no crazy old Indian hanging around. We found the car. You go back to your camp," Wilkins growled.

Fergus remained partially stooped over. "How do you know this is not where I was going? Perhaps I will make this my camp."

"Stick around, Fergus," O. T. invited. "We could use the help. I'd like to keep ever' pair of eyes we have until we find his brothers."

"They got tracks leadin' in all directions. I cain't tell which to follow." Wilkins circled the car. "All they had to do was sit still and wait. What were they thinkin'?"

"Let me see the lantern," Fergus requested.

"You ain't gettin'. . ." Wilkins glanced over at O. T. Then he handed the Paiute the lantern.

Fergus, bent over at the waist, held the lantern inches off the ground. His head was barely above the lantern. He circled the abandoned Thomas motorcar three times in that position.

"What's he lookin' for, all bent over like that?" Ace fumed. "We're wastin' time."

"I suppose he's lookin' for clues about your brothers." O. T. leaned up against the front fender of the car and watched the old man orbit the car.

Wilkins edged next to O. T. "Well, he's lookin' all wrong. He ought to make a wider circle."

The old Indian stopped in front of O. T., still stooped over.

"What do you see down there?" O. T. asked.

"Dirt."

"Any clues?"

"Perhaps."

O. T. leaned over and studied the ground beneath the lantern. "Why are you still bending over?"

"I can't stand up."

"What?"

"My back went out," Fergus reported. "I can't stand up."

"This is ridiculous!" Wilkins fumed. He grabbed the lantern and hiked several steps north.

O. T. put his arm on Fergus's shoulders and the palm of his other hand on the lower part of the old man's back and slowly tilted him up.

"Thank you very much," Fergus sighed.

O. T. crossed his arms and felt the cool slick silk of his shirt sleeves. "You're welcome."

Wilkins marched back. "Did you find anything in the tracks? I think maybe someone went over this way."

Fergus scooted over. "Which of your brothers repaired his left boot heel with horseshoe nails?"

Ace spun around. "Trey did that. How did you know?"

Fergus rubbed a brown, crooked finger across his lips and studied Wilkins's face. The lantern light did little more than illuminate three dusty men's faces and seemed to be swallowed up in the desert darkness.

Wilkins marched up within inches of the Paiute. "I asked you a question. How did you know about the horseshoe nail in Trey's boots? Maybe you know more about my brother's disappearance than you let on."

Fergus didn't back away an inch. His voice was so deep it was gravelly. "You remind me of Major Ormsby," he declared.

Ace Wilkins stepped back a foot. "Who the blazes is Major Ormsby?"

"He grossly underestimated the Paiute. You never heard of the Pyramid Lake War?" the Indian challenged.

"What war? What's he babblin' about?" Ace tugged his hat low in the front. "I'll give him a war!"

O. T. grabbed Wilkins's wrist just as he reached for his revolver. "What do you make of the tracks with the horseshoe nails in the boot heel?"

Fergus's smile revealed large, yellowed front teeth in the flickering shadows. "He was walking straight south toward the Montezumas."

"By himself? He wouldn't go off and leave a wounded brother." Wilkins released the grip of his revolver, and O. T. pulled his hand back.

"You did." Fergus's tone was matter-of-fact.

Wilkins leaned against Skinner as if trying to get at the Indian. "I went for help!" he boomed.

"Maybe that's what your brother is doing," O. T. offered.

Ace stared out into the dark night. "Straight south? Why would he go there? And where's Deuce?"

Fergus pointed to the right. "Someone went northwest."

"Northwest? Why would he do that? That's the direction we came from."

"Two men leaving in the opposite direction are more difficult to follow than two men leaving in the same direction," Fergus explained. "Even Paiute children know that."

Wilkins paced in front of the motorcar. "Are you tellin' me my brothers split up and went two different ways so that no one would follow them?"

"Perhaps."

"I don't believe that for one minute!"

The Indian shrugged. "It doesn't matter to me. They are not my brothers."

Wilkins yanked the lantern off the dirt. "Well, I'm going to make a couple wide circles. An old Indian with a bad back can't find anything. Are you coming with me?"

"I'm going to stay with my rig," O. T. replied. "I can't afford to wander off and lose my team. Come back and tell us what you found. Then we'll all head in that direction."

Fergus stood alongside O. T. "There is no reason for an old Indian with a bad back who can't find anything to go with you."

Wilkins stormed off, the lantern in his left hand, his revolver in the right.

The other two stood in the moonlight next to the motorcar. "Well, if I can see my way over there, I reckon I'd better tend my mules," Skinner announced.

"I am going to sleep. It has become my greatest delight. Sleep is the Creator's gift for the very young and the very old. The backseat of this motorcar looks quite vast. If I can crawl up there, I will sleep in comfort."

O. T. walked slowly in the dark, brushing his hand along Ada's back as he proceeded to the front of the team.

"Hey, Wall-Walker," Fergus called out from the motorcar, "have you got a sulfur match on you?"

"Have you taken up smoking?" O. T. laughed as he returned to the motorcar.

"I never gave it up. There are merely times when I have no tobacco," the Indian announced.

The Paiute sat high on the back cushion of the rear seat. The black silhouette of Indian, motorcar, and desert projected a bizarre image. "What are you doin' way up there?"

"I did not like the feel of the cushion. Would you strike a light for me?"

O. T. stepped up on the running board and lit a match. He held it over the foot space in the backseat.

"Deuce and Trey!" he gasped.

The old man pulled his knees up under his chin. "Are they dead? I do not like to touch dead bodies."

O. T. surveyed the two men crumpled up between the front seat and the back. "No, it looks like they were coldcocked and dumped in here." He stood on the running board and shouted out into the night. "Ace? Ace! . . . We found them!"

He heard no reply and could not see the lantern in any direction. "Where did he get to? Can you see him?"

Fergus stared down at the men. "Are you sure they are not dead?"

O. T. struck another match. "They're breathin', all right."

Fergus let his feet down on the seat cushion and crawled out of the motorcar, carefully avoiding the two unconscious men. "A man should never lie down until he can see where he is lying. I could have gone to sleep on a pile of dead men."

O. T. lit another match. "They aren't dead, but they did lose their boots and their pistols. . . . No, the guns are tossed in the front seat. Who would coldcock two men for their boots and leave the guns?"

"Someone without shoes," Fergus replied.

The match flickered out. O. T. stepped down beside the Indian. "You wouldn't happen to know someone like that, would you?"

"I know many people like that. But I did not take the boots. I am wearing moccasins. I didn't know they were here. Are you sure they are not dead?"

"I'm sure." O. T. looked out into the darkness of the desert. "Ace!" he hollered. Then he turned to Fergus. "How could he get out of shouting distance so quickly?"

"I will go find him and bring him back," Fergus offered. "I do not choose to stay with the dead."

"They aren't dead!"

"They might be soon. I will go."

"Fergus, make some noise. Don't go sneakin' up on him. He's got his pistol, and he's jumpy. He'll pull the trigger and then investigate later. I'll see if I can bring these two around."

With repeated striking of matches for light, O. T. tugged Deuce to a sitting position. His right arm was splinted with an axe handle and wrapped with linen strips. Trey sported a big blue lump on his forehead just above his right eye. O. T. soon had them sitting in the backseat as if they were dozing off on a lazy Sunday drive. Then he pulled the wooden bucket from the side of the wagon and filled it half full of water. Standing on the running board, he tossed water into the face of Trey Wilkins.

Wilkins sputtered, cursed, and reached for his empty holster. "What the . . ."

"Trey, it's me—O. T. Skinner. Me and Ace came out for you."

Holding his forehead, Trey Wilkins struggled to stand in the open touring car.

"Where's my gun? Where's Ace? Where are my boots?" He clutched his head and flopped back down in the leather seat.

O. T. tossed the rest of the water on Deuce Wilkins, who shouted and launched a clenched left fist at Trey, connecting in the shoulder.

"Why'd you do that?" Trey hollered.

"Where are my boots?" Deuce struggled to stand. "Who's there?"

Trey remained seated. "It's Skinner. You know, the family man with the mules and the wagon? He and Ace came back for us."

"Where's Ace?" Deuce shouted.

"Ace took the lantern out on the desert to look for you. Your pistols are laying up here in the front seat," O. T. explained. "As for your boots, I have no idea what happened to them."

"Them Indians," Trey muttered. "They took 'em."

"What Indians?" O. T. asked.

"Three Diggers came through here beggin' for food, but we chased them off. They must have come back and bushwhacked us. What else did they steal?"

"We can't tell in the dark. We'll have to wait until Ace comes back with the lantern."

"I can't believe they stole our boots," Deuce griped. "We can't even chase 'em down barefoot."

O. T. thought about how good his new boots felt. "That might be the reason they took 'em."

Both brothers gingerly climbed down out of the motorcar until they stood alongside Skinner.

"How's your arm?" O. T. asked.

"It hurts like Hades when I bump it up against anything. I ain't never goin' to crank one of them engines again," Deuce declared. "But right at the moment this lump on my head hurts even worse."

All three men froze in place when a muffled gunshot exploded to the southwest.

"Ace is in trouble!" Trey shouted.

"Oh, no! He's gone and shot Fergus!" O. T. groaned. *Lord, maybe Lucky Jack is right. I shouldn't have anything to do with men like this. He was just an old man trying to survive from day to day like the rest of us.*

Deuce looked to the southwest. "Who in blazes is Fergus?"

"An old Paiute who helped us locate the motorcar," O. T. explained.

Deuce paced in the darkness. "Maybe he's the one who stole our boots."

O. T. lowered his voice to almost a whisper. "He was wearing homemade moccasins."

"We've got to go help Ace," Trey insisted.

"He's the only one with a gun," O. T. explained. "It's Fergus who needs help. I'll go check it out. You two wait here by my mules."

"It's a cinch we ain't goin' to go hikin'," Deuce declared.

"Do you have a gun?" Trey probed.

O. T. inched his way up the side of the darkened arroyo. "What for? I don't intend to shoot anyone." *Lord, I'm glad I left the shotgun with Dola, because I would be sorely tempted to plug Ace Wilkins if he shot that old man.*

Skinner slowly climbed up the side of the dark arroyo. When he reached the top, he spotted a lantern light about half a mile away. Walking as fast as possible across the rolling hillside, he headed toward the light.

At a hundred yards he thought he could see two men.

At fifty yards he could make out both Ace and Fergus.

Ace Wilkins led the way, carrying the lantern, stepping lightly and mumbling. Fergus strolled behind him carrying a pistol by the barrel, the grip pointed toward the stars.

At twenty-five yards Fergus called out into the darkness. "Is that you, Wall-Walker?"

"Yes . . . what happened? What was that shot?" O. T. marched close enough to be in the lantern light. "What happened to your boots, Ace?"

"Them Diggers took 'em, and he did nothing to help!" He turned around and noticed Fergus holding the pistol by the barrel. "Give me that!" Wilkins jerked the revolver out of his hand.

"They were Mojaves," Fergus declared. "Some of that Colorado River bunch that left the reservation and moved up here."

"I'll shoot ever' one of them," Ace muttered.

"What happened?" Skinner asked.

"They ambushed me," Ace insisted.

"I think he stumbled into their camp, and they captured him. When I got there, they were discussing how much of his things to steal. One of them wanted his trousers."

"They're going to be dead. Ever' one of them is dead!" Wilkins fumed. "I'll hunt them down. I'll shoot them."

"You goin' to go after them barefoot?" Fergus probed.

"If I have to."

"That's up to you," O. T. said. "I'm goin' back to Goldfield. I have a family to take care of. You want me to tow in your motorcar or just leave it out here?"

The three hiked back along the ridge of the arroyo.

"Slow down—my feet is tender," Ace complained.

O. T. walked slowly enough to stay in the lantern light. "Fergus, how come those Indians only stole boots? I'd think they would want the guns and other gear."

The old man rubbed his big leather-tough ears as if it would help him hear. "The Mojaves are not dumb. They know that white men will chase them if they steal too much. So they try to take things that won't be worth the effort."

"They made a grave mistake when they took on the Wilkins brothers," Ace asserted.

"They haven't had any trouble so far," Fergus pointed out.

"They snuck up on me in the night," Ace fussed.

"How could they sneak up on you? You had the lantern," the Indian insisted.

"You know what I meant!"

"They wanted to steal the lantern too. I talked them out of it," Fergus revealed.

"How did you do that?" O. T. questioned.

Fergus yawned and stretched his arms. "I told them that it belonged to my friend, the Wall-Walker. They seemed quite impressed."

"The Mojaves know about that?" Skinner was amazed.

"It is their desert." The old Paiute spoke as if his answer would solve all confusion.

"They weren't impressed enough to give me back my boots," Ace ranted.

"Fergus," O. T. quizzed, "how far will those three be by daylight?"

"With good boots on, they could be all the way to the Silver Peak Range."

"And from there?"

"The White Mountains . . . the Mojave . . . the Sierras—who knows. You will not find them. If the army cannot find them and take them back to Parker, barefoot men will not find them."

Ace Wilkins now trudged twenty feet behind them.

"Were those boots expensive?" O. T. called back.

Ace stopped, set the lantern down, and brushed something off the bottom of his foot. "It ain't the boots; it's the principle."

"Well, ever' day you and your brothers tramp around in the desert looking for old, dirty boots is one more day you ain't workin' that good-payin' job in Goldfield." Skinner kept trudging out into the darkness. "I ain't real smart, Ace, but at some point you boys have to ask yourself how much a pair of boots is worth."

The sun was straight above their heads and the water in the keg almost gone when they rolled down the Tonopah road into the outskirts of Goldfield. It didn't take long for word to spread. By the time they reached the intersection of Main and Crook Streets, almost every saloon had emptied, with patrons huddled on the boardwalks as if watching a parade.

Fatigued, Ada and Ida plodded slowly down the street. O. T. Skinner drove the wagon, his worn denims tucked inside the new boots. His silk shirt still looked fancy, though now frosted with gray alkali dust.

Beside him, with a ridged straight back, was Fergus. In his lap lay the sawed-off .45-70 Trapdoor rifle with patterns of brass upholstery tacks in the stock. The feather in his black wide-brimmed felt hat was the same white color as his hair. His pointed chin and flat nose were held high as if in triumph.

Behind the old farm wagon, a heavy rope led to the bumper of the Thomas motorcar. Ace and Trey Wilkins sat in the front seat. Deuce huddled down in the back with his splinted arm well out of sight.

From the boardwalk, no would could tell that all three were barefoot.

But everyone could see they were mad.

# EIGHT

Dola awoke with a small girl's blonde head on her lap. She stroked the sunken cheeks lightly. *Lord, I once heard a missionary talk about the famished street children of Bombay. Poor little Caitlynn. I pray that her spirit has not been as starved as her body.*

The single lightbulb still illuminated the room, but the windows indicated that daylight was turning the night sky to light gray. The hospital lobby felt sterile and stuffy. Dola's left leg was numb, and her right one was starting to cramp. Her stomach growled, and she could almost taste scrambled eggs.

*I need to get back and help Rita Ann with breakfast . . . but I can't leave Jared and Caitlynn.* She patted the young girl's matted hair and tried to comb it gently with her fingers. *I can't leave her at all. Lord, I know she deserves better than this, but I can't just blame her father. Times are tough for some of us. Right smack dab in a town full of folks making it rich, some are barely gettin' by. And some . . . Well, some aren't getting by at all.*

She looked over at Jared asleep in the oak chair.

*I'm amazed he hasn't started stealin' food. He's a strong boy. He'll survive somehow. But I don't know about Stella. Or Caitlynn.*

There was a muted banging noise.

Dola glanced toward the back room where she supposed the operation was still taking place. *It sounds like they're doing surgery with a hammer.* She sat up and tried to listen more intently. *No . . . it's outside.*

Dola gently laid Caitlynn's head down on the Morris chair and limped quietly over to the window facing the street. Feeling slowly came back into her leg. She could not see who was on the boardwalk directly beneath the window, but even in the shadows, she thought she caught a glimpse of Stella Rokker.

She pulled the side pins on the small-paned window and yanked it up. "Stella?" she called.

The girl popped out onto the street, as did her brother Danny and a massive man wearing a tattered blanket wrapped around him like a giant cape.

"Mrs. Skinner?" Stella called. "Where's Mama?" The faded dress hung straight down on the young girl like a dishrag lapped over a spoon.

Dola leaned out the window and attempted to speak without waking those in the room behind her. "She's up here in the hospital. You can come up the stairs on the end of the building."

"You ain't got no right to bring my wife to this hospital!" Elias Rokker blustered, holding the blanket under his chin with one hand.

"Mr. Rokker, I will not shout out a window to any man. If you'd like to come upstairs, we can continue this conversation." Dola stepped back and slid the window down.

*No right? Mr. Rokker, you have no right to treat your wife like you do. No right to starve your children. No right to drink yourself into a stupor every night. Lord, I have no idea why You even created this man, let alone allowed him to get married and father children! You know that I try very hard never to question Your wisdom, but I must admit I am completely stumped about this matter.*

Dola returned to the big chair and resumed her place with Caitlynn lying across her lap. She poked the twelve-year-old in the chair next to her. "Jared . . . Jared. Wake up—your daddy's here."

He was on his feet before his eyes were fully open. "Daddy? But how's Mama? Are they through?"

Dola glanced at the lobby door. "They haven't come back yet. Stella, Danny, and your daddy are coming up the stairs now."

Jared ran over to the door just as Danny burst through. "How's Mama?" Danny asked anxiously.

"She's having surgery," Jared reported.

Stella scrambled into the room. "Is she goin' to die?"

"That's up to the doctor's skill and Mrs. Skinner's prayers," Jared said.

All three Rokker children scooted over to Dola just as Elias Rokker stormed in. Dola could smell the filth and whiskey. The old wool blanket had a hole in the middle of it, and Rokker had jammed his head through the hole. He wore the blanket like a poncho, his red underwear showing, and he was still barefoot.

He tramped over to Dola as if dressed in a Sunday ready-made suit. "Where's my wife?" he demanded.

Dola leaned back in the chair and stroked Caitlynn's back, but she refused to look up at the man. "The doctor believes her appendix has ruptured. He's operating on her now."

Dola noticed that the second toe on his right foot had been broken and was pointing sideways. "He cain't do that. I never gave him permission!"

Finally she glanced up at his bloodshot brown eyes. "Mr. Rokker, you were passed out drunk, and your wife was about to die. I didn't think we would need your permission to save her life."

He rubbed his grubby mustache, and specks of dirt and grime flaked onto the blanket. "She weren't that bad off."

Dola studied the face of each child. *They seem to be holding their breath as if anticipating an explosion.* "How do you know?" she challenged. "You were unconscious."

He scratched the back of his neck. "I ain't payin' for this hospital. No, sir, they don't get one dime out of me!"

"I already paid for it." *How in the world can the father be so fat and the mother and children so thin?*

"You did?" He picked his nose with his thumb, and Dola looked away.

Jared cleared his throat and swallowed hard. "Mama was in terrible pain, Daddy. We thought she was dyin'. We had to do somethin'."

Mr. Rokker ran massive fingers through his black and gray hair. His face was flushed. "You had no right to—"

"Mr. Rokker, if I found a kitten with a badly cut paw, I would patch it first and ask whose cat it was later. Certainly I'm allowed to treat Mrs. Rokker as well as I would an animal."

He pointed a finger with a dirty nail at Caitlynn. "What's my baby girl doin' in your arms?"

"She's sleeping. We had to separate her from her mother durin' surgery. This is the only way she would settle down. Would you like to sit down and hold her? I'll be happy to stand."

Rokker waved her off and spun around toward the nurse's desk. "No, she pitches a fit when I hug her."

Dola studied the backside of the large man. *Perhaps she has a sensitive nose and objects to the stench. Lord, forgive me. I'm failin' so miserably to care about this man. I would imagine Mrs. Rokker is about the only one on earth who ever cared for him.*

He didn't turn back but seemed to be talking to the empty desk across the room. "Where's my wife?"

Dola found she could count Caitlynn's ribs even as she rubbed her back. "The doctor and nurse are with her—"

He spun back around and waved his fingers only inches from Dola's face. "I want to talk to the doctor, and I want to talk to him right now!"

"Here he comes!" Jared called out as a sweaty and tired Dr. Silvermeyer emerged from the back room.

His vest was gone, and his white shirt sleeves were rolled up to the elbows. He stared at all the people in the lobby. "My word, was there a stage accident?"

Elias Rokker stalked over to the five-foot, four-inch white-haired doctor. "You've got my wife back there."

The doctor gaped at the blanket-draped man, pulled his glasses off, and rubbed the bridge of his nose. "You're the husband?"

"Yep, and I'm a tellin' you, you ain't goin' to touch my wife. I came to take her home."

Now Dola could see how puffy his lips looked. Each word seemed to pop out of his whiskered mouth like a bubble.

Dr. Silvermeyer reset his glasses and unfastened the top button of his sweat-drenched white shirt. "I'm afraid it's impossible to take her home."

Stella burst into tears.

Jared's mouth dropped open. "She ain't . . ."

"No, no." The doctor raised his hands to silence them. "Your mother's in satisfactory condition, so far. Mr. Rokker, your wife's appendix ruptured. I was able to remove most of it and get her stabilized. But the next twenty-four hours are critical. I just don't know how much poison it sent through her system. It looks as if she has not eaten well in a long time and is very weak. You should have brought her days ago."

When Rokker folded his arms across his chest, they seemed to be shelved on top of his massive stomach. "I didn't know nothin' about it."

The doctor rubbed his nose and then stepped back away from Rokker. "She mentioned she'd been hurting for several days."

Arms still folded, Elias Rokker paced the room. "Well, I ain't payin' for nothin' because I didn't agree to it."

Dr. Silvermeyer glanced over at Dola. "Some men test my concept of divine wisdom in His creation," he admitted.

"The Lord and I have been discussin' the very same topic," she replied.

Rokker huffed back over to them. "What are you two talkin' about?"

Dr. Silvermeyer retrieved his coat, vest, and tie from the back of the oak chair at the nurse's desk. "Mr. Rokker, I do not know if your wife will pull through this. But I do know I've done all I can for now. If she survives, it will be because Mrs. Skinner brought her here in the middle of the night and was insistent that I treat her. Would that the world was peopled with folks who cared that much for their neighbors. Now I am very tired. I need to clean up, drink some strong coffee, and begin a busy day."

"When can we go see Mama?" Jared asked.

"Miss Greer will come in when Mrs. Rokker is ready," the doctor announced. He headed out the door.

While the children huddled near Dola, Elias Rokker flounced about the room like a caged buffalo. "She should have told me she was sick. She don't talk to me. Sneakin' around behind my back. Why didn't you kids wake me up? You knew better than to do somethin' like this behind my back. Jared Wayne, I was countin' on better from you. It ain't right. I'm the husband. I'm suppose to make the decisions."

Caitlynn sat up in Dola's lap and silently watched her father stalk the hospital lobby. When he rambled by where she huddled, the young girl sheepishly called out, "Hi, Daddy!"

He spun on his heels. "Where did you get that new dress?" he barked.

Caitlynn threw her arms around Dola's neck and buried her face.

"It's not a dress; it's a pillowcase. I could not bring your precious five-year-old daughter to the hospital stark naked. And I'm sorry to admit, I don't own an extra dress to give her, so I did the best I could." Dola struggled to her feet, still carrying the young girl.

"Mr. Rokker, in all my days I have never, and I do mean never, known any man who so neglected his family or showed less love or concern for his wife. My only explanation for your existence is that the Lord must want you as a horrible example to others. But I have no idea why your wife and children must put up with this."

"I don't surmise I have to listen to you," he groused.

"Let me tell you what I surmise. I surmise this is the exact same message your conscience gives you ever' wakin', sober minute of your life. That's why you try to stay drunk all the time. You don't deserve this family, Elias Rokker, and you know it!"

It was as if he had walked out of a dark cave into the bright sun of noonday. His anger dissipated, his eyes closed, and his shoulders sagged. His massive, unclothed arms began to quiver. He clenched his fists until they were white.

Dola held her breath.

Then he opened his mouth.

And moaned.

"Oh . . . oh . . . I'm so scared. I can't lose her. What would I do? Oh, what would I do?"

The burly man began to sob. Tears streaked his dirty beard. "I can't live with myself now. . . . Without her . . . I would die. . . . The children would be orphans. . . . Oh, Lord, what am I goin' to do? What am I goin' to do?"

Stella threw her arms around him. "It's okay, Daddy. It's okay. . . . Mama ain't goin' to die."

Danny was next to hug him. "I'm scared too, Daddy. I'm really scared. I don't want Mama to die."

Jared tugged on his father's arm. "It's all right, Daddy. Mama's going to pull through. Mrs. Skinner prayed for her. The Lord will take care of us."

Caitlynn squirmed out of Dola's arms and, chin down on her chest, crept over to her father, bit her lip, then finally spoke. "Do I look pretty in my new dress, Daddy? Mrs. Skinner says I look pretty."

Elias Rokker opened his mouth, but all he could do was nod his head and sob. He scooped her up with one massive arm, and she clutched his neck and kissed his greasy, dirty cheek.

Huddled in the middle of the room, the Rokker family didn't see

Miss Greer enter the back of the lobby. Dola scooted next to the nurse, who ushered her to the back room.

The nurse's white dress was sweat-soaked. "Is that man her husband?" she asked.

Dola felt sloppy with her hair down on her shoulders. She fought the urge to brush it back. "Yes, those are her children as well," she offered.

"Where are his clothes?"

"I'm not sure he has any right at the moment."

The nurse folded her arms across her chest. "Everyone has clothes!"

"Not everyone, Miss Greer," Dola murmured. "Some of us wear our entire wardrobe every day. How is Mrs. Rokker?"

"She is in terrific pain, but she seems determined to endure it. It's just a matter of waiting to see how her body fights off the poison in her system." The nurse led Dola past several curtain-draped empty beds. "She wanted to speak to you before she talked to the children."

"She did?"

The nurse pointed to bed #4. "She insisted. You go on in and chat while I explain her condition to her family."

Dola padded toward the bed and peeked around the curtain. Lying on her back under clean white cotton sheets was an exhausted-looking Mrs. Rokker. Even with her face scrubbed and her mostly gray hair combed, she looked fifty.

*I've never seen a woman look so worn out. Lord, I know she's not any older than I am. Is that the way I look to others?*

She stood by the woman's bed. One sunken eye and then the other blinked open. A thin, bony hand reached out from under the sheet. Dola took the ice-cold hand and squeezed it lightly.

"Mrs. Skinner . . ."

"I'm Dola."

"And I'm Nellie. I want to thank you, but I'm feared I'll start cryin' and won't be able to stop."

Dola patted her hand. "Nellie, don't worry about thanking me. You would have done the same if the tables had been reversed."

Nellie glanced up at the high hospital ceiling as if reading a script. "But I wouldn't have had the money for the surgery. The nurse told me you paid for it."

"Now, honey, the Lord's in charge of finances. Let's just leave that to Him. Right now you need to rest, eat, and regain your strength."

Nellie clutched Dola's hand, pleading with her eyes and her words. "But the children . . . What about my children?"

Dola patted the top of the woman's hand. "They are all fine. They are all in the lobby with your husband."

Like an earthquake rolling along a mountainous fault, the lines across her forehead wavered, then tightened. "He's here at the hospital?"

"Yes, he is."

"Is he drunk?"

"No."

"Is he clothed?"

"Well . . . he does have a blanket wrapped around him."

Mrs. Rokker turned her head away and stared at the white curtain. "It's humiliating. If it weren't for the children, I would be better off dead."

"Don't you talk that way. After all, a man who hikes across town dressed like that when he's sober sincerely cares about his wife."

Mrs. Rokker turned back toward Dola. "Did he say that?"

"He's so worried he's in tears."

"Elias doesn't ever cry when he's sober."

"He's sober. And I can guarantee he's crying. He needs you to pull through. They all need you."

Nellie Rokker's eyes were now locked onto Dola's, pleading for support. "Where's my baby?"

"She's with her father."

"She doesn't like to be away from me."

Dola took a damp cloth draped over the white-enameled head-board and wiped Mrs. Rokker's forehead. "She's growin' up, Mama."

Nellie Rokker closed her eyes. "Does she have on any clothes? That ol' dress was beyond repair. I jist didn't know what to do."

"She's wearing a cute little silk dress that looks strangely like a pillowcase."

Her eyes still closed, Nellie sighed. Tears trickled down her cheeks. "I hurt."

"The doctor said you just need rest."

"He also said the blood poison could kill me within hours. I wasn't as unconscious as he thought. Still, this is a comfortable bed. I can't remember a decent bed and clean sheets." She blinked her eyes open. "You'll need to get back to your family."

"Yes, I suppose so. I'll go and let your family come see you."

"Will you come back?"

"Yes, but it may not be until tomorrow."

"I don't know how many days I have. I'd like to see you again. Are you still planning on leaving for California tomorrow?"

"Oh, my . . . tomorrow? I'm not sure. But I will certainly come back to see you before we go."

The Rokker family paraded past her in the big room as she pointed out bed #4. When she reached the lobby, Miss Greer was instructing the day-shift nurse.

"Mrs. Skinner, one moment, please." She finished the conversation with the other nurse and joined Dola at the door. "I'll walk down the stairs with you."

The two women were about the same height and same age. But Miss Greer walked with her shoulders back, chin high, and head perfectly level. Her face looked wrinkle free. So did her hands. Dola could not remember when her own hands had looked so youthful.

When they reached the bottom stair, the nurse touched Dola's elbow. "Mrs. Skinner, I owe you an apology. I'm afraid I acted rather rudely and callously when you first came in."

"It was the middle of the night. I'm sure you were tired." Dola threw her chest forward and shoulders back, but was not sure that it made her look any different. The plain dress still hung very similar to Caitlynn's pillowcase dress.

"I'm not very good at extemporaneous things. I know I should be more flexible."

"Miss Greer, I promise you I will not give it another thought. Will there be additional costs?"

"The doctor said he would talk to Mr. Rokker about them. I do hope that man gets some clothes on."

"I'm not sure Mr. Rokker has any funds."

Conversation died while a freight wagon rumbled by. The nurse stepped to the edge of the boardwalk. "Is your husband really the Wall-Walker?"

Dola stood alongside her watching the morning traffic. "Yes, he is."

"I heard Jug Cherry tried to shoot him off the wall, but he kept right on packing out those casks of water. Is that true?"

"I have no idea. Orion didn't seem to remember to tell me about that." *Someone was shooting at my husband, and I didn't even know about it!*

"It would have been a sight to see. Everyone in town is very grateful . . . except for Mr. Cherry. He is a loud, obnoxious, violent man. But I suppose you've heard all those stories about him." She turned to the right when they reached the boardwalk. "Good-bye, Mrs. Skinner."

"Good-bye, Miss Greer." *Just what stories are you talking about? Did he really try to shoot Orion while he was drawing water from a public well? Why is it that everyone in town knows more about my husband than I do? Lord, bring that man home safely.*

The early morning boardwalks were filled mainly with men in a hurry to get somewhere. Most were dressed in riveted denim britches and long-sleeved cotton shirts and were toting round tin lunch buckets. Most ignored her completely.

*There are times, Lord, when being plain is very comfortable. I certainly will turn no head and tempt no man. I like that very much.*

Dola had walked only a block when a carriage pulled up beside her. She tried to ignore it.

"Mornin', Mrs. Skinner."

A relaxed smile broke across her face. "Oh . . . good mornin', Mr. LaPorte. Don't you ever sleep?"

The big man pulled out a blue bandanna and brushed off his boots. "I'm on my way home right now. I had a very productive night for my first venture into driving a hack."

"I trust you didn't spend your entire time giving free rides."

"No, ma'am. Can I give you a lift? I would guess you haven't slept much either."

"Thank you, I'm tired enough to accept it." She started to climb up in the front seat next to him.

LaPorte waved his arm. "Mrs. Skinner, would you mind sitting back there. It will look like you hired me, and folks wouldn't talk as much."

Dola paused. "Mr. LaPorte, are you embarrassed to have me ride next to you?"

"Eh, no, ma'am . . . it's just that some folks in this town don't want black men being that chummy with white ladies."

She pulled herself up into the front seat. "I find prejudice a luxury I cannot afford. Besides, I believe most of that crowd will still be asleep, don't you, Mr. LaPorte?"

"I reckon you're right about that."

"Right at this moment, Mr. LaPorte, I'm so tired I could lay down in the middle of Main Street and fall asleep. I reckon I'd even ride with the devil if he promised to keep his hands to himself."

LaPorte slapped the line on his horse and lurched out into the street. "I cain't believe you said that," he laughed.

"Nor can I. I must be even more tired than I imagined."

"How's Mrs. Rokker?" he inquired.

"She's recovering from emergency appendix surgery. If she has enough strength, she should do well enough. Thanks to you, we got her there in time."

"That's good . . . that's mighty good. She surely is a thin, sickly thing. Now you take my Omega, she is a healthy-sized woman. I like 'em that way. Eh, nothin' personal."

Dola leaned back on the seat cushion and closed her eyes. "I look forward to meeting your wife."

"After I get some sleep, we might just come over. You two can talk about raisin' children and . . . and alligator boots. They surely do look nobby on you, Mrs. Skinner."

Dola was so tired she felt very little control. "I have a question for you, Mr. LaPorte."

"Ma'am?"

"Orion is a trustin', true man. The thought of the origin of those boots probably did not cross his mind. But I want to know—did they come from a woman who worked at a brothel?" *I've never even used that word with Orion. Dola Davis Skinner, shame on you. Lord, I'd better go home.*

LaPorte turned the hack west on Columbia Street. "You're probably right. Does it matter where they're from?"

Dola knew she was blushing and purposely stared across at Columbia Mountain. "I just don't think I could wear a soiled dove's boots."

"You know, I figured my Omega would say the same thing when I told her where I got them. But you know what she said? She jist raised that round nose of hers and said, 'Well, the devil's had them long enough. It's time for the redeemed to enjoy them.'"

A wide smile broke across Dola's face. "I don't know if it's just that I'm tired or that you're such a persuasive fellow . . . but I reckon I'll wear them just to keep them out of the devil's hands."

The sun was breaking over Columbia Mountain when she climbed down from Lucian LaPorte's hack. From the street she could see a table full of people behind her tent. A barefoot Tommy-Blue met her at the edge of the lot. His hat was pulled down across uncombed hair, but his face looked fairly clean.

His blue eyes sparkled. "Mama, Rita-Ann cooked breakfast, and she burnt the eggs!"

"Oh . . . my." She glanced back toward the men and didn't spot anyone who looked disturbed over the food.

"Mama, Mama, Mama, Mama, Mama!" Punky squeaked as he ran toward her and leaped into her arms.

When she picked him up, she could feel a sharp pain in the lower part of her back. *Lord, may I never complain about Punky's weight again. He is nice and healthy. And that is certainly better than the alternative!* "Well, young man, the eggs on your chin look just fine." As she strolled up to the table with the toddler on her hip, all three men stood.

"Mornin', Mrs. Skinner," Lucky Jack called out. "Heard you had a rough night."

"How's Mrs. Rokker, Mama?" Rita Ann queried.

"She had her ruptured appendix removed. Now we'll just have to wait and see how she heals." Dola looked at her oldest daughter standing by the stove.

*Her hair is braided and perfectly curled on the sides of her head. She wore my clean apron. Her old faded dress is neat and clean. Her eyes survey her domain. She is the queen over everything and everyone within her sight, and she doesn't even know it. Someday, Rita Ann Skinner, you will rule kingdoms.*

"How is your breakfast, men?" Dola asked.

"It's hot, tasty, and satisfying." Wasco grinned.

"You will notice they didn't say delicious," Rita Ann pouted. "I think I built too hot a fire. The eggs got a little brown. Of course, Lucky Jack took one bite and asked me if I would marry him." Her pout turned to a giggle.

Dola stared at the men. "Is that true, Mr. Gately?"

The blond-headed man with dancing blue-gray eyes shoved his hat back. "Oh, yes, ma'am, but she turned me down flat. It's a sad day when a man is so quickly rejected."

"And I say that girl is one smart young lady," Charlie Fred laughed. "She has a discernin' eye."

"I told him, 'Yet hasty marriage seldom proveth well,' just like Gloucester in *Henry VI*," Rita Ann reported.

Dola stooped and put the barefoot, squirming Punky on the ground. When she straightened, a sharp pain burned its way down her left leg. She took a deep breath. "How did Mr. Gately reply to that?"

"He said, 'And ruin'd love, when it is built anew, grows fairer than at first, more strong, far greater.'" Rita Ann giggled. "But I told him I'm not going to get married until I'm sixteen."

"Sixteen?" Dola gasped.

Rita Ann carried the coffeepot to the table. "You were sixteen when you married Daddy."

"I think she's got you there, Mrs. Skinner," Wasco teased.

"She ain't goin' to be sixteen for a long time," Tommy-Blue insisted.

Dola stared at her beaming daughter. *It will come much too soon. Much too soon.*

Lucky Jack finished off his coffee and stood up. "We'd best head out. We've been doin' nothin' but drillin'. Now we have to set some charges and see what we've got."

"Daddy's going to assay my pay dirt today," Tommy-Blue reported.

"That's good, son. You're a hard-workin' boy. It must run in the family," Lucky Jack said.

Dola stood at the head of the table. "We will need to bring your lunches out to—"

"Mama," Rita Ann interrupted, "I fixed their lunches and already loaded them into their buckets."

"You did?"

Rita Ann nodded her head. "I, eh . . . didn't go back to sleep but sort of stayed up and fixed some things."

"You see?" Lucky Jack laughed. "She's the girl of my dreams."

Dola waved her finger at the man. "You start dreamin' about my daughter, and you never get another meal from me, Lucky Jack."

"Whoa," Charlie Fred called out, "when the mama bear shows her teeth, it's time to leave."

"I didn't mean to growl." Dola tried to smile, but didn't want to show her dimples. "Well, perhaps just a little. I'm a little too tired to have much self-control."

"Say," Lucky Jack called out, "how about us finding an awning to stretch over the table? That would give the dining room a little shade."

"And keep the rain out of our soup," Wasco added.

"It don't never rain here," Charlie Fred groused.

"That's okay—I don't like soup." Wasco laughed.

After the men left, Dola and Rita Ann started to clear the dishes. "Do you have any hot water boiling?"

"Yes, Mama. I tried to remember everything."

"I'm proud of you, darlin'."

"Is Mrs. Rokker really going to be all right?"

"We'll have to wait and see."

"Mama, don't worry about Lucky Jack. He was just funnin' me."

Dola slipped her arm around her daughter's waist. "I know it, honey."

"Besides, he's not my type. At least, I don't think so. I want someone who is brave and honorable and trustworthy and loves the

Lord and holds the door open for me when I go into the bank and cradles me tender when I'm upset and cryin'."

"Now that, young lady, sounds an awful lot like your father."

"Yes. I want a husband who is just like Daddy. But I think there aren't many of them like that, are there?"

"No, honey, not very many."

"Mama, can Punky help me with my claim?" Tommy-Blue asked.

"Yes, but don't let him scoop dirt onto his head."

Corrie wiped plum jam off her chin onto the sleeve of her plain brown dress. "Mama, can I go and visit Mrs. Marsh? I haven't seen her come out of her tent today."

"Yes, but don't get in her way or annoy her."

When they finished the dishes, Rita Ann slowly took off the apron. "Mama, I really like cooking. To see the look on the men's faces when they enjoyed what I cooked—that's really fun, isn't it?"

"Yes, it is. And you can stop being twenty and go back to being twelve now."

"I like being older."

"It will happen soon enough, darlin'. Now how would you like to go in and take a little nap on our feather mattress?"

"I'd love to. How did you know?" Rita Ann questioned.

"Because that's exactly what I'd like to do. I'm so tired I could sleep on top of this table."

"There's room for two in here," Rita Ann called out from the tent flap.

"I do believe you're right. It's time for us ladies to take a rest."

Rita Ann's grin was from ear to ear. "That's the first time you ever referred to 'us ladies.'"

"Well, it won't be the last, darlin'."

Dola knew she would not sleep.

Not with the sun burning brightly above.

Not with Punky playing out in the yard.

Not with the worry about Nellie Rokker on her mind.

Not with Orion somewhere out on the desert with the Wilkins brothers.

Not in a hot, stuffy tent in a wild and dangerous place like Goldfield.

She was wrong.

And this time she was way too tired to dream.

"Skinner, come out of that tent right now!"

Mother and daughter sat up on the bed at the same time. Dola brushed her hair back with her fingers. *I haven't even done my hair up today. It's not a good time for visitors.*

"Who is it, Mama?" Rita Ann whispered.

"I'd better go see, darlin'. You lay back down and rest."

Dola swung her legs over the edge of the bed and tugged on her boots.

Rita Ann did the same.

"You heard me, Skinner—I'm callin' you out!"

"What does he mean, callin' me out?" Dola asked Rita Ann.

"He wants to challenge you in a gunfight. Remember when Stuart Brannon in *The Bordertown Sheriff* had to confront that wicked man named Traver, and he—"

Dola tugged on her second boot. "And what did Pop Brannon tell us about those books?"

Rita Ann rolled her eyes. "He said they were mostly lies."

"Except the part about Uncle Everett."

"But, Mama, all fiction is mostly made up, but that doesn't mean it doesn't hold some truth."

"I'm givin' you to the count of ten, Skinner," the man shouted.

"I'm impressed," Dola whispered. "From the whiskey slur in his voice, he doesn't sound like the type of man that can count to ten."

"Aren't you scared, Mama?"

"I'm absolutely too tired to be scared. When I'm this tired, I get frivolous and silly."

"Mama, you've never been silly in your life."

"How about the time I made the chicken costume and chased that pack of dogs out of the barn?"

Rita Ann burst out laughing. "Okay . . . okay. Every once in a great while you are really silly."

They both stood up.

"Did you get taller?" Dola asked.

"Not since yesterday, Mama."

"Well, maybe I'm just getting shorter."

"This is your last chance, Skinner!" the man screamed.

"I do wish I had on that chicken costume right now!" Dola led her twelve-year-old out through the tent flap. She shaded her eyes with her hand. "Which Skinner did you want to talk to? I'm Dola Skinner, and this is my daughter Rita Ann."

The man rubbed his week-old black beard. His nose was the same round shape as his head. Both his neck and his nose were flushed. He had a short-barreled saddle-ring carbine in his hands. His felt hat was covered with dark gray alkali dust. "What? Where's that water-stealin' Wall-Walker?" he yelled.

Tommy-Blue and a dirty-headed Punky emerged from their hole and scooted over to the crates next to the tent. "Daddy didn't steal any water. Ever'one knows the water at Rabbit Springs is free. How can you steal free water?" Tommy-Blue said.

"He ruined my business, that's what he did," the man shouted.

"Are you Mr. Cherry?" Dola demanded.

"Yep. And I had me a good business before he came to town."

"If he did something illegal, why don't you consult the sheriff?"

"'Cause I'm goin' to handle this myself. Is he in that tent?"

"No," Dola replied.

"Well, I don't believe you." He took several steps toward them. "I'm goin' to look for myself."

Dola folded her arms and blocked his path. "If you do, I'll get the sheriff to arrest you for breaking and entering."

He waved the gun at her. "For entering a tent?"

"This is our home," she insisted. "I don't imagine the law specifies what material the house is made of."

His face was now as flushed as his nose. "Lady, that's the lamest threat I ever did hear in my life." He took a step toward the tent.

"Mama, is this shotgun cocked or not?"

Dola and Jug Cherry looked over at Tommy-Blue, who had pulled the shotgun from one crate and laid it on top of another. Both barrels were pointed at the man's midsection. The boy's fingers were on the triggers.

"Tommy-Blue, you be careful," Dola shouted. "It certainly looks cocked. What do you think, Mr. Cherry?"

"Now, boy, jist back away. Mind your mama. . . . You—you could get yourself hurt!" he stammered.

"Are you really going to break into our tent?" Tommy-Blue asked.

"Eh . . . is your daddy home, son?"

Tommy-Blue shook his head.

"You wouldn't lie to me, would you?"

Tommy-Blue shook his head again. "I don't lie."

"Well, in that case, I won't need to look in the tent." Cherry swallowed each word hard. "Now tell the boy to back away from the shotgun."

"Take your fingers off the trigger, darlin'. You don't want to shoot that gun. The recoil would give you a big bruise."

"A big bruise?" Cherry mumbled. "What do you think it would give me?"

The boy released his fingers but kept his hand on the receiver. He made sure the barrel kept pointing toward the man. Cherry backed up toward the long table. "I reckon I kin just sit here and wait for him. Me and the Wall-Walker have a matter to settle, and that Ace Wilkins left town last night, so he ain't got nobody to go his play."

"Daddy's bringing all three Wilkins brothers into Goldfield this morning. I believe they'll be along any minute," Rita Ann announced. "And I don't lie either."

"Don't anyone in this family lie?" Cherry murmured.

"What's the ruckus down here?" a woman's voice shouted from up the slope of the lot.

Mrs. Marsh and Corrie walked up behind the man. Their neighbor carried her own ever-present shotgun. It was pointed at Cherry's head.

"Who are you?" he cried out.

"That really ain't none of your business," Mrs. Marsh snapped. Dola was surprised to see her dressed in a stylish Eton jacket lined with white silk. Her daringly short skirt was four inches off the ground. "Put that carbine on the table," she demanded.

The man kept the carbine in his hand. "You think women and children can disarm me?"

"Doesn't look like you have any choice, Mr. Cherry," Dola put in.

"I ain't puttin' down my gun, so make your move."

"What's goin' on, Mama?" Corrie asked. "Who is this man?"

"I think he's a lame thumper!" Punky shouted.

"What did he call me?" Cherry asked.

"A claim jumper," Corrie explained.

At those words Mrs. Marsh leaped forward and shoved the shotgun into the back of the man's neck so forcefully that he dropped his carbine in the dirt and raised his hands. "I ain't no claim jumper!" he protested.

Rita Ann stooped and plucked up his carbine. "Well, Punky's only two," she replied. "Sometimes he lies."

"What are we going to do with him, Mama?" Corrie asked.

"There's a grave dug in the middle of this lot. I say we shoot him and roll him into it," Mrs. Marsh huffed.

"What? You can't . . ." Cherry sputtered.

"No, that wouldn't be the Christian thing to do." Dola glanced around the yard. "This man came to visit with my husband, so I believe he should get his visit. We just need a place to keep him until Orion gets home."

"We could pull off his britches and chain him down in an anthill!" Tommy-Blue suggested.

"Boy, where did you learn to talk that way?" Dola scolded.

"You told me that's what happened to Uncle Everett one time," he gulped.

"Yes, well, that was only to get you to fall asleep. We are not going to chain him to an anthill. But we do need a secure building to lock him in."

"Perhaps a rock one will do," Mrs. Marsh suggested.

It took several minutes and severe threats from the business end of a shotgun to coax Jug Cherry into the outhouse. It only took a few seconds for Tommy-Blue to nail the door shut.

"You cain't do this!" Cherry screamed.

"We just did," Dola replied. "If you persist in screaming, you will only get thirsty. I'm sure my husband will be home in an hour or two."

"An hour? What am I supposed to do in here for that long?"

"I suggest you contemplate the direction your life is going and change your ways. Prayer and meditation might be nice. Or perhaps you would like something to read. I'm afraid all our newspapers are several weeks old."

"I don't want anything to read! Let me out of here. This is illegal. You cain't do this!"

"Would you like me to summon the sheriff, Mr. Cherry?" Dola queried.

There was no reply.

She and the others walked back down toward Tommy-Blue's hole.

"What are we goin' to do, Mama?" Corrie asked.

"If Daddy doesn't get back soon, we will leave him there for a short while and then turn him loose, without his gun, of course," Dola explained.

Mrs. Marsh gave Dola an admiring look. "Corrie Lou told me about Mrs. Rokker's surgery. I can't believe I slept through everything. Ever' since she brought me those groceries, I've been sleeping better."

"That's wonderful," Dola said. "And you are dressed very fashionable today."

"I haven't worn this since Mr. Marsh died."

"You make me feel plain."

"And you make me feel old and miserly. Little Corrie said Mr. Rokker lost his clothes."

Dola nodded. "Yes, and I'm not sure what the story is on that."

"Well, my husband was about the same size, and I've got a couple of suits that are just gettin' in the way. You suppose he'd take them off my hands?"

"Yes!" Dola clapped her hands. "Oh, that would be wonderful, Mrs. Marsh."

"I could take them to him at the hospital," Rita Ann offered.

"Yes, that would work. Corrie could go with you," Dola insisted.

"Why, Mama? I can do it by myself," Rita Ann reasoned. "You said I was acting more mature."

"That's exactly why you need little sis," Dola asserted.


The alley behind Comstock Boot & Saddle was crooked, narrow, and strewn with trash. But the Wilkins brothers insisted that O. T. drive the team, towing the motorcar, down the alley to the store's back door so they might exit without anyone seeing their unbooted feet. Fergus continued to sit up straight as if in a parade, though there was no one in the alley to watch.

O. T. glanced back at the three disgruntled brothers. "Are you sure you want me to park the motorcar at our place?"

"I don't ever want to see this thing again," Ace fumed. "You can have it."

"If you didn't want it, why not just leave it out in the desert?" O. T. asked.

Ace Wilkins unstrapped a large leather trunk from the back of the motorcar. "I've been wonderin' the same thing," he called out. "I reckon 'cause we'd be saying it beat us. But if we drag it to town and dump it, then we're gettin' even. Anyway, it's your pay."

O. T. handed the lead lines to Fergus and climbed down. "I don't want anything for bringing you in."

"Well, you ain't gettin' anything but a yard toy, as far we're concerned," Deuce remarked as he stacked a wooden box on the step.

Trey handed O. T. a greenback.

"I don't need no five dollars," he protested.

"It ain't for you; it's for the mules," Trey insisted. "They did all the work. You jist rode along. Give 'em a couple of nights at the livery with some fresh hay and grain, and they'll be mighty thankful."

O. T. tucked the bill in his britches pocket. "You're right about that. This is for Ada and Ida."

After stacking a large pile of supplies on the back step, the Wilkins brothers entered the boot shop. Ace turned at the door. "Thanks, Skinner, that's the second time you treated us better than we deserved. I don't forget things like that."

O. T. climbed up next to the Paiute. "Fergus, put down that Trapdoor. You're the motorcar driver now. You got to crawl back there and steer that thing out of the alley. It don't trailer well without someone at the wheel. Have you ever driven one of those?"

"No, but often I have sat in the ones in my front yard."

"That's better than me," O. T. told him. "It looks like all you have to do is sit there and turn that wheel back and forth."

"I will do it."

O. T. looked back, making sure they didn't clip the edge of McCaffrey's Meat Market as they pulled into the street. However, he failed to pay attention to traffic in the street. The Tonopah stage was forced to a sliding, passenger-tumbling stop to avoid a collision, as was a Ford motorcar that bounced along in the opposite direction.

Drivers of both rigs screamed and cursed as the wagon-towed Thomas crept out into the street. The commotion emptied nearby stores. Soon a large crowd poured out to view the spectacle.

Fergus smiled and waved to the crowd in triumph.

"You better hurry up, Wall-Walker. That there Indian in the motorcar is about to ketch you!" one man hooted.

"You got a two-mule-power engine in that Thomas?" another shouted.

"Hey, they finally invented a motorcar that don't need no gasoline!"

But it was a high-pitched feminine voice that O. T. heard most clearly.

"Daddy!"

He stopped the wagon in the middle of the street. The motor-car rolled to a stop behind him. Again teamsters yelled and cursed. A dark-haired girl with bangs flopping in her eyes dashed through the crowd and out into the street. "Daddy!"

"Corrie, darlin', what are you doin' here?"

"Can we ride home with you?"

"We?" He glanced up. Rita Ann and the Rokker children streamed out of the crowd.

"What have you all been up to?" O. T. inquired.

"I'll tell you on the way home," Corrie explained.

"Is that a real Indian?" Danny Rokker asked.

"Kids, this is my good friend Fergus. He's a genuine Paiute Indian," O. T. announced.

Jared Rokker whispered something to Rita Ann. "Can we sit in the motorcar, Daddy?" she asked. "We've never been in a motorcar."

"I reckon you can," O. T. offered. "It will be parked over at our place awhile. Of course, the motor's broke, and it don't run."

"You mean, it's ours?" Corrie asked.

"The Wilkins brothers gave it to us," O. T. explained. "But we don't have any use for it. We surely ain't draggin' it all the way to California."

"We have a motorcar!" Rita Ann shouted as she led the whole gang to pile into the high backseat of the touring car.

All except Corrie.

"Can I sit with you, Daddy?" she asked.

"Of course, darlin'. I need someone to tell me how this whole gang came to be downtown. I reckon you all had a nice peaceful night last night."

She clutched his arm and leaned her head against his shoulder. "You reckoned wrong, Daddy."

When O. T. reached lot #124, he swung the parade wide and towed the motorcar into the middle of the lot next to Tommy-Blue's diggings.

"Tommy-Blue, this is our motorcar. Isn't it the most beautiful motorcar in the world?" Corrie shouted as she jumped out of the wagon.

Dola met him with a hug in front of the team of mules.

"You missed me?" he grinned.

"I always miss you, Orion Tower Skinner." She glanced back at the motorcar. "This is really ours?"

"It's broke, and the Wilkins brothers wanted to dump it. They said the kids could use it for a yard toy."

"That's a dramatic yard toy." Dola stared at the old Indian who approached. "Does it come with a chauffeur?"

"Fergus, this is my wife, Mrs. Skinner. Dola, this is Fergus, a Paiute Indian who helped us last night."

The Indian flashed a warm, yellow-toothed smile. "It is an honor to meet such a courageous woman," he said.

"Courageous?" she quizzed.

The smile melted away slowly. "Among my people, it takes great courage for such a young, attractive woman to marry such a plain, old man."

Dola curtsied. "And it takes a wise Indian to flatter a woman at lunchtime."

"Not wise—hungry," he answered.

"Mr. Fergus, would you stay and join us for lunch?"

"If you insist."

"I do."

"Then I will postpone my other plans," he announced.

"What had you intended to do?" Dola asked.

"Go hungry."

O. T. slipped his arm around Dola's shoulder and gave her a squeeze. "Corrie Lou filled me in. We both had exciting nights."

"Thus far Goldfield is not boring."

Tommy-Blue ran up. "Daddy, can we go to the assay office now?"

"Yep. Go get your sample ore. That's just where I'm headed."

"You'll eat lunch first, won't you?" Dola asked.

"I'll be back," O. T. replied. "I want to put Ida and Ada in a livery. The Wilkins brothers insisted on paying their board. We'll need them strong before we push on to California."

"When do you plan on us leavin'?" Dola pressed.

"As soon as the mules are rested and we can buy supplies. I thought we would board the mules two days. That tollhouse man, Jug Cherry, is spoutin' off. I figure we'll jist stay over on this side of town and pull out before he comes a callin' on us."

"Cherry! . . . Oh, my!" Dola gasped.

"What's the matter?" O. T. prodded.

"I forgot all about him."

O. T. scratched the back of his neck. "Cherry came by?"

Dola chewed on her lip. "He's still here."

"Where?" O. T. spun around to survey the property.

Dola pointed toward the back of the lot. "Eh . . . we sort of locked him in the outhouse."

# NINE

The sound of a motorcar backfiring drew their attention to the street. A man with a badge pulled over and climbed out of an open-top black Ford. "Are you the one they call the Wall-Walker?" he asked as he approached.

O. T. went to meet him.

"Mama, your olive crock is all full of dirt," Rita Ann reported as she toted the heavy ceramic jar out of the Wilkins brothers' motorcar.

Dola continued to gaze at the lawman. "It will wash up."

"You want us to dump out the dirt?" Rita Ann pressed.

"Yes, that would be nice. Then we'll clean it up," Dola murmured. She strained to listen to the men's conversation.

O. T. read the badge. "You the sheriff?"

"Yep."

"What can I do for you?"

The lawman looped his thumbs in his gray vest. "Have you seen Jug Cherry?"

O. T. rubbed his stubby beard. "I haven't exactly seen him yet, but I'm told—"

"He's been drinkin' all night and threatenin' you bodily harm." The sheriff surveyed the lot. "When the bartender at the Eureka Saloon took up for you, Cherry pulled a knife and cut his arm. So now I have to arrest him."

"Is the bartender all right?" O. T. glanced down and noticed that his boots were in better shape than the sheriff's.

"Wasn't much of a wound, but I'll toss Cherry into jail for a day jist to sober him. That is, I would, if I had a cell. The new jail isn't finished, and the old one is filled with union organizers today. I'll have to chain him to the desk or something. I jist wanted to warn you in case he staggers over here."

"Mama, can I use your olive crock to carry my sample pay dirt to the assay office?" Tommy-Blue asked.

Dola pulled her gaze away from the lawman. "What? Dirt? No, not the crock. It's not for dirt."

"It was full of dirt."

"Well, you take the old bucket. I'm going to wash the crock."

"But the bucket handle is busted! I can't carry it full."

"I'm sure Daddy will be able to manage."

"It ain't a very nobby way to tote ore," he whined.

"We aren't very nobby people. I'm not lending my dishes out for dirt." She waved him off and strained to listen again.

O. T. and the lawman were strolling toward the table. "Sheriff, when I said I hadn't seen Cherry, that's true. But let me finish. He came over here and threatened the wife and kids, so they shut him up in the outhouse."

"They what?" The sheriff stared around the yard.

Dola scurried over to them. "He was threatening us with his gun, so we nailed him into that rock privy, Sheriff. Orion just got here, and I was going to let him decide Mr. Cherry's fate," she declared. She found herself looking at her worn, very plain dress. *If I could buy a yard of new material and make myself an apron, it would certainly perk up my wardrobe.*

"I was jist headin' up that way," O. T. added.

The sheriff shook his head. "I've got to see this."

"Daddy, can I go with you and Tommy-Blue to the assay office?"

Corrie called out from behind the steering wheel of the abandoned Thomas.

"Surely, darlin'. As long as it's all right with Mama."

"She said I should stay here and help her and Rita Ann cook."

"Then you mind your mama. Don't go playin' me against her."

"Look, Daddy!" Punky sat in Corrie's lap, his hands on the steering wheel. "Punky drives!"

O. T. laughed. "You're doin' a fine job there, son."

"Who's the Indian?" The sheriff nodded toward the old man sitting at the table with a mound of food on a tin plate.

"His name is Fergus. He's a friend of mine."

"Don't let him steal you blind."

"Sheriff, when you're as poor as we are, there jist ain't nothin' nobody wants," O. T. replied.

They hiked past the car, the hole in the ground, and over to the rock privy. An overdressed woman with a shotgun stood near the back property line.

O. T. tipped his hat. "Mornin', ma'am."

She eyed the sheriff as if selecting a chicken in the hen house. "Mornin', Mr. Skinner. I see you brought the sheriff to arrest this claim jumper."

"I ain't no claim jumper!" Cherry yelled from inside. "Is that you, Sheriff?"

The lawman looped his thumbs in his vest pockets. "It's me."

"You've got to get me out of here."

"Why?" the sheriff prodded.

"It ain't right."

"I don't know. I mean, the cell's a tad small, no doubt, but it has all the amenities," the sheriff noted.

"That ain't funny," Cherry protested.

"All right, I'll let you out. But I'm takin' you to jail."

"What for?" The words filtered out through the half-moon opening carved in the wooden door.

"Attemptin' to murder the bartender at the Eureka Saloon."

"I jist sliced his arm. I didn't try to kill him."

"That's for the judge to decide."

"When do I get to see the judge?"

"Maybe tonight, maybe tomorrow. We got eight union organiz-ers that got in a fight over at the Tever Mine Extension. He's got to rule on each one of them separately. I got 'em packed four to a cell, but we'll squeeze you in."

"You cain't do that!" he screamed.

"Why not?"

"'Cause I got in a fight with a union man last night."

"Did you slice him too?"

"A little. They'll kick my head in if you put me in there," Cherry complained.

The sheriff stepped up closer to the door. "You ain't got many friends in this town, Cherry. Did you ever think about leavin'?"

"I been givin' it some thought."

The sheriff turned to O. T. "Skinner, I'll give you three dollars if you keep him locked up overnight."

"I don't need you to pay me," O. T. protested.

"If I don't pay you, you can't do it. I have records to keep, and I get three dollars a day to house and feed prisoners. That money has to go somewhere."

O. T. shrugged. "Whatever's fair."

"You're in luck, Cherry," the sheriff hollered. "The Wall-Walker said he'd board you and let you stay in his privy."

"You cain't do that," Cherry pleaded.

The sheriff turned to O. T. "Surprisin' how bein' locked in a privy sobers a man. Well, Cherry, take your choice—the crowded jail cell or—"

"Okay, I'll stay. But it's hot and smelly in here!"

"And I reckon we'll need to use it pretty soon," O. T. added, as he surveyed the lot. "Can I jist chain him to that motorcar for a while?"

The sheriff pulled out a white linen bandanna and wiped his forehead. "Yep, that will work."

"Can I shoot him if he tries to escape?" Mrs. Marsh called out from her lot.

"Sheriff, that woman's crazy!" Cherry screamed from the outhouse.

"Ma'am, if he breaks out of his chains, you may shoot him on sight," the sheriff shouted.

"Don't tell her that. She'll do it! Ever'body in this town is against me!" Cherry hollered.

"You've made your tollhouse money. Maybe it's time for you to leave town," the sheriff suggested. "But you aren't goin' to do it until the judge sets your fine. Now I'll go get the Wall-Walker some leg irons and wrist irons out of my car."

O. T. walked with the sheriff back to the street. "I've got me some errands to run. Maybe I'll have Fergus watch him."

"Don't matter to me," the sheriff reported. "I don't care if he escapes. Just so he leaves town. I don't want him pesterin' people anymore."

By the time O. T. and Tommy-Blue left for the livery and the assay office with the half-filled broken-handled bucket on the wagon seat between them, Mr. Cherry was wearing leg chains fastened to the back bumper of the motorcar. He sat in the dirt, but Tommy-Blue's diggings tarp provided him some shade. He held a tin plate in his lap and devoured the large lunch that Dola provided.

The boarding price was two dollars a night for two mules, cash in advance. That gave Ada and Ida shade, water, and hay. They left the farm wagon at the livery and started walking downtown.

O. T. placed the wooden bucket on his shoulder as they hiked

along the sidewalk. The sun was past halfway in the sky. Heat radiated out of the ground like a thick river of air to be waded through.

Half a dozen men lounged on new wooden benches in the shade
under the wooden awning of the Central Nevada Assay Office.
O. T. nodded to them as he and Tommy-Blue approached the door.

"Hey, ain't you that Wall-Walker?" one of them asked.

"That was yesterday," O. T. smiled. "I retired."

"You got water in that bucket?" another called out.

"Nope. I've got dirt."

"Well, shoot," an older, gray-haired man with drooping mustache joshed, "there ain't as much demand for dirt as there is for
water."

"You reckon I should have stuck with my former profession?"
O. T. said.

The men began to whoop it up.

"Let us buy you a drink," one shouted.

"I heard he don't drink. It's against his Christian principles,"
another noted.

"Well, there ain't nothin' unchristian about sody water, is there?
We'll buy you and the boy a root beer," the old-timer offered.

"I appreciate the invite, boys," O. T. responded, "but I'm afraid
the kids at home would pitch a fit to be left out. Might be better off
if me and the lad took a pass on that."

O. T. and Tommy-Blue walked into the assay office. Two men
were busy at a lab table in the back.

Tommy-Blue peeked out from under his floppy-brimmed hat. "I
like root beer, Daddy."

"I know, son, but we got to be fair with them at home. We treat
ever'one the same. You know that."

The nine-year-old spied a glass case along the side wall. "Look
at those nuggets, Daddy! Can I go look at that case?"

"I reckon. Jist as long as you don't touch nothin'."

"Look at that one. It's as big as my fist," Tommy-Blue called out.

"And that one . . . Look at this one! It's in the middle of a quartz crystal."

"Mr. Skinner, I believe?" a man said.

O. T. looked up to see the gray-haired Daniel Tolavitch. "You remembered me?"

"You helped me with my water barrel and liberated Goldfield from the oppressive water tolls. You're the talk of the town this week. Of course, next week it could be a prospector, speculator, bartender, or soiled dove. But this is your week. What can I do for you?"

"We need you to assay this sample." O. T. lowered the bucket to the table.

"Didn't know you were scratching for gold like everyone else."

"I'm not. It's Tommy-Blue that's the prospector."

The boy's nose was pressed against the glass case. "Look, Daddy, look at this one. Oh, man, it must be the shiniest, prettiest nugget in the entire world!"

O. T. leaned over the table and spoke softly. "Mr. Tolavitch, I need a favor. The boy's set on gettin' an assay. Now I don't want to take your time, and frankly I can't afford your services. But I was wonderin' if I paid you a dollar, could you write an official-lookin' report? You know, one of them describin' the contents of the sample and such. There ain't no gold in this sample. It came from right over in one of them city lots on the east side of town. But it would mean a whole lot to Tommy-Blue to have an official assay to tuck in his scrapbook."

"Be happy to do it, Mr. Skinner."

"Like I said, all I got is a dollar." O. T. pulled out the only coin he had in his pocket.

Mr. Tolavitch waved him off. "That's not necessary. I'd be happy to . . ."

O. T. shoved the coin into the man's hand. "You probably don't need my dollar, but I need to give. The boy needs to learn that a man has to pay his way in this world."

Tolavitch tightened his black tie. "All right, I accept the payment."

"Thank you."

"Now . . ." Mr. Tolavitch shoved the coin back into O. T.'s hand.

"Why did you do that?" O. T. asked.

"Mr. Skinner, I know you probably don't need my dollar, but I need to give it. I need to remind myself that a businessman must pay for the services rendered. That's for your assistance with the water."

"But—"

"Yes, sir, Mr. Skinner," the man said loudly. "I'll have this assay done by late afternoon."

Tommy-Blue pulled his face away from the glass. "You will? Today?"

"Your daddy and I are friends. I'll rush it right through," the chemist told him.

"Say," Tommy-Blue whispered, "this assay is secret, ain't it?"

"I won't tell a soul about the results," Tolavitch promised.

"Thank you very much." Tommy-Blue turned back to the case. "Tell me, mister, how much is that shiny nugget on the top shelf worth?"

"The one that's as big as a sweet potato?"

"Yes, sir. It has all them shiny facets. It's beautiful."

Mr. Tolavitch went over and opened the case and pulled out the rock. He handed it to Tommy-Blue.

"Wow, Daddy, it's really heavy! I bet it's worth a fortune. I bet it's worth a—a hundred dollars!"

"Young Mr. Skinner," Tolavitch lectured, "I'm going to give you an important lesson in prospecting."

Tommy-Blue's eyes grew wide. "Are you goin' to tell me how I can find one of these?" he gasped.

"Even better. I'm going to give you that one."

Tommy-Blue's eyes grew wide, and he held his breath. He

glanced at his father with a don't-pinch-me-or-I-might-wake-up expression on his face. "Really?" he choked.

"Yes," Mr. Tolavitch declared. "Because it isn't worth one penny."

Tommy-Blue stared at the nugget. "What?"

"It's iron pyrite, son," Tolavitch explained. "Fool's gold. It looks nice on the outside, but it isn't worth more than a granite pebble. Now you take that worthless thing out of my office and keep it with your prospectin' gear. From time to time pull it out and look at it and say, 'This is phony. I want the real thing.'"

Tommy-Blue danced from one foot to the other. "You really goin' to let me keep it?"

"It's yours."

O. T. reached out and shook the man's hand. "Thanks, Mr. Tolavitch. It means a lot to the boy."

"I get ten of those in here in a week. They get tossed into the cesspool leach line out back. That's all they're good for. Let him enjoy it."

Father and son strolled out on the sidewalk in front of the assay office. They stopped near the now-empty benches.

"Is it really worthless, Daddy?"

"I reckon so. Mr. Tolavitch knows his business."

Tommy-Blue studied the nugget. "Well, I like it anyway."

"I believe you're right. It *is* very nice-lookin'."

"Look, Daddy, there's a crate that says 'Wall-Walker.' One of those men must have left you something. I wonder where they all went?"

O. T. looked up and down the fairly busy sidewalk, but he couldn't spot any of the men. He peeked inside the crate.

"What's in there, Daddy?"

"It looks like a whole case of root beer."

"Really?" Tommy-Blue bent low and peeked into the wooden case.

O. T. stood up and looked around. "Count them up for me, son."

"There's twenty-four of 'em! Daddy, I've never seen so many root beers in my life. Can we keep 'em? Can we?"

"Well, there ain't no one to give them back to. So I reckon I'll tote them home. You carry the bucket."

"And my nugget. I bet this is about the most beautiful worthless nugget in the whole world! Can we have the root beers as soon as we get home?"

"No, I think we'll wait until after supper this evenin'. We'll just sit back peaceful-like and watch the sun go down while drinkin' our root beers." The case felt heavy on O. T.'s raw shoulder. "Don't that sound nobby?"

The first thing O. T. did after lunch was give Dola a kiss on the cheek. The second thing he did was go into the tent and fall asleep.

Two men from Millard's Canvas & Awning stopped by just after Dola had washed the lunch dishes. They brought a used thirty-by-fifteen-foot brown canvas awning with Mojave Desert dirt permanently embedded in it. They set it up on two fourteen-foot center poles at each end of the table. They used ten five-foot poles, sisal rope, and twenty-five tent pegs to secure it.

Tommy-Blue and the Rokker children were inspired to move the old awning that had provided shade over his diggings. It now was stretched over the motorcar to cool it off enough to be played in even during the heat of the day.

There was no breeze, and the heat was still stifling, but now Dola and Rita Ann could sit in the shade and slice carrots for supper.

The pan of carrots was nearly full when a big, clean-shaven man in a three-piece suit marched up the road carrying a loaded wire crate on his shoulder. He looked slightly familiar. When he turned into their lot and hiked toward them, Dola knew she had met him somewhere. It was his eyes that made her stare.

Then Caitlynn shouted, "Daddy! Daddy!" She ran to his side.

She didn't lift her arms, but he scooped her up anyway. The silk pillowcase dress now had a hearty frosting of desert dust. The other Rokker children piled out of the motorcar and ran to his side.

"Mr. Rokker, you look very nice in that suit!" Dola called out.

"I ain't had on one of these in ten years," he admitted. "But it surely beats wearin' a blanket."

Stella scooted up to his side and rubbed the sleeve of his coat. "You shaved, Daddy."

"Got me a haircut too."

"How's Mama?" Jared asked.

"She's sleepin' most of the time. Doc says tonight will be the test."

"What's in the basket, Daddy?" Danny probed.

Mr. Rokker set it down on the table. "It's groceries."

"Really?" Stella licked her thin, chapped lips. "For us?"

"Yes and no. Let me explain." He stepped up to the table and dropped his chin. "Mrs. Skinner, I cain't believe I have to ask you another favor. You've been doin' nothin' but helpin' us since the hour you came to town. But I want to spend this evening and night with my Nellie at the hospital."

She didn't wait for him to pause but blurted out, "Can I watch the children for you, Mr. Rokker?"

He looked up with a wide grin full of crooked teeth. "Yes, ma'am, I was hopin' and prayin' you'd say that."

"Why can't we go sit with you and Mama?" Stella asked.

"I'm . . . I just couldn't . . . If somethin' happened and she . . . You cain't because . . . because . . ." he stammered. His panicked green eyes pleaded with Dola.

"Because your mama needs lots of rest to get well, and she loves all of you so much she wouldn't want to sleep if you were there. She'd just want to stay awake and visit. And that wouldn't be good, would it?" Dola asserted.

Elias Rokker took a deep breath and nodded his head. "Mrs.

Skinner's right. Now these groceries are for Mrs. Skinner, 'cause she has to do all the cookin'.'"

"Oh no, Mr. Rokker, I wouldn't dream of—"

"Mrs. Skinner, them is honest groceries."

"Oh, I didn't mean to imply—," Dola began.

"Giving you those groceries makes me feel like a husband and father," he explained. "I ain't felt that way in a long time. Don't take that away from me."

"No, Mr. Rokker, I surely won't. Thank you for the supplies."

"You're welcome."

"Did you get a job, Daddy?" Jared asked.

"Well, after the Skinner girls brought me these clothes, Dr. Silvermeyer said I could use the hospital tub to clean up. He even gave me two bits for a shave and a haircut. After I was cleaned up, I was walkin' by Peterson's Feed Mill, and a man was strugglin' to unload 140-pound sacks of oats. He offered me five dollars to help. It was one of those tandem rigs pulled by seventeen mules and three horses. So I pulled off my coat and vest and went to work."

"That's wonderful," Dola replied.

"Said he'd like me to do all his loadin' and unloadin' on a permanent basis, provided I stay sober."

"He knows about your drinking?" she probed.

"I reckon everyone in town does. They're talkin' about only two people downtown—the brave Wall-Walker and the fat, stupid drunk wearin' long johns."

"Oh, I'm sure you're exaggerating," she insisted.

"No, ma'am, and it don't bother me. They're right. And I don't honestly know if I can be any other way. But I've got one more chance. If it don't work this time, I'm goin' to lose . . ." He looked at the girl in his arm and couldn't complete the sentence.

"Are you cryin', Daddy?" Caitlynn asked.

"I bet he got some dirt in his eye," Dola explained. "Did that ever happen to you, darlin'?"

Caitlynn nodded her head and clutched her daddy's arm.

"You Skinners are pure gold," he mumbled. "I reckon I'll go up there and thank Mrs. Marsh for the clothing."

"I'll go with you," Corrie volunteered. "Me and Mrs. Marsh are very good friends, you know."

"Mr. Rokker," Dola added, "you will stay for supper before you go back to the hospital, won't you?"

"Yes, ma'am."

"Corrie, would you invite Mrs. Marsh to come to supper tonight also? There's no reason for her to eat up there alone."

Rokker took two steps and then turned back. "Who's the man chained to the motorcar, and why is that Indian sitting cross-legged with a Trapdoor guarding him?"

"It was a very exciting adventure," Jared explained. "Rita Ann can tell you all about it."

Like a burly pied piper, Elias Rokker carried Caitlynn and led six children to the back of the lot. Only Punky opted to stay under the awning with his mother.

Dola plucked him up and sat him on the table. "Well, little darlin', how would you like to cut carrots with me?"

He pointed to the bowl. "Punky eat carrots!"

"You want to eat one?"

He nodded his head.

"You promise you won't take one bite and throw it into the dirt?"

The small sandy-blond head nodded up and down.

Dola took a slice about two inches long, dipped the end of it in a bowl of molasses, and handed it to him. He took one bite and then spat it out on his shirt. He cocked his arm back with the rest of the carrot in his hand.

"No, you don't, young man! You eat that carrot!" Dola scolded.

Punky bowed his head, retrieved the bite off his shirt, and crammed it into his mouth.

"That's better," his mother encouraged.

228 ◆ Stephen Bly

He looked up with a sheepish smile and continued to chomp the raw carrot and lick the molasses off his lips.

She had just uncrated the new groceries when the parade returned across the lot. Mr. Rokker toted a huge green steamer trunk.

Corrie ran up to the table first. "Mama! Mama, Mrs. Marsh gave us a whole trunk full of clothes."

"What do you mean?"

"Well, when we came up and said we wanted her to come eat with us so she wouldn't have to be alone, she started to bawl and then gave us this trunk."

"What's inside?"

"She saved all her daughter's clothes since the day she was born."

"Mrs. Marsh has a daughter?"

"That's the sad part. Her daughter was killed up in Alaska when the ice jam on the Yukon River broke loose," Corrie reported.

"Oh, my."

Rita Ann scooted up next to Dola. "Mrs. Marsh said we could keep any of them or alter them if we wanted to. She's been hanging onto them waiting for someone to give them to. She decided now is the time."

"Can we open it up and look at them?" Stella asked.

"I need to continue to fix supper for all of us," Dola explained. "So why don't you open the trunk out here and sort through things out on the table where we all can see them. I'm sure some just won't be alterable. But perhaps each of the girls can find one item to wear. Wouldn't it be nice for everyone to have another outfit?"

Caitlynn turned loose of her father's leg and crept over toward Dola. "Mrs. Skinner, do I have to give my pretty purple dress back?"

Dola reached down and hugged the little girl. "No, darlin', you get to keep that dress forever."

The tiny, round brown eyes were still sunken above the thin cheekbones, but for a moment Dola saw them flash.

"I'm never, ever goin' to take it off," she pledged.

Dola looked away and rubbed her nose on the back of her hand. When she turned back, Mr. Rokker had retired to his tent.

Danny, Jared, and Tommy-Blue climbed into the car and pretended to drive to Dinuba.

Punky seemed content to sit on the table and maul his carrot as long as it occasionally got dipped into molasses.

Rita Ann, Corrie, Stella, and Caitlynn pulled all of the clothes out of the trunk and piled them on the end of the long table. Then they propped the steamer trunk behind the crates next to the tent and made a dressing room out of it. For the next hour they giggled, sang, and tried on every piece of clothing that halfway fit.

Dola could tell the styles were ten to twenty years old. She could smell the cedar chips that had been used to discourage the moths. She knew that many of the dresses were sewn for Alaska, not the Nevada desert, and could never be worn in a hot climate. Still she marveled at how much fun four barefoot girls were having.

She had the fire going in the stove, which now had shade because of the huge awning. The carrots were just starting to cook. The white beans had finished soaking, and the cornbread batter waited in a covered container. The aroma of baked ham would have filled the room . . . if they had had a room.

"Look at this one, Mama," Rita Ann called out. "It must have been one of her last dresses. It's way too big for me."

The bright yellow dress dragged the ground, the sleeves were down to her fingertips, and the collar was scooped enough to slip off her shoulder.

"Can I keep this one until I fill it out? It's so pretty. I will fill it out, won't I, Mama? Corrie said I'd always be skinny like you, but I think I'll fill it out someday," Rita Ann rambled on.

Dola glanced down at her faded brown dress hanging straight like a sack. *Skinny like me? Plain and skinny. Children are so honest.* "Oh, darlin', I pray you'll continue to turn out as beautiful on the outside as you already are on the inside. But I don't think you should save that dress. It will be too far out of style."

"Then why don't you wear it, Mama?" Rita Ann suggested.

"Oh, yes, Mama," Corrie called. "You wear it."

"I don't need another dress. I already have two, remember?"

"But you're saving your good one to wear to church after we get to Dinuba. You haven't worn it in a long time," Rita Ann replied.

"Well, I'm not growing out of my old things like you girls are. But fold it and leave it here. I know a woman in the hospital who might like to wear something new when she comes home."

"Oh, yes!" Stella laughed. It was the very first time Dola had ever heard the girl laugh. "Look, Mrs. Skinner," she continued. "There's a red one just like it—only a little bigger!" She held up a bright red dress with yellow embroidered flowers.

"That is the reddest dress I've ever seen!" Dola exclaimed.

"It's for you, Mama!" Corrie squealed. "Try it on, please."

"Oh, my, no. . . . I would die of embarrassment if I wore something that color. It's beautiful, but I couldn't . . . It takes a very special lady to wear that."

"You're very special, Mama," Corrie insisted.

"I meant special-looking. I'm skinny and plain, remember?"

A molasses-lipped Punky looked at her. "My mama's purdy!"

"Oh, you are one smooth-talkin' two-year-old, but I am not going to wear that bright red dress."

Rita Ann folded the dress neatly. "I'll put it right here on the table, Mama."

Each of the four girls selected one dress or outfit from the trunk. Stella's green dress with lace was much too formal for living in a tent on the desert, but she insisted on wearing it, even if it dragged in the dirt.

Rita Ann's selection was a smart, fairly straight steel-gray skirt with the remnants of a bustle in the back. And she chose a lacy white blouse with a large black bow at the neck. Dola knew it would take considerable alteration to make it look neat and proper on Rita Ann. She also knew Rita Ann would never wear it any other way.

Corrie's selection was a simple blue gingham dress with a full skirt. She would need to hem up the skirt at least a foot. "I wanted a dress that wouldn't slow me down when I'm running," Corrie explained.

The tiny dress that Caitlynn selected was hand-knit of loose-woven wool yarn, bleached white, with horizontal multicolored silk ribbons woven into the material.

"Isn't it pretty?" Caitlynn asked.

"Darlin', that is without a doubt the fanciest dress I've ever seen in my life. But you don't want to wear it out here too much. It will get so dirty. You can save it for Sunday school and church."

Stella hung her head. "We don't go to church. Daddy says all they want is our money."

"Well, we don't have any money, so that can't be what they want from us," Dola told her. "I think most churches just want to tell us about the Lord. Money isn't all that important."

"We always find a church to go to," Rita Ann explained. "That is, if we aren't camped out in the wilderness. God deserves to be worshiped no matter where we are."

"And we always sit in the back row," Corrie declared.

Dola studied her daughters' faces. *Lord, I look forward to going to church and not feeling embarrassed about the way we look. We'll march up to the front and sit down, and people will say, "My, what an attractive, well-dressed family."*

She sighed deeply.

*Lord, forgive me for my pride. After all You've done for me. I am truly ashamed.*

"Maybe you can go to church with us on Sunday," Rita Ann suggested. "Then we will have a place to wear our new dresses."

"After you put the rest of the things back into the trunk, I want each one of you to borrow some of Rita Ann's paper and write Mrs. Marsh a thank-you note."

Caitlynn hung her tiny head. "I can't write."

"That's all right, darlin'. I meant the older ones. Stella can—"

"I don't know how to write neither," the ten-year-old admitted.

"Daddy knows how to write and read," Caitlynn added.

"Well, that's okay," Dola consoled. "Rita Ann can write it for all of you."

"Could you teach me how to write?" Stella asked.

"Well . . . eh, yes, I will if the Lord decides He wants us to stay here awhile. But you can learn that in school this fall."

"Daddy says we move too much to make school worthwhile."

"Perhaps things will be different this year," Dola encouraged her.

"How will we know if the Lord wants us to stay here, Mama?" Corrie asked.

"That's a very good question I don't have the answer for. But I believe He'll show us if that is His plan."

Stella hiked out to the motorcar with Caitlynn hanging on her arm. They made the boys all crowd into the front and pretend to be chauffeurs.

Corrie and Rita Ann set the table for fifteen.

"We don't have enough crates and chairs," Rita Ann announced.

"Some will have to stand."

"The boys want to eat in the motorcar."

"Who ever heard of people eating in a motorcar?" Dola scoffed.

Rita Ann studied the place settings. "How about Fergus and Mr. Cherry?"

"Oh, I forgot all about them. Corrie, go give Mr. Fergus a break for a few minutes. Perhaps he's hungry again."

"Do I get to hold his Trapdoor rifle?"

"You most certainly do not!"

A few minutes later the old Paiute laid his gun on the table and sat down on a crate next to the stove. "Do you make good coffee?" he asked.

"Why don't you try some and see?" Dola smiled.

He leaped up and grabbed a tin cup. "If you insist."

"I do."

"Thank you very much."

"You're welcome."

"Look, Mama, here come Mr. LaPorte and some lady," Rita Ann called out. A couple in a hack with the top down rode up the street.

"It must be his wife," Dola said.

"I think I will return to my post." Fergus wandered off with his coffee.

"She looks very pretty," Corrie observed as she returned to the table.

Mrs. LaPorte wore a calling dress of a striking shade of purple velvet, trimmed with an exquisite "fancy" of marabou. From her black lace hat two long black ostrich feathers curled down directly behind her left ear.

Dola studied the woman as she approached. *Mrs. LaPorte is my exact opposite. She's dark; I'm pale. She has a strong, dramatic face; mine is nondescript. Her hair is black, with natural curls; mine is a washed-out gray-brown, straight as a string. Her figure is ample; mine is as curvaceous as a fence post. Her clothes reflect glamour; mine reflect bacon grease. Lord, I'm not complaining about how I look. It's just . . . sometimes comparisons are a little too graphic.*

Corrie met the couple as they hiked across the dirt lot to the awning-covered table.

"Mrs. Skinner, this is my wife, Omega. Omega, honey . . . Mrs. Skinner."

Dola held out her hand. "I'm glad you stopped by! Call me Dola. I hear we have some boots in common."

Mrs. LaPorte sat on a crate in the shade and pulled off her long black gloves and began to fan herself. "Honey, ain't these about the most comfortable boots you ever wore?"

"They certainly are."

"Rich folks can afford to be comfortable. Did you ever think about that? It's us poor folks that have to make do with whatever."

"Now, Omega darlin', don't you start that poor-folk talk. We got all we need," her husband chided.

"There's something we don't have," she answered. Then she turned to Dola. "We been married eight years without any children, and, Lord knows, we've tried."

Dola blushed.

"Looks like you been addin' to the place." Lucian pointed at the motorcar.

"It doesn't run, but the Wilkins brothers gave it to O. T. It's something for the kids to play on."

Lucian leaned forward. "Frankly, Mrs. Skinner, your husband should watch himself with the likes of such men. They got a reputation."

"They've always treated us fairly. And I don't believe they're wanted by the law," she argued.

"Maybe not. But if you keep stickin' your hand in a rattlesnake hole, sooner or later you'll get bit."

"And if you keep pushin' your nose in someone else's business, they won't invite you back to visit," Omega retorted.

"You're right there, darlin'." Lucian pulled a toothpick out from behind his ear and began to chew on it.

"Of course I am. I'm always right."

Lucian grinned but didn't respond.

"What's your baby's name?" Omega asked.

"His birth name is Silas Paul, but everyone just calls him Punky."

"I like that. Come here, li'l darlin', I need the practice," Mrs. LaPorte coaxed.

Punky immediately crawled across the table to the woman's outstretched arms. He sat in her lap and studied her face. Finally he reached up a fat finger and touched her lips.

"Red!" he declared.

"That's right, honey. I wear red lipstick. If I had pretty lips like your mama, I wouldn't wear lipstick either."

Dola smiled. *You are a very gracious woman. Flattering but gracious.*

Punky reached around and touched the dangling earrings. "Red!" he again announced.

"Yes, someday I'm going to get me a red dress and—"

"Oh . . . my!" Dola blurted out. "Rita Ann, hand me that dress."

Dola took the dress and handed it to Mrs. LaPorte. "I want you to have this."

"You what?" Mrs. LaPorte's eyes widened as she set Punky on the table. She unfolded the dress.

"It's for you," Dola announced. "I got it free, and it—it's not my style. You have to accept it. Doesn't she, Mr. LaPorte?"

"Well, I reckon if you took the boots, she's got to take the dress," he concurred.

Omega stood up and held the dress up to herself. "It's beautiful! Oh, my, oh, my, oh, my. It needs to be . . . let out in a place or two, but I love it." She held it up to her neck and paraded in front of her husband, batting her long, black eyelashes. "Lucian, honey, what do you think?"

"I think I ain't goin' to let you wear it out of the house—that's what I think," he gruffed.

Mrs. LaPorte sat down and folded the dress in her lap. "Oh, my, you made my day, Dola. I can't thank you enough."

"Perhaps you two would like to stay for supper. Mrs. Marsh who lives back there gave us a trunk of clothes that belonged to her daughter. That was one of them. She's coming, so you could thank her directly."

"Looks like you already have a gang eatin' here. Why, I know some cafes that don't serve a supper this big," Lucian roared.

"With this kind of setup, you ought to open a cafe," Omega suggested. "If you needed some help, I'd come work for you." She turned and glared at Mr. LaPorte. "I certainly don't have anything else to do during the day."

"Is that Mr. Cherry chained to the back of that motorcar?" Mr. LaPorte questioned.

"Yes, it is."

"And the Indian?"

"His name is Fergus. He's a friend of Orion's."

"Where is your husband, Mrs. Skinner?" LaPorte asked.

"He's catching up on sleep. I'll go wake him."

"Let him rest," Lucian insisted. "I just about worked him into the ground yesterday. He deserves it."

"Looks like you have some more customers!" Omega pointed toward a buckboard that rumbled down the road from the east and pulled over to their lot.

LaPorte jumped to his feet. "Is that Charlie Fred?" he gasped.

Dola wiped her hands on her apron. "Yes. Do you know him?"

"Know him? He's my cousin. I didn't know he was in Goldfield!" LaPorte stood up as the dusty, dirty men approached. "Are you still alive, Charlie Fred?" he boomed.

"Lucian! Omega! Well, I'll be! Did Aunt Belinda send you to find me?"

"Find you? If I'd known you were in Goldfield, I would have moved to Alaska!" LaPorte boomed.

The two black men threw their arms around each other.

"You jist perked up an otherwise disastrous day," Charlie Fred reported. "You got coffee there, Mrs. Skinner?" he asked.

"Rita Ann," she called out, "would you pour coffee for any who want it, please?"

"'I can nothing say, but that I am your most obedient servant.'"

"Thank you, noble Helena." Dola plucked Punky off the table

and set him down on his bare feet. "You run out there and play with Tommy-Blue, darlin'. And don't put dirt in your hair."

The men scooted crates up into the shade next to the table and began to sip their coffee.

"Nice awning," Lucky Jack declared.

"Oh, it's wonderful!" Dola agreed.

"It's a good thing we ordered it this mornin'," Wasco noted. "It was about the last thing that went right."

"Oh, dear." Dola waited for them to continue.

But they glanced up at Mrs. Marsh as she hiked down from her tent toting her carbine. "I saw the crowd and figured it was gettin' time for supper," she announced.

"The men got here early today, so it will still be awhile," Dola reported, "but you're welcome to join in the conversation."

The older woman brushed off the top of a crate and sat down, the shotgun flopped across the lap of her gray dress.

"Mr. and Mrs. LaPorte, this is Mrs. Marsh. I believe you men all met Mrs. Marsh yesterday."

"You been stalkin' any more privies?" she grinned.

Lucky Jack roared. "I'm glad you don't hold that against us."

"You make one move in my direction, and I'll blast you," she declared. The grin was gone.

"How did you men get so dirty this afternoon?" Dola asked.

Lucky Jack shook his head. "That's what we were about to explain. It doesn't look good for The Rita Ann Lease. We set off our charges, and the whole mine tunnel collapsed. One shaft after another went down like dominos. We were outside, and we tried diggin' back in to get our gear, but couldn't make it."

"What are you goin' to do?" Dola asked.

"Retire, I reckon. We cain't afford the big diggin' equipment, and by the time we hand-dig that tunnel back out, our lease will expire," Lucky Jack said.

"You're going to abandon The Rita Ann Lease?" Rita Ann grimaced.

"You'll always be close to my heart, darlin'," he teased.

"I can't believe you could just walk away," Rita Ann pouted.

"It's not like they left you buried in a mine shaft," Corrie interjected.

Wasco plopped down his coffee cup. "Yeah, this faro dealer from up at the Tonopah Club is in town. A guy named George Wingfield, and he's offered us $5,000 for the lease. He's got the machinery and the crews to dig it back out in a hurry."

"That seems like a lot of money," Dola replied.

Lucky Jack shook his head. "We borrowed $10,000 from the John S. Cooke Bank in Tonopah. We're in the hole if we sell it for $5,000."

"Perhaps you could sell this lot to help pay them back," Dola offered.

"We might have to if nothin' else works, but we have until January to pay the bank," Lucky Jack replied.

Mrs. Marsh folded her arms and left the shotgun in her lap. "Do you three boys really know anything at all about mining?"

Wasco took another sip from his coffee cup and shook his head. "Just enough to go broke, I reckon."

"Well, I got a deal for you to consider," she announced.

Lucky Jack raised his eyebrows like a gambler searching for an inside straight. "Ma'am?"

"I've been sittin' back there for two years tryin' to sell that mine my husband left me. I ain't had no luck. Now I'll give you boys until January to dig in it, and we split the earnin's four ways."

Wasco pointed to the desert around the table. "There ain't no gold over here, ma'am."

"Not on top the ground. But I'm talkin' about a shaft fifty feet down," she explained.

"Where?" Charlie Fred quizzed.

"Under my tent," she announced. "My husband discovered pay dirt two days before he died, but I cain't get anyone to give me a fair price."

"After that close call today, I think we're about ready to retire from mining," Lucky Jack informed her. "Seein' that tunnel explode was unsettlin'."

LaPorte leaned over to Charlie Fred. "But how are you going to pay back the bank?"

"We talked about leavin' the state and never comin' back," his cousin replied.

Mrs. Marsh pointed back at her tent. "Mr. Marsh had it stepped and laddered clear down to the cross shaft. Why not just come take a gander? I've got a lantern and a box of miner's candles."

Lucky Jack scratched his head, then sipped some coffee. "I reckon it wouldn't hurt."

Mrs. Marsh, gun in hand, led the three men back up to her tent. With the sun hanging low over Malpais Mesa, their shadows cast a hundred feet to the east.

Omega turned to see a young girl in a purple silk dress staring at her. "Well, just who is this?" She opened her arms, and the child immediately ran over and buried her head in Dola's lap.

"This is Caitlynn Rokker, our neighbor's girl," Dola explained. "Her sister Stella is in the green dress, and her brothers Jared and Danny are with our son Tommy-Blue in the motorcar. They're drivin' to Dinuba to look at a vineyard."

"I thought all the children were yours," Omega declared.

Dola shook her head. *If you think I look worn out now . . .*

"Can I help you with supper?" Omega offered. "I'll be insulted if you turn me down!"

"I'm not going to insult you. We've got hungry men here. Let's see what we can do to speed it up," Dola replied.

"I hear Daddy!" Caitlynn called as she ran toward the front tent.

"How is Mrs. Rokker doin' this evenin'?" Lucian asked.

"Fair, I think," Dola called out from the stove. "I need to go visit her—perhaps tonight."

"I'll give you a lift down to the hospital if you need it," LaPorte offered.

"Just what in blazes are those two doin' here?" A sleepy but suit-clad Elias Rokker glared at the LaPortes as he approached the table.

Lucian jumped to his feet. Dola could hear Omega grind her teeth.

"Mr. Rokker, I'm glad you're awake." Dola hurried to stand between him and Lucian. Both men were at least twice her size, and she felt like a weed in a forest of massive oaks.

"I said—," Rokker boomed.

"I believe everyone on the east side of town heard what you said, Mr. Rokker," Dola countered. "Let me introduce them to you. This is Mr. and Mrs. LaPorte. They are friends of ours. Actually Mr. LaPorte's cousin, Charlie Fred, is one of the men who owns this lot and so graciously allows us to camp here for free."

Rokker looked stunned. "He's black?"

"Well, yes, now that you mention it, he is. Fortunately for us, he allows us to stay here anyway. And Mr. LaPorte is the man who generously gave your Nellie and me a free ride to the hospital. Without his quick thinking and timely help, we could have very well lost her."

"He did?"

"I sort of saw you last night when I came by to help out," LaPorte added. "But you were—eh, sleepin'."

Dola noticed Rokker's dark eyes soften.

"I was passed out drunk," he mumbled.

"Mr. LaPorte was just inquiring about your wife's health," Dola noted.

"He was?"

"I trust the surgery went well," Lucian commented. "When I last saw her, she was in agonizing pain."

"Well, eh . . . thanks for askin'. She's still hurtin' a lot, and eh, well, the doc says the poison might still get her." Rokker turned away from the table and wiped his eyes.

"Me and the wife have been prayin' for her," LaPorte declared.

"I appreciate it," Rokker mumbled without looking back.

"Mr. Rokker, supper will be ready in about fifteen minutes," Dola offered.

He kept staring across the lot. "I reckon I'll go take me a look at that motorcar. I ain't ever goin' to have enough money to own one myself, but I'd like to see it close up."

They watched Rokker and Caitlynn hike to the middle of the lot.

"You're a fine mediator, Mrs. Skinner," LaPorte said. "You handled that better than I would have."

"Mr. Rokker is a broken man. He's failed at everything, including as husband and father. I figure this situation with his wife will either give him another chance or destroy him completely."

Omega stepped over to Dola and whispered, "Don't he ever feed his kids?"

"They've been goin' through lean times."

"That ain't lean, honey—it's starvation." Omega returned to the pot of white beans on the stove. "Makes you wonder, don't it? Why does God put children into some families and keep 'em out of another? I don't have no answer for that, do you?"

Dola stared at Rita Ann and Corrie setting the table. "No," she murmured. "I have no answer either."

"Now ain't this something!" Lucian called out. "I do believe the Wilkins brothers are ridin' this way. This is kind of like sittin' on the rail at the O.K. Corral or being at the courthouse during the Lincoln County War. Take a good look, Omega—we might be seeing history unfold before our eyes."

"Corrie!" Dola called out. "Go wake up your daddy—now!"

# TEN

O. T. knew Corrie had told him several things when she ran into the tent, but the only thing he could remember was that he had some friends outside. Although buttoned, his silk white shirt draped over his denim britches as he jammed on his hat, ignored his boots, and wandered out of the tent barefoot. The yard bustled with kids, a prisoner, an Indian, neighbors, and a well-dressed black couple.

"Lucian! Glad you could stop by. You must be Mrs. LaPorte. How long have you been here?" he probed.

"A little while, but we aren't the reason you got woke from your nap." Lucian pointed to the three men in a buckboard wagon stopping behind LaPorte's hack.

"The Wilkins brothers?" O. T. rocked back on his heels as he felt the powdery dirt warm his toes. "I'm surprised they found a wagon and a team for sale so quickly."

"Nobody said they bought 'em," Lucian mumbled.

O. T. strolled around the tent to greet the men. "Boys, you look better shod than earlier in the day."

"You don't, Skinner," Trey said.

"You caught me nappin'. It's a wonder you all aren't sleepin' yourselves." O. T. wiggled his toes in the fine desert dirt.

"We slept in that good-for-nothing motorcar, remember?" Ace said.

O. T. scanned Deuce Wilkins. "You get that arm patched up?"

"It's set and splinted. I reckon I'll have to wait to use it much. Probably a good thing I can shoot with either hand."

O. T. turned and ushered them toward the awning-covered table and cookstove. "You know my wife. These are our friends, Mr. and Mrs. LaPorte. You boys will stay for supper, won't you?"

"No!" Dola blurted out.

O. T. stared at his wife. "I cain't believe you said that. You ain't never turned no one down before."

Dola wrung her hands together as if drying them off. "Look around the yard, Orion. It's filled with children and neighbors. And any minute now Lucky Jack, Wasco, and Charlie Fred will come hiking down from Mrs. Marsh's."

Trey Wilkins's hand went for his holstered revolver.

"Are they up there visitin'?" O. T. questioned. "I didn't know they knew her."

"We can't have the Gately-Wilkins feud bust out at our supper table. There are children . . . and, eh, women and . . . well, it's just not right." Dola took a deep breath. She could feel her lip begin to quiver. She turned to her husband with pleading eyes. "I'm scared, Orion. I'm tired and I'm hot and I'm sweaty and I'm scared. A drunk like Jug Cherry is enough for one day, but now we have six professional gunmen and a ten-year-old feud. I don't know if there really is a time and a place for everything, but this is not the time nor the place." She gasped for each breath, trying not to cry.

O. T. put his arm around her shoulder and pulled her close. "She's right, boys. I'm still a little groggy from the nap. You're welcome to our table most any time, but you and Lucky Jack have to settle your fracas some other place. Hope you understand."

Ace left his hand on his revolver and studied Mrs. Marsh's tent on the neighboring lot. "We didn't come by to cause trouble, ma'am. If they stay hidden in that tent, we'll be on our way out of town."

"The Wilkins brothers are leavin' Goldfield already?" LaPorte quizzed.

Mrs. LaPorte silenced him with a well-placed elbow.

"Yep. Things didn't turn out the way we figured," Ace admitted.

While Ace remained next to the table, Deuce strolled over to the stove, placing it between him and the back of the lot.

"What about those good-payin' jobs you got lined up?" O. T. asked.

"Turned out to be a little different than we were told," Ace explained.

Dola stepped back, took a deep breath, and brushed a spray of hair out of her eyes. "Oh?"

Trey meandered back among the crates and laid his pistol on top of one, pointing the barrel toward Mrs. Marsh's tent. "We was told we had jobs guardin' gold shipments," he said.

Ace's brown eyes narrowed as he surveyed the yard. "What they really wanted was for us to guard the mine against any miners who go on strike or try to organize a union."

"You don't like that kind of work?" Dola asked. Her mouth was so dry her tongue almost stuck to the top of it.

Ace stretched his fingers out as he talked, as if preparing for a piano recital. Never once did he take his eyes off the Marsh tent. "No, ma'am, contrary to a lot of rumors, we don't go up against unarmed men. Never have. Never will."

"Guardin' a gold coach means that the only ones we have to fight against is them comin' after us," Trey called out. "Ain't nothin' wrong with that."

"And there ain't nothin' wrong with facin' down some armed bushwhackers like Gately," Deuce added from over next to the stove.

"Mrs. Skinner, it was your husband who convinced us not to take that job," Ace continued.

"I don't remember ever talkin' about it," O. T. said. He leaned against the edge of the table, his back toward the upper end of the lot.

Ace took off his hat and ran callused fingers over his bald head. "We got to thinkin' that most of them miners is just ordinary fellas livin' up and down one of these streets. Some of 'em are family men with a wife and kids like you. Then Trey said, 'What if we look around someday, and one of them strikers is Skinner? We goin' to shoot him down dead and then go tell his wife and kids?' No, sir," Ace concluded. "They can hire someone else. But I ain't goin' to make a livin' threatenin' unarmed, innocent men. At least, not anymore."

"But that ain't why we came by," Trey reported. "Mrs. Skinner, we wanted to get that diggin' sample out of your olive crock and be on our way."

Dola glanced back among the crates trying to remember which one now housed the crock. She felt her forehead tighten. "What kind of sample?"

"Me and Deuce didn't have nothin' to do while we waited for Ace to come back and fetch us," Trey reported. "So we did a little explorin' over in the Weepah Hills. Came across some ground that showed a little promise. We aren't prospectors, but it looked like it would pay. We thought we'd assay it, and then if it proved decent, we'd go out and poke around a little as long as we was down in this desert."

"You don't plan to look for Mojaves wearing your boots, do you?" O. T. probed.

"Nope. But if they wandered into camp, they'd wish they hadn't," Deuce reported.

"We didn't have any sample buckets, so we just filled up your crock," Trey said. "Then we was so embarrassed comin' to town with no boots, we forgot to unload it with our gear. We'll clean it up for you now and be on our way."

"Oh, no!" Dola exclaimed. "I didn't know it was a sample. Rita Ann said it had some dirt in it, and I told her to dump it out."

"You did?" Trey gasped. "Where did she dump it?"

"I have no idea," Dola said.

They all looked out to the middle of the lot.

"Rita Ann!" O. T. called out.

Just then Lucky Jack Gately and his partners emerged from Mrs. Marsh's big tent.

"I think maybe it's time for you to leave," O. T. suggested to Ace.

"Too late for that. We don't back down, Skinner. Never," Ace grumbled. He cocked the hammer on his revolver.

"Not with the children here!" Dola insisted.

"Are you lookin' for us?" Lucky Jack hollered from the top of the lot.

"Maybe it's time to get this over with, Gately," Ace shouted.

"Mother!" Corrie called out.

Dola sprinted to the motorcar where a stunned Elias Rokker seemed frozen in place, staring at the gunmen. She grabbed his arm. "Mr. Rokker, help me get all the children behind the crates."

Fergus sat crossed-legged on the running board of the motorcar facing away from the conflict. His brass-tacked Trapdoor rifle lay across his lap. Jug Cherry dove under the Thomas motorcar, still chained to the back bumper. When Dola got the children back of the crates, she saw Lucian and Omega LaPorte peeking out from behind the cast-iron stove.

"Make your move, Lucky Jack. You ain't got no dynamite in the dark this time," Ace shouted.

Gately had his revolver pointed in the direction of Ace Wilkins. "And you can't shoot us in the back like before, Wilkins. It don't make no difference, but I didn't toss that dynamite. It ain't my style."

"Somebody blew Pete Phillips off to his eternal reward," Ace yelled, as he inched his way out from under the awning.

"And that's why I quit. I didn't run away guilty. I walked away disgusted," Lucky Jack explained.

"You know who did it?" Trey hollered.

"Yep."

"You goin' to tell us?" Ace demanded.

"Nope." Lucky Jack led Wasco and Charlie Fred slowly down the gradual slope of the long lot. "That ain't my style either."

Dola positioned herself in front of the crate and the children. "Where's Punky?" she asked Corrie.

"Tommy-Blue said he was sleepin'."

Dola glanced back at the tent. *He might be the only person who slept though the last great gun battle in the West.*

Ace Wilkins raised his arm and took aim at Lucky Jack. "Well, I didn't shoot Two Nose in the back either. We'll take you on face to face ever'time. You know that."

"Do you know who did shoot Tully in the back?" Wasco yelled out.

"Yep, we do. But we won't tell you. That ain't the way we do things," Trey asserted as he pointed his revolver at Charlie Fred.

"Then it looks like we better settle it up right here and now," Gately said as he cocked the hammer back on his pistol.

"Wait a minute," O. T. shouted out as he strolled out to the empty space between the two gangs. "You been feudin' for ten years over somethin' neither of you did?"

"It's way past that, Skinner. You wouldn't understand," Lucky Jack insisted.

"No, I don't reckon I would." O. T. positioned himself exactly in the line of fire between Lucky Jack and Ace Wilkins. "I'm just a simple man. You aren't talkin' what's fair, what's just, what's legal, what's loyal. You're just talkin' about shootin' each other out of a habit of hatin'. You made a practice of wantin' to kill each other and don't know how to break it."

"Don't get involved, Skinner," Ace insisted. "Lucky Jack is right. You're bein' foolish. You don't know what's goin' on here."

"Well, at least you agree on somethin'—that I'm a fool. But even a fool wouldn't sacrifice his life for nothin'. If you're goin' to get yourself killed, make it over somethin' important," O. T. insisted.

"Get out of the way, Skinner, or you'll get yourself shot," Deuce screamed.

O. T. spun back toward him. "You mean you'd shoot an unarmed man?"

"Move!" Trey Wilkins yelled.

"How about you, Lucky Jack? Wasco? Charlie Fred? Would you shoot an unarmed man?" O. T. challenged.

"Don't press it, Skinner," Wasco called back.

"It's jist a foolish yes-or-no question. I want to know. Will you shoot an unarmed man?" O. T. demanded.

"No, I ain't goin' to . . . None of us are goin' to shoot you," Ace said.

"Then I'm goin' to stay right here."

"That's the dumbest thing I ever heard of!" Lucky Jack yelled.

"If I was smart, I wouldn't be in Goldfield. If I was smart, I wouldn't be draggin' my poor family all over the West. If I was smart, I'd have my wife dressed in satins and livin' in a fine house. If I was smart, I would have never given you three a free ride nor spent the night pullin' the Wilkins brothers out of the desert. No, sir, this might be dumb, but no one ever accused me of being smart." O. T. was barefoot, his shirt untucked, but his shoulders were thrown back and his head held high.

"Orion, you're scarin' me and the kids. Please come over here," Dola pleaded.

"Dola, honey, I don't aim to scare no one, but there's jist some things a man's got to do. These boys understand. They've said they were doin' what they got to do. Well, so am I."

"This is crazy!" Ace Wilkins declared.

O. T. nodded. "Yes, sir, it is."

Suddenly Punky crawled out of the backseat of the car and toddled out to where O. T. stood. "Daddy, Daddy, Daddy!" His hands were held high.

"Punky, no!" Dola yelled. "Come here . . . come here, darlin'!"

She shot a panicked glance back at Corrie. "I thought you said he was in the tent."

"No, I said he was sleepin'."

O. T. took off his hat and brushed back his gray hair. *I got to do the right thing, Lord. You know that. O sweet Jesus, I hope this is the right thing.*

He reached down and picked up the toddler.

"You got to move now, Skinner," Lucky Jack called out. "You wouldn't imperil your own kid."

"How can I endanger him? I'm not the one holding a gun," O. T. said. "It will be your bullets that strike us."

Lucian LaPorte let out a deep sigh from where he and Omega crouched behind the stove. "Well, I'll be," he mumbled. "He's goin' to stay. . . . He don't bluff." LaPorte stood up and hiked out toward O. T.

"Lucian, where are you goin'?" Omega called out.

"To join a friend," LaPorte declared.

"Where do you think you're goin'!" Charlie Fred called out.

"To keep your mama from losin' her baby boy!" LaPorte replied. "I don't want to be the one to tell Aunt Bertie that I stood by while her boy died."

He came alongside O. T. and Punky.

"I can't believe you came out here," O. T. murmured.

"I can't believe it either. Skinner, you're either the bravest man or the dumbest fool I ever met," LaPorte sighed.

Elias Rokker stepped out from behind the crates where he and his children had been cowering. He began to hike out to Skinner.

Caitlynn, barefoot and wearing her purple silk pillowcase, dashed out and grabbed his massive hand and walked with him.

"Get back," Deuce Wilkins hollered. "You don't know what you're doin'."

"I know I ain't never done a brave thing in my life," Rokker puffed. "I reckon it's time."

Fergus tossed his rifle into the front seat of the motorcar and held his head up as he marched over to join the others.

"We'll shoot you, Indian," Wasco screamed.

"It is better to die with friends for a good cause than to die in your sleep out on the desert all alone," he stoically replied.

"Well, I ain't goin' out there," Jug Cherry yelled from his position under the car, his wrist still chained to the bumper. "Ever'one of you is stupider than okra on a Sunday afternoon!"

O. T. shifted Punky to his other arm and glanced over at a nervous, perspiring Lucian LaPorte. "Okra on a Sunday afternoon?" A slight smile broke across his face. "What is that suppose to mean?"

"Don't look at me. I hate the slimy stuff. It must be an insult," Lucian said.

"We're givin' you one last chance, Skinner. You got to all move aside now!" Lucky Jack demanded.

"Can I go stand with Daddy?" Corrie asked.

Dola glanced at both daughters and Tommy-Blue. "Come on, children. We'll all go stand by Daddy."

"Get back!" Ace yelled. "Trey, don't let them get out there."

"I cain't stop them," the youngest of the Wilkins brothers replied.

"This ain't no parlor game!" Ace hollered.

"We don't have a parlor, Mr. Wilkins," Dola replied.

Stella, Jared, and Danny Rokker trailed out to stand alongside their father.

Omega LaPorte picked up the folded red dress and hiked out to her husband.

"Where do you think you're goin'?" Charlie Fred screamed.

"I ain't sure where I'm goin', but I'm goin' to take this red dress with me," she retorted. "Besides I didn't like squattin' over there all by myself."

"You're all crazy. You act like you're from—from the moon!"

Cherry screamed from under the car. "Unfasten me before the bullets start flyin'."

"I'm goin' to pass on joinin' in," Mrs. Marsh shouted down from her position next to the rock privy. "I reckon someone has to survive jist to write it all down. Like Mrs. Dickerson at the Alamo."

The mixture of men, women, and children stood shoulder to shoulder, dividing the lot in half like a human fence.

The Wilkins brothers, guns drawn, stood by the table and crates.

Lucky Jack, Wasco, and Charlie Fred kept their positions halfway between Tommy-Blue's hole and the outhouse.

It grew quiet as everyone stood and stared and waited.

Dola looked at O. T.'s set square jaw as he faced the Wilkins brothers, his back to Lucky Jack and gang. *Lord, he's penniless, barefoot, unshaven, and his shirt is untucked. Yet I'll follow him anywhere, stand beside him anytime, and risk everything at his word.* She could feel the tears stream down her cheeks. She held Corrie's hand and put her arm around Rita Ann's shoulder.

"'Lord, what fools these mortals be,'" Rita Ann murmured. "What do we do now, Mama?"

Dola brushed tears back, sniffed, and wiped her nose on her dress sleeve. Then she glanced back at the stove. *Well, I'm not goin' to ruin supper, no matter what.* "Deuce Wilkins, would you stir those beans, please, or they're goin' to burn."

"What?"

"None of us want to eat burnt beans. You stir them right now!" Dola insisted.

"I cain't. My right arm's busted," Deuce asserted.

Dola folded her arms across her thin chest. "Well, put down your gun and stir them with your left hand."

"I ain't puttin' down my gun. That would give Gately the advantage."

Dola spun around to the top of the lot. "Wasco, put down your gun so it will be fair."

"What?"

"You heard me," she shouted. "Put it down now. You don't want your supper to burn!"

She watched as he and Deuce lowered their revolvers.

"This is the stupidest thing I ever watched in my life!" Cherry shouted from under the motorcar. "It's like one of them bad dreams when you et too much eggplant and mushrooms."

"Don't forget the cornbread," Fergus probed. "I do not like burnt cornbread either."

"Oh, he's right." Dola waved her arm as she spoke. "Trey, you go take the cornbread out of the oven."

"We ain't cooks!" Trey complained.

"But you don't like burnt cornbread. This is that new kind that fluffs up like a caky biscuit. I've got two pans full in the oven, and if you don't pull them out, they'll be about as tasty as a buffalo chip," Dola fussed. "Now hurry."

"I can't lay down my—"

Dola spun back to the other side. "Oh, for heaven's sake. Charlie Fred, lay down that gun too so we won't have to eat burnt cornbread."

When the men laid their guns down, Trey scooted over to the oven. "The door handle's hot!" he yelped.

"Use a tea towel," Dola instructed.

"What about this ham in here?" Trey yelled.

"Is it dry? Does it have any liquid in the pan?" she asked.

"No, ma'am."

"Then you'll have to baste it with a little of that mustard and molasses concoction."

"What?"

"Take that little pan of sauce and brush it on the ham. You do plan on eatin' supper with us, don't you?"

"Not all of us will be hungry," Ace yelled back.

"Well, those who are should have a nice, hearty meal," Dola hollered.

Trey squatted down next to the oven and smeared some sauce on the huge ham roast.

The voice was new . . . loud . . . and it came from the street. "My, this looks like an interesting game."

O. T. looked up. Daniel Tolavitch climbed out of his carriage and hiked toward Ace Wilkins.

"Stay back, mister!" Ace growled, still pointing his revolver toward Lucky Jack.

"Look, I just wanted to deliver—"

"Do you have my assay?" Tommy-Blue yelled out from his position next to his father.

"Yes, I do."

"Well," Tommy-Blue hollered, "did I hit pay dirt?"

Mr. Tolavitch pulled several folded papers out of his suit coat pocket. "Yes, you did, son."

"I knew we had rich diggin's!" Tommy-Blue shouted as he and Danny Rokker began to dance around.

"Where did he find gold at?" Lucky Jack called out.

Tommy-Blue pointed to the big crater behind the motorcar. "In my hole!"

"Actually, son," O. T. cautioned, "Mr. Tolavitch was just pretendin' to do an assay, and he—"

Tolavitch stomped past Ace Wilkins and right up to Tommy-Blue. "No, I went ahead and ran a real assay on your sample. Look at this report."

"Get out of there, mister," Ace growled.

"Wait a minute," Lucky Jack called out. "This is our lot. That means it's our sample."

"It will run $800 to a ton or better," the assayer said.

"Pay dirt!" Tommy-Blue shouted.

Mr. Tolavitch studied the ground. "There might not be too much of it. It all depends on where its origin is."

"The origin is up here on my place!" Mrs. Marsh shouted. "I told you this was a good lead, and nobody listened." She came bounding down from the outhouse. "Gately, didn't I tell you it was rich? You better assay a sample from my place."

Mr. Tolavitch barged over to the table and laid out the papers. "Well, everyone come over here and look at this report!"

Everyone hesitated, staring at each other.

"My word, no game is that important," Tolavitch called back. "Call it a draw. Now come on and look at this! It's about the best assay I've ever seen in Goldfield."

It was O. T. who took charge. "Dola, you go up and gather Lucky Jack's and them's guns. I'll hold onto the Wilkins brothers' guns. Then we can all look at the assay report without anyone gettin' shot. It would be a shame to have anyone die on top of an undeveloped gold mine."

"What about it, Ace?" Lucky Jack called out.

"The whole thing was goin' on a runaway train anyway. This thing ain't over. I'll kill you later, Gately." Ace handed his gun to O. T.

The men and children huddled around Mr. Tolavitch and his assay report.

Dola, Mrs. Marsh, and Omega gathered near the stove.

"This could be quite a nice claim," Tolavitch announced.

"I told you!" Tommy-Blue shouted. "I told you. Do me and Danny get finder's fees?"

O. T. slipped his arm onto his son's shoulder. "This land belongs to Lucky Jack and—"

"Of course you do, son," Lucky Jack promised. "Right, boys?"

"They found it for us," Wasco laughed. "They get paid—that's certain. A man's worth his wages, and that goes for boys too."

"I reckon a 10-percent finder's fee," Charlie Fred announced.

"Ten percent? Wow!" Tommy-Blue exclaimed. Then he turned to his sister. "Rita Ann, what's 10 percent?"

She brushed dust off the sleeves of her dress and pushed her glasses back up on her nose. "Well, if they find a hundred dollars' worth of gold, after expenses are taken out, you and Danny would split ten dollars of it."

"You mean we would both get five whole dollars!" Tommy-Blue gasped.

"Could be you'll get a whole lot more than that," Mr. Tolavitch informed him.

"This is gettin' us nowhere," Ace mumbled. "Skinner, this don't involve us. Jist give us our guns, and we'll pull out."

"But don't you want to stay for supper?" Dola queried.

"I thought you didn't want to feed us."

"Only because Lucky Jack and them are here," she explained. "It's almost dark. Won't you please stay?"

"Before we lose daylight, I need to take a look at this young man's test hole," Mr. Tolavitch added. "I was quite surprised to find that soil type this close to Goldfield."

Tommy-Blue led the troupe, minus the women, to his hole in the ground. "Here it is," he beamed. "It would have been deeper, but we only had one broken shovel between us."

Tolavitch climbed down into the hole. He picked up some of the desert dirt and ran it through his fingers. "This is strange. . . . Very strange. . . . Are you sure your sample came from here?"

Tommy-Blue wiggled his bare toes in the loose dirt. "Yep, it came from right down there at your feet."

"Well, it just can't be." Tolavitch took some of the dirt and placed it on the end of his tongue.

"He eats dirt!" Corrie gasped.

O. T. nodded. "Yep. I reckon little Punky is a natural-born assay man, ain't he?"

"This isn't the right soil," Tolavitch declared.

"What?" Lucky Jack questioned.

"That's what troubled me. Most of that sample had a higher alkali content, like out on the flats or over in the Weepah Hills."

"Weepah? Our sample was from the Weepah district!" Ace exclaimed.

Corrie hung her head. "It's all my fault," she announced. "Mama told Rita Ann to dump the dirt out of the crock, and Rita Ann told me to do it, and I rolled it over here and dumped it out in Tommy-Blue's dumb ol' hole in the ground."

"You mean, that's *our* sample?" Deuce whooped.

Trey snatched up the report from Wasco's hands. "You assayed *our* sample?"

"Can you find it again?" Tolavitch asked.

"All we got to do is backtrack through the . . . wind and sand and alkali and . . . Hey, the old Indian knows," Deuce asserted. "He can lead us there!"

Fergus smiled. "Finder's fee—10 percent."

"We ain't goin' to—," Deuce fumed.

"Sounds fair to me," O. T. interrupted.

All eyes focused on the Wilkins brothers.

"All right," Ace relented, "if he helps us locate it, he gets 10 percent."

"Does this mean we don't get nothin'?" Tommy-Blue complained.

"We still got us a nice hole," Danny consoled him.

"Maybe we'd better get goin' while there's still a trace of daylight," Deuce suggested.

"Why don't you all go runnin' out into the desert and leave me the food," Cherry hollered. "I'm starvin' down here!"

"Mr. Cherry's right," Dola called out. "Everything's ready. We have plates for everyone but not enough chairs. You boys will have to eat in the car anyway."

"Mr. Tolavitch, can you take a real sample from our hole?" Tommy-Blue insisted.

"I'll do that, son," Tolavitch agreed.

"You might as well pull off your coat and eat with us in the meantime," Mrs. Marsh insisted. "You ain't leavin' without a sample from my place too. The ore down there looks good. Ain't that right, Gately?"

"She's right," Lucky Jack concurred. "I don't know if it's $800 a ton, but it looks better than the $10,000 lease we just blew up."

O. T. glanced over at Lucky Jack. "The Wilkins brothers might have a richer sample, but they ain't exactly found the spot yet."

"Quite true," Mr. Tolavitch remarked. "Many a prospector has struck pay dirt and was never able to relocate the claim."

"Say, did any of you ever hear about that lode of Mexican McGuire's down in Madres?" Deuce Wilkins began.

"Hey, I knew Mexican McGuire down in El Paso," Wasco responded. "One night he got to drinkin' and got real melancholy about dyin' young and drew a map right on top of a faro layout for me and the dealer to look at."

"What happened to the map?" Ace Wilkins asked.

"The faro dealer took it, but the next night he and McGuire tried swimmin' their horses across the Rio Grande, and they both drowned. No one has seen that map since."

"Do you remember any of it?" Trey Wilkins asked.

"Ever' bit of it," Wasco declared.

"How come you never told me about that?" Lucky Jack pressed.

Wasco shrugged. "What difference does it make? Mexico's got that there revolution goin' on, and there are so many banditos around the Sierra Madres. I reckon it would take half a dozen reckless armed gunmen to safely go in there and search for it."

Lucky Jack glanced over at Ace. For the first time, the oldest of the Wilkins brothers cracked a smile. "Well, shoot," he said, "if neither of our diggin's prove rich, we'll jist team up and go down there to take a little of Mexican McGuire's gold."

Lucky Jack started to laugh. "At least down there we could kill each other in peace without some crazy Wall-Walker and his wife gettin' in our way!"

"I appreciated you not shootin' anyone," Dola said. "It would have ruined a very good supper. Now everybody hike back to the table and grab a plate. It's time to eat."

For four hours on a hot desert evening, the liveliest place in Goldfield, Nevada, was the lantern-lit old oak table under the dusty canvas awning on lot #124. The entire ham was devoured, most of the beans, and every crumb of cornbread. The only pie that was left was on Punky's bibbed coveralls. Twenty-four six-ounce, amber root beer bottles stood empty on the big table. But there was considerable boiled spinach left over.

Gradually the crowd began to disperse. Omega LaPorte volunteered to assist Dola in all food preparation and cleanup in the future in exchange for meals for her and Lucian. Then they gave Elias Rokker a lift to the hospital to sit through the night with his wife. He rode off hunkered down in the backseat, his hat pulled low over his eyes, ill at ease about accepting hospitality from a gracious black couple.

Rita Ann gathered all the children in the Skinner tent to act out *The Merchant of Venice* as she read the text. After several moments of careful deliberation, she cast herself both as Portia and Shylock.

Mrs. Marsh retired to her tent, happy that at last someone was taking her claim seriously. "I'm going to move my tent down by that motorcar," she had announced. "Then the boys can have free rein to develop the mine. I might even build me a cabin."

After Jug Cherry finished his supper, he was chained so he could sleep in the backseat of the Thomas motorcar. He claimed it was more comfortable than the bridal suite at the Imperial Hotel in Denver. He wouldn't reveal how he came upon such information.

The Wilkins Brothers would not wait for morning. They rumbled off into the desert night toward the Weepah Hills, with Fergus wearing a smile and toting a sack of leftovers. He sat at the back of the buckboard, his legs drooping over the tailgate, brass-tacked Trapdoor across his lap.

Lucky Jack, Wasco, and Charlie Fred didn't leave until they brought up three different samples from the fifty-foot level of the Marsh claim. They went back to their old lease for the evening but planned to move the entire camp over to Mrs. Marsh's lot.

At the suggestion of Elmira Marsh and to the absolute delight of a dark-haired ten-year-old girl with drooping bangs, they decided to call it The Corrie Lou Lease.

Because he waited for all the ore samples, Mr. Tolavitch was the last one to leave. Dola and a lantern-carrying O. T. walked him out to his rig.

"Mr. Tolavitch, you know you're invited to take meals with us anytime," Dola offered.

"Mrs. Skinner, you've got the best restaurant in town. I'd be pleased to dine here. But you're going to have trouble the first big sandstorm that blows through. My partner and I might be able to put you up a little building, if you'd be interested in running a more substantial eatery."

Dola glanced over at O. T. "Oh, I don't think we're going to be around too long. We're on our way to Dinuba."

"It was just a thought. There's a lot of men making money in the mines who would pay two dollars a meal for food like that," Tolavitch informed her.

"They got to be makin' a lot of money to pay that price!" O. T. exclaimed.

"Just in case you do decide to stay, think about my offer. I know a fella who can put a building up in a week. Or perhaps we can find one already built."

"We are kind of figurin' on pullin' out for California in a few days," O. T. added. "I've got a brother in Dinuba, and I need to—"

Daniel Tolavitch cut O. T. short. "Skinner, I don't mean to be messing with your plans, but I'd like to offer you a job."

"I don't know nothin' about assayin'. I didn't get much beyond readin' and writin' in school."

"Orion has very nice penmanship," Dola bragged.

"Let me tell you the deal," Tolavitch said. "The assay business is booming right now, but it might not last forever. It can go bust in a matter of days. It's so good right now that I don't have time to go to the mines and bring in the samples or hand-deliver the assay reports. But that's what everybody wants. They are scared to death some messenger is going to switch samples or peek at the reports and tell everyone in town. I need someone to tote samples and deliver reports for me."

"But they won't want me to tote their valuable samples and papers."

"That's where you're wrong. Because right now you're the most trusted man in Goldfield. I know I trust you."

"Why is that?" O. T. asked.

"Because you're too smart . . . or too dumb . . . to go after the gold. And you're hard-working. And you don't bluff down."

"How do you know that?"

"You're the Wall-Walker. Some say that makes you the bravest man in town. That's quite a compliment. And once what happened this afternoon gets around, your status will be legendary . . . at least until next week."

"You mean this ruckus we had out here in our yard?" Dola questioned.

"Ruckus? That was the Gately-Wilkins feud comin' to a head. Folks have been talkin' about that ever since the Paradise Valley War shot itself out. This was the last big rivalry in what's left of the Old West. You stopped the whole thing, unarmed and barefoot. Till the day I die I will never forget that scene. Now what about that job?"

"What kind of hours would Orion be working?" Dola asked. "He doesn't work Sundays. We need to go to church."

"I don't work Sundays either, ma'am. There would be long hours when we're busy and short ones when we aren't. Kind of seasonal. If you could only give me a week, two weeks, two months, or two years, I'll take it. Any of it. You're the one I need."

"I'm sure you could hire someone else, Mr. Tolavitch."

"That's where you're wrong. It's either you, or I have to do it all myself. Think about it. Who am I goin' to hire in this town to go get samples from the Wilkins brothers? And what if they don't like the assay? You're the only man I know who could deliver it with a smile and have 'em laughing before you left camp. You'd probably tote them one of Mrs. Skinner's pies, and they'd end up thankin' you for comin'. Everybody else would get tarred and feathered. I need you, Skinner. It's your calling."

"I appreciate your confidence, Mr. Tolavitch. Me and Dola would like to ponder it a night, if you don't mind."

"Why don't you join us for breakfast, Mr. Tolavitch," Dola offered. "We can tell you our answer then."

"I do believe I will."

They watched the assayer drive west in the dark desert night.

"A whole lot happened today, Mama," O. T. said.

They walked hand in hand toward the almost clean oak table.

"What do you think we should do?" she asked.

"I don't believe I've ever been at a place where folks wanted us to stay so much."

"Goldfield is a horrible place," she sighed. "Dust, dirt, heat, greed, gambling, drunkenness, and a red-light district that covers six blocks."

"You know about that?"

"Omega was quite graphic in her descriptions."

"Not exactly the kind of place to put down roots and raise a family," he concurred.

"Absolutely not."

"Then you think we should move on?"

"Definitely," she asserted. "In a little while . . ."

"In a little while?" he questioned.

"I can't leave with Nellie Rokker so critically ill. And you're a good influence on Elias. Surely you see that."

"I hadn't gave it much thought," he said. "So you think we should stay until she pulls through?"

"She will do fine; she's got to. But it will take some weeks. Perhaps we can put some meat on her children before we leave. Besides, Mr. Tolavitch needs you. You heard him. No one else can do the job like you, Orion Tower Skinner. When was the last time a business couldn't get along without you? When was the last time a town needed you? It's your calling. Maybe the Lord has led us to Goldfield."

O. T. shook his head. "Hard to imagine the Lord leadin' anyone to a place like this."

"Even Sodom had righteous Lot and his family."

"But that town got its due."

"Not for quite a number of years," she countered. "Now I'm not saying we should stay years. I really want to go to Dinuba. But a few more weeks wouldn't hurt."

"You promise not to turn back and look when we leave?" he chided.

"I promise. This place doesn't need any more salty pillars."

O. T. pulled off his hat and laid it on the table. The desert air had only slightly cooled off, but every degree less felt good. "Ada and Ida could use the rest," he murmured.

"I had a crazy idea watchin' how the kids love playin' on that motorcar," Dola blurted out.

O. T. plopped down on a crate and motioned for her to sit on his knee. "Don't tell me you want to tow that motorcar all the way to Dinuba?"

"No, but what about repairing it and driving it to California?" She put her arm around his neck. "Wouldn't that be something to drive up to Pegasus' place in a motorcar?"

"I don't know how to fix a motorcar," O. T. cautioned. "I don't know anyone who does."

"It was just a thought." She ran her finger lightly around his ear.

"But if we did get it fixed, I suppose we could tie Ada and Ida on behind. I surely ain't goin' to leave them in Goldfield." O. T. slipped his arm around her waist. "I think decidin' whether to stay would be easier if this place had some green grass, trees, and a shady park someplace. It's such a desolate land."

"That's why they need you, Orion." She ran her hand along the sleeve of his smooth, cool silk shirt. "It's desolate in climate and in spirit. It's not just a job; it's your unique calling."

"There must be others could do the assay job. It's jist that ever'one is so busy tryin' to find gold that they don't have time to help others."

"And you have no interest in gold?" she teased.

"Darlin', I've looked around Goldfield for two days, and I figure I'm the richest man in town already." He leaned over to kiss her cheek, but she held him back with the palm of her hand.

"Perhaps we shouldn't waste any more kerosene," she grinned.

"Yes, ma'am." O. T. reached over and turned off the lantern.

When the light finally flickered out, she slipped her arms back around his neck. Her lips met his.

They were soft.

Tender.

"I imagine you're worn out," he whispered.

"I seem to be regaining my strength," she murmured.

Again their lips met.

And the tent flap flew open.

"Mama? Daddy? Are you out there?" Rita Ann called out.

"We're out at the table, darlin'," O. T. replied.

"What are you doin' in the dark."

"What do you think?" he laughed.

"But . . . you just did that yesterday!"

"It's habit-formin'."

"What do you need, honey?" Dola called out.

"You have to do something with Punky and Caitlynn. They are constantly not paying attention and messing up my performance."

"*Your* performance?" Mrs. Skinner challenged.

Rita Ann had one pigtail unfastened and draped under her nose like a mustache. "I mean, our performance. Can I send them out with you?"

Dola stood up. O. T. struck a match and relit the lantern. "Send them out, darlin'."

With giggles and squeals, two barefoot children dashed out of the tent. Punky toddled over to O. T. Caitlynn hopped into Dola's lap. There was a little round tummy pushing against the purple silk pillowcase dress.

"So you two were messing up big sister's Shakespeare?" Dola asked. "That is a serious crime around here."

O. T. began to laugh.

"Hey!" Jug Cherry yelled out through the dark. "Cain't you two knock off all that jabberin' and turn that light off? A man's got to get some sleep. Tomorrow's a big day for me. I need my rest."

O. T. jostled Punky on his knee as he reached over and once again turned off the lantern.

Dola hugged the silk-clad Caitlynn Rokker to her chest and whispered, "Tomorrow's a big day for all of us."

For a list of other books by
Stephen Bly

write:

Stephen Bly
Winchester, Idaho 83555

# OLD CALIFORNIA

*They were women of courage in a land and time that would
test the strength of their faith*

Though at 19 Alena Tipton is a confident entrepreneur, her heart is restless to fulfill its divine calling. But it could lead her away from the place—and the man—she loves.

Martina Swan's marriage was supposed to be perfect. So why is she fighting a devious bank and outlaws by herself, with the most difficult battle—learning to forgive and love again—still ahead of her?

Christina Swan is still seeking to find her place, her man, and her calling. The answers will come in one incredibly surprising way after another as she struggles to be obedient to God's leading.

BOOK 1: *The Red Dove of Monterey*
BOOK 2: *The Last Swan in Sacramento*
BOOK 3: *Proud Quail of the San Joaquin*

# HEROINES OF THE GOLDEN WEST

They've come West for completely different reasons, but what Carolina Cantrell, Isabel Leon, and Oliole Fontenot are about to discover is that moving to Montana Territory will change their lives, their dreams—and their hearts—forever. With robberies and shootouts, love and romance, life in Montana is anything but dull for these Heroines of the Golden West.

BOOK 1: *Sweet Carolina*  BOOK 2: *The Marquesa*
BOOK 3: *Miss Fontenot*

# THE AUSTIN-STONER FILES

Lynda Dawn Austin's sophisticated. New York city life as a book editor has prepared her for just about everything—except a certain charmin' rodeo cowboy and the rugged territory he's guiding her through. Join them as they travel the West in search of lost manuscripts, stolen chapters with treasure maps, and missing authors.

Now if only they can find everything they're looking for before danger finally catches up with them!

# CODE OF THE WEST

You'll be on the edge of your saddle until the very end with feisty Pepper Paige and her cowboy Tap Andrews. She's determined to keep him next to her and away from danger, but he's got a knack for finding trouble behind every tumbleweed. Together they discover courageous faith, a deepening love, and the meaning of second chances in this wild six-volume ride. The Old West will never be the same!